JACKIE GAY was born in Birmingham in 1962. She has published one novel, *Scapegrace*, and has co-edited three anthologies of short stories including *Hard Shoulder* (Tindal Street Press, 1999), which won the Raymond Williams Community Publishing Prize. She is currently working as an artist in healthcare and community settings.

To Joan
Hope you enjoy it —
Keep writing
Lots g love
Jackie
xx

Wist

Jackie Gay

TINDAL STREET PRESS

First published in 2003 by
Tindal Street Press Ltd
217 The Custard Factory, Gibb Street, Birmingham, B9 4AA
www.tindalstreet.co.uk

Typesetting: Tindal Street Press Ltd

A CIP catalogue reference for this book is available from
the British Library.

ISBN: 0 9541303 4 0

Printed and bound in Great Britain by
Biddles Ltd, *www.biddles.co.uk*

For Dad, who never flinched

Acknowledgements

I would like to thank my dear friend and esteemed editor, Emma Hargrave – keep the faith!

Part 1

Twins

'I tried to get my mind to settle by looking back . . .
and thinking it all through. After a while I stopped,
having succeeded only in recalling the facts, and they
were so starkly real that I could draw no conclusions
from them.'

Joe Simpson, *Touching the Void*

1

Romany says that Ty made his mind up then, during the minute or two we lingered in the bookshop before following him through Greenwich Park up to the observatory. I'd known it was coming for months, a cloud banking up along my horizon, and I could have stopped her then, over the coffee-table picture books of mountains and deserts and dark-eyed women wrapped in pink saris. I could have said, 'No, Romany. You can't.' But we moved quietly up the path. The wind was blowing in hard from the sea, tree-shadows slapped onto the path in front of us, daffodils bent horizontal. By the time we got to the top they were going together. Off, away, looping around the world, destination everywhere. Romany snatched a quick glance at me and I felt it, too; the billowing under her ribs as she rushed him across the courtyard. Their bodies touched and static crackled in the air; excitement caught by the wind, bouncing off the walls, the thrashing trees. She spoke to him and he nodded – *yes yes yes* – and they looked down over the green slope of the park to the waning river, winding its way out of London and off into the world.

'We're out of here!' yelled Romany, one foot on either side of the prime meridian. 'Yess!'

Someone clapped; Ty took a little bow.

'She knows that,' said Ty, coming to my side, nudging me. 'Don't you, Katie?'

'You come too,' said Romany. 'We'll find a way.'

'I want *letters*,' I said. 'You must write to me. Every day, OK?'

I knew that they were half gone already. Wanted only to be sat in a café, making plans. Tables papered with books and maps; country-shapes in bright blue and orange: seas, river basins, mountain spines. But I'd come to see the museum; to look at the clocks, sextants and telescopes which first allowed us to set off across oceans confident of return, wiser and stronger for the wandering. I watched the movements of Harrison's chronometers – more regular than a heartbeat, built to bear heat, cold, the sudden pitch of a forty-foot wave – and felt a lurch of my own. How do people stand this? This leap away; free-falling with nothing but a dream of leaving and flimsy, rose-tinted impressions of what might lie ahead.

All Romany wanted was to get off, to go. I'd heard nothing else through the winter.

'Maybe I could get Ty to come with me, that'd sort it. Mum and Dad might even be happy for me, then. But he just sits and reads about the world. Nothing wrong with that, like . . . but . . .'

I could have held her back. She knew it and waited, the decision was mine. 'He'd probably jump at the chance,' I said.

'Let's see if I can't tempt him, then.'

In the Greenwich Observatory I watched the clocks as Ty and Romany stood spinning a globe, fingers brushing the raised ridges of the Himalayas, grazing the frozen plateau of Tibet. Their bodies leaned towards each other and a streak of sunshine jumped through the window above them, a fuzzy golden spotlight. That's it, I thought. They're going to leave me.

I smiled at my sister and my best friend as the banking clouds hissed and spat.

2

Romany is in India. No delays – I checked on Ceefax. The plane is on the ground, Mumbai airport, they'll be disembarking now – sucked through customs and pushed out into the hot air where a man in dun-coloured pyjamas is smoking a beedi. 'Taxi?' he'll say. 'A hundred rupees downtown?' They'll squeeze in, wondering if this is a good price and whether the corroding Morris Oxford can possibly make it out of airport-world – India style – into the unimaginable streets of outer Bombay.

Romany is my sister. Chosen sister, blood sister, soul sister, twin. Together every day since she landed on our doorstep six years ago, fifteen, brooding and suspicious, stinking of street life and contempt. And before that, too, in spirit, in soul. We have the same faces, see. We look at each other and can feel our selves in another body, each other's history in our own bones. She was even wearing my clothes when we met: squatting on a bridge over the canal, begging, with my clothes and my face, and in ten seconds our lives changed for ever.

It was all an accident, of course. Neither of us was meant to be there.

We know the details, the facts; they're lodged in our joint archives like a wedding or the birth of a baby. She wakes under a blanket of rubbish in a corner of the market,

11

shivers, begs a cup of tea; up to New Street to catch the morning commuters but someone's puked in a long, agonizing trail all the way down the ramp, and Romany gets the dark glances even though, as she says, her stomach could never hold that much puke in a million years. I wake up queasy, feverish, under my own blanket of papers and books; plead off school – those looks from Mum – but the wind and the sun outside nudge me from my bed and I've read everything in the house two or three times. I can quote the damn things. She runs into Tom and a litter of puppies – 'I'll have one,' she says, 'he'll help me get fed tonight' – and heads up to Broad Street to try her luck. I'm restless – a curse, a saviour, a little bit of both – only a short hop into town, but the bus routes have changed and I'm landed in Five Ways, dust and scaffolding right down to the library. Aching and sweating, up on to the bridge, *spare change spare change*. Rifling for coins, stumbling, seeing my face, her seeing mine.

'That's my jumper,' I say. 'I made that.'

It still makes us laugh now; Romany imitates my indignation well. But I loved that jumper, couldn't believe it when Mum gave it to the charity shop.

'You can talk,' she said. 'You've got my face.'

I could be you in the clicking of heels past us; *you could be me* in the wake sloshing below. Then a scrambling and yipping from the pup and Romany was gone before the copper even saw her – they won't have begging up there, she told me later, it's all private land – leaving me stranded on the bridge but in my head running off, the hot pup's heart beating, my whole body linked by invisible string to her.

Mum had seen her, too, hanging around the Bull Ring begging with the other street kids. She followed Romany round the back of a burger van and said, 'Come and stay with us. Kate has always wanted a sister.'

'Kate?'

'My daughter, Kate Jackson. You look just like her.' Mum stopped, took a breath. 'Unless you've got somewhere else –?'

'Have I fuck,' spat Romany, stuffing stale bun crusts into her mouth. 'Ask me if I'm bothered.'

She vanished behind bolts of silk and suiting. We kept seeing her though; on the street, in the park, squatting at the edge of the market selling grubby friendship bracelets. She reared at the sight of us – we might lasso her, drag her inside – but Mum wasn't fooled. Said she'd seen that look on my face plenty of times, had enough doors slammed in her face not to be put off by a bit of scowling. 'That girl needs us,' she said. I wasn't sure. Anyone who could survive out there on the jagged streets, dare to sleep without walls – curled in a doorway, lips murmuring silently – didn't need anything from us. Now Mum smiles when her friends ask if she's worried about Romany going off travelling around the world. 'Romany can look after herself,' she says. 'And Ty's with her of course. Nice lad. His mother phoned last week, asked me all these questions like she was filling in a form.'

I tune in to Romany; her face pressed up against the window of the taxi. Bumping through the *jheel*, inside the bubble of the broiling taxi, right into the biggest slum in Asia. Romany will be a sponge, soaking up everything. Pictures of the goddess Lakshmi swinging from the driver's mirror, cows munching bananas in the middle of the traffic. But what is Ty thinking? Does his hand hover over Romany's sweating back, as she leans forward to chat to the driver?

Six months after that first eye-lock Romany knocked on our door, 34 Mount Street. The day next door's cat had two perfect kittens – twins; it seemed significant to everybody. Spring, but cold. Romany was shivering, teeth clacking. I said to her later, 'You could have spent the winter here, you know.' She knew which was our house, but something stopped her: pride perhaps. Don't need nothing or no one me.

'Are you OK?' I said, stupidly, as she swayed on the step.

'No,' she said, staggering into the hall, passing out half-way down.

Everything went frantic then. Mum tumbled down the stairs and Dad got on the phone and Dr Finnegan arrived with his black briefcase. I squirmed inside my skin, seeing her prodded and poked and tutted over like that. And the image of her face falling past me flicked through my head. Sliding down white and drawn, like a ghost of myself from a dream.

We didn't match our faces properly till much later. She was so sick people turned away when they saw her. Stomach ulcers, bronchitis, ringworm, lice, terrible sores on her feet and ankles. They had to amputate one of her toes in the end, crushed under a bus as she'd scarpered from market security. Mum berated her tenderly – 'Why wait until you're practically dead before coming to us?' – and was rewarded by Romany's measurable recovery. As she got better she told us her stories. Common ones, I guess, if you let yourself hear them: running from children's homes, foster homes, dyeing her hair to dodge the police. The stories punctured holes in the small, safe world I'd created. I could never again pretend to not know what was out there.

She told us wild stories too. Rescued from a dustbin as a baby; her dad an Arabian prince, her mum dying tragically in childbirth. Mum tried to separate the strands, untangle the truths. But me and Dad and Romany just elaborated; re-knotted the rope. Foundling, faerie child, changeling,

14

stray. Left under a gooseberry bush in a basket in the rushes. What did it matter? She was with us now. She had a mum and a dad who'd always be there for her and a sister whose face matched her own.

We sat in front of the mirror, comparing, while the black kittens Hutu and Zulu batted at our feet. Dark hair, dark eyes – hers slightly more so than mine. Skin – hers pale but gaining colour fast, mine slightly sallow; Mediterranean looking, people said, often asking if I was adopted when they saw my sandy-haired parents. Perhaps I was a changeling, too. Narrow cheekbones, narrow noses, wide mouths; Romany's wonky grin, my smile more wary. If we tried to pull the same face we never could, but would occasionally catch each other's expression and think, that's me. Her face looks just like mine. 'Well,' we said, 'whatever's out there now we've got each other, deal?'

'Protection, man,' said Romany. 'That's what a girl needs in these crazy times. Someone on your side, no matter what.'

No matter what?

Deal.

Spit on our palms and write it in blood.

They'll be in downtown Colaba now, where even buildings have to fight for space. Streets choked with chai stalls and sweet trolleys, honking trucks and *tuk-tuks*; shrines, flowers, cows, dogs, kids, people everywhere, hanging out of windows and on to the roofs of buses. They'll be trying to find a room, lucky if they get a cardboard partition, a latch on the door. Negotiating unknown streets, Romany's senses popping, Ty more cautious, I guess. He's not city born, not like Romany and me. Came to Birmingham from Northumberland on a college exchange. I bumped into him in the library and we fell into conversation as easy as blinking. He was only supposed to be here for a few months but never went back. We used to tease him – 'What have you done up there, Ty?' – and he'd say, 'Why would I want to leave town now I've met up with you two honeys . . .'

Oh, he's a charmer, is Ty. I've never seen his manner slip, sometimes wonder if it could. Perhaps he simply came out gurgling winningly, like some babies do. One thing's for sure, though, Romany will know. By the end of this round trip she'll know all about him.

*

A postcard and a letter! 'Listen!' says Mum, rushing back from the front door. 'Dear Mum and Dad and Kate and Hutu and Zulu . . .' She stops, scans the rest of the card.

'Come on, Mum,' I say, curbing the urge to snatch the letter and hole myself up.

Arrived in Bombay – what a place! – spent first few days trying to work out left from right before heading down to Goa on the boat. Jet-lagged but HIGH! Wish you were here. Miss cats, bed and Marmite as well as you, you and you.
Love and kisses, R.

Mum peers at Romany's writing as if she can read more into it, the loops on her ys, the way her vowels all slide into one another. She's back with us, briefly, for the first time since those manic days before they left. Hugging the stair walls as Romany dived up and down, grabbing and discarding mementos, spreading maps out on the floor, drunk on the glamour of mile-high mountains and ancient cities. Then to Heathrow where an unheard-of relative of Ty's appeared and clapped him on the back. We were all in floods – including Dad, who never misses the chance for a good cry. Then this 'uncle' arrives and emotion ricochets between his hand and Ty's back, curiosity stilling our tears.

'Who was he?' said Mum, but Ty was halfway to the paper shop, heading for a copy of *Time* with a picture of Hindu pilgrims on the cover; black hair, red robes and glinting white teeth.

Dad gets the map out and traces his finger down the coast-line from Bombay to Goa. We pin it up on the kitchen wall next to an old RECLAIM THE STREETS poster, coloured string marking their route.

I finger the letter, tucked in my pocket now. Mum notices and her mouth droops, the lines at the corners of her eyes too. Her face falls like this sometimes; if she caught sight of herself in the mirror she'd pull it up.

'You coming swimming with me today, Kate?' she says.

'Don't fancy it much.'

Dad unfolds his newspaper but doesn't read it. 'How's the course going this term, then?' he says.

It takes a while to get away from Dad's questions, but I think I convince him that I'm doing more than mooning about, missing Romany. Everything's the same in our room; her pinboard of photographs, her globe, her maps of the world. A map – a Birmingham *A–Z* – was the first thing she picked up when she came to live with us. During her sickness Mum hissed at me, 'Take some books in. It can't be good for her sitting there staring at the walls.' Then she froze, anguished. 'Oh my God,' she said. 'I wonder if she can read?'

'Can you read, Romany?' Dad's voice boomed up the stairs.

'If I feel like it,' said Romany.

I took her in a pile of magazines and sat on the end of her bed.

'I can hear you moving about at night,' she said.

'Oh,' I said, 'sorry, only I . . .'

'It's OK,' said Romany. 'Gives me the creeps, a room to myself, tell you the truth. Can't we share?'

Mum was dead against it, but Romany said let's just do it anyway, so our stuff began to merge across the two rooms – Romany's few clothes and her bag of carefully guarded scraps. Eventually Mum moved the beds around, admitting defeat. We had a space that was ours. I came home from school to find Romany in my room, grinning and reading the A–Z.

Those first few weeks were hard for Mum, not knowing what her impulsiveness would bring. Romany could run off, they mightn't be allowed to adopt – had she invited chaos into our lives? And Romany's presence, ticking away upstairs, distrustful of adults, of mums and dads. She didn't trust the house either: the carpeted floors, the instant heat, the cupboards of food. I'd find her downstairs gorging herself, stuffing food into her pockets, secreting cheese triangles into her bag where they'd squash and mingle with dead matches and knots of hair.

'Come back to bed,' I'd say. 'It'll still be here in the morning.'

'Only if you promise me,' she said.

I pull the letter out of my pocket. Postmarked MUMBAI, INDIA, 6TH OCTOBER 1996, and peppered with scrawls and stamps as if it's been through many hands to get here:

Dear Kate

I'm here! We're here. Sitting on a mattress in this bug-ridden, airless hole they call a room – noise and heat sliding through the walls. And this is luxury – seems like half of Bombay is homeless, living on a pavement, a doorway, snatching some sleep balanced on a ducting pipe. Tell you what, the street kids of Brum could learn a thing or two out here.

I can't tell you what it's like, Kate, to be here at last after so much dreaming. Ever since we got on the plane I've just felt so free. Got to try and describe it to you, borrow your way with words so you can feel it too. We circled over London, the city below with the ribbon of river, lights flickering messages to outer space. But then we were off, east towards the sunrise, the earth moving around underneath us. Cocooned for nine hours then stumbling out into the laser-bright sunshine, so tired I could've just curled up like a cat and slept on the floor. Into a taxi and through the swamp to the city. Leprous hands rattling on the windows of the taxi, schoolgirls in starched dresses waiting for the bus, red ribbons braided through their hair. White frocks from the slum, an everyday Indian miracle. I'll never manage to keep clean here, Kate. I couldn't even do it in Birmingham . . .

I imagine me doing it. Travelling – India, Africa; the moon or Mars or Jupiter. Easy – piece of piss, as Romany would say – you just close your eyes or pick up a book. But I'm edgy without her, need distraction. I could play my flute perhaps, but won't settle to proper practice. Romany knows I'll be conjuring the journey up for myself, sitting on this wide window ledge where she always used to find me.

'Where you been off to then?' she'd say, snatching back the curtain. 'Come on, spill . . .' And we'd share the details of our day, our dreams.

She said we'd still be together, whatever. But how can that be true when already I feel the sting of the time and space between us?

3

Romany trusted me right from the start. Maybe it was our faces.

'When your mum pounced on me I was like, *scarper*,' she said. 'Her clothes all perfect and that teacher's voice? I thought, oh yeah, what's your game?'

We eyed each other, laughter bubbling. Delicious laughter; just for us. We were fifteen and conspiracy against the rest of the universe was really possible. Only *you* understand the way things are; see the greenness of every grass blade; feel the heat of injustice, the rush of connection. But now there are two of you.

'Half the people on earth were twins in the womb, you know,' I said.

We drove Mum and Dad nuts finishing off each other's sentences, but the change in us both was so remarkable that no one complained. An only child, I'd grown up to be solitary, most comfortable with my books and dreaming. I grated against people's expectations, building up a head of resentment that Romany burst, spectacularly, the first day she came to school with me. She hadn't had much schooling, but was clever and determined and wasn't having any of the remedial class.

'I'm going in with Kate,' she said. 'Throw me out in two months if I haven't caught up.' The teachers couldn't get over how hard she worked, but I knew her hunger for it, for something to arm herself with. 'Kate showed me the way,' she said.

A line from her letter. *There're so many faces here like ours. I keep thinking I've seen you.* Then she went on and on about Ty, an instant hero, apparently. Everyone's luggage stranded in Moscow and Ty the one to sort it out. She's made up, she says, feels she can really trust him. She has to, out there where it's just the two of them, now. Where what's happening is as intense as the midday sun on the gluey streets of Bombay.

Romany's in love. That's what she says, not in words, but the feeling rises like musk from the paper. In love with the stars, the jewelled Indian ladies, with *bhelpuri* and *channa* and chai and Ty. I can feel it, snaking across oceans and deserts, over Europe in a flash, up the M1 as a streak of light. *Ty's transformed*, she says. He's bought cotton trousers, ties a scarf around his head to guard against the heat. His skin is browning and his muscles stand out as the fat falls off him. They sleep together on the deck of the ferry as it slips through the Indian Ocean, fishing boats with Sinbad sails rolling on the swell.

A recollection of him, reaching above me to fetch a book down, dried sweat marks in the armpit of his T-shirt, red-blond hair flopping round his face. 'Hi,' he said, 'I'm Ty – I've seen you around a lot in here.' I was reading up on globalization – his eyes gleamed, he said we *had* to join the Greenpeace demo which was leaving soon from the Union steps. His T-shirt had a graphic of a solar system on it, a big YOU ARE HERE arrow nudging the densest section.

'You reckon you're insignificant in the greater scheme of things, then?' I said, cheeky for me.

'We're *all* insignificant,' he said, 'compared to what's going on out there.' He meant out there generally, but I thought he was talking about the demo and that impressed me. Here was someone who thought things could change.

He took me to meetings, on marches. Mum and Dad got all excited: they'd always hoped I'd be an activist, sent me off to junior CND when I was a kid. I could just imagine them getting out their demo photos from the seventies and Dad taking Ty out to the workshop to show off his latest eco-gadget. But I found the meetings strangely dispiriting, riven by rivalries and burgeoning egos, and was happier when Ty and me would just read and work together. We both loved the release of the library, leaving your baggage at the door, turning to a fresh page. The Central Ref. was one of the top reasons Ty stayed in Brum. 'Not counting you, of course,' he said, tipping his head. I thought the tip was ironic, to mock his smooth delivery, but then his head twitched again, involuntarily.

'It's a tic,' he said, unembarrassed. 'Used to be quite bad. Doesn't bother me much now.'

Romany had finished her course in Performance and was 'experimenting'. Running nights for DJs and performance artists with names like Dreamers of the Day; hours quizzing Mum and Dad about collectives, sustainable communities, and then off to paint damp warehouse walls, rig up lights, write vengeful rants and get trashed in the name of revolution. As soon as she'd settled into our household she was itching to get out; did anything to earn money once she'd decided to go – bars, waitressing, office jobs, early morning cleaning in offices.

'It's not you I want to get away from,' she said. 'Never. But I've got choices now, possibilities, a life. I'm going to survive, not end up a corpse in a stairwell or a ghetto crack-whore.'

'I wish you wouldn't talk like that, Romany,' Mum would say. 'You'll give me nightmares.'

'You don't know how close I came,' said Romany.

'I think I do,' said Mum.

She wanted to learn, to party, but most of all she wanted adventure. A step into the unknown, the fear-thrill of a mountain or a desert or an unmapped city. The first time she went abroad – a school trip to Italy – she stood on the Ponte Vecchio, letting the pattern of untranslated words fall around her. A street artist sketched her in charcoal and turned her into a proud gypsy, wrists twisted, about to dance. She loved that picture; it's on our wall, here in our bedroom, her charcoal eyes watch me as I move around the room.

A week goes by. No letters – delays in the post, I tell myself. Autumn is slipping away. I try to distract myself, work hard on a Chaucer essay, go to the pictures with Dad and shopping with Mum – she spoils me, spoils herself. The cats come in from a hard morning's mystery – stalking frogs, catching mice – and fall asleep in a black heap of paws, tails, ears and whiskers. Their bead-bright eyes follow us, identical faces up on the counter mewling for food, then off scampering up the garden, whiskers twitching, finding adventure right under the next bush.

Then a letter. A letter from Ty . . .

Dear Kate,
A picture of Goa for you. Beaches, palm trees, a warm breeze; a Portuguese-style hut for a bedroom, with a fan and a boy to bring lemonade. We have seriously slowed down.
   Typical conversation:
   Me: What do you fancy doing today?
   R: (stretching) Oh, I dunno. Swim, maybe?
   Me: Yeah. In a bit. (Waves lap the shore, women stalk the beach, pineapples and melons and trinkets in baskets on their heads. Birds calling in the trees, a motorbike coughs, the horizon is steady and blue.)

23

R: (Who is dozing off) We could go for a walk later.
Me: Are you hungry yet?
The sea is like a big warm bath and last night the moon was so bright it cast our shadows on the white sand . . .

I want to be there next to the gently breathing sea. Relaxing with them; a spiced breeze blowing around our heads. But I'm not; I'm here on my window seat looking out over the back gardens, threaded together by yellowing walls, spindly wild flowers clutching at the bricks. *Secret Garden* walls, where hedgehogs burrow and cats doze – one of them is there now, tail twitching.

. . . Not sure where we're going next. The old India-hands say, go north, to Bengal. The younger ones say, south, to Kerala, the backwaters, to Kovalam for sun, sand and techno. How about Sri Lanka, the Hima-laya, Burma, Thailand, the Far East? Romany says we should just go down to the bus station, close our eyes: eeny meeny miney mo.

How's everyone back there? We're thinking about you all – your dad in the workshop and your mum pounding around Handsworth Park, you on the window seat.

Anyway, it's hot and the sea is calling.
Much love,
Ty xxxx

A deal's a deal, Romany. You taught me that. Can't trust someone who welshes on a deal. Dad squeezes my arm and says she's just got caught up in it all, it doesn't *mean* anything. I know I should stop thinking about them, get away from her maps and her globe and her charcoal eyes. Mum needs a break, too; even more running and gym and swimming since Romany left; she doesn't bother to ask me along to the pool any more.

'Shall we go to Frieda's?' she says and I say 'Yes!' too loudly, too quickly. Dad can't come, though: Braxton's Nuts, Bolts and Fixings for the World can't manage a day without him, apparently. 'He'll be glad to get shot of us,' says Mum.

Frieda is Mum's oldest friend; she lives far out on the Norfolk coast, no more land until Scandinavia. Every year her outcrop is eaten a little more by wind and tide; she only survives because the rock her house stands on is a geological freak. Her sons joke about building her a bridge across the water that will soon reach round her like a moat. You can hear it at night, water wriggling into the fissures under the house, slapping, hissing, trickling. I plan our route, conjure up the sea, the wind blowing in from Siberia, nipping the tough black thorns that cling onto Frieda's rock.

'She's barmy,' says Mum, while we're stopped for lunch. 'You'd think she'd never heard of global warming.'

'I wonder if the boys'll be there?' I say.

I hope so, I say to my reflection in the mirror in the toilets; to Romany, wherever she may be. Frieda's sons are my friends, we grew up together. Romany nearly had a fling with Chrissy a year ago, but they couldn't go through with it in the end. They tried to kiss, but ended up scrapping like the cats instead. 'Brothers and sisters – like that,' I said, looping one finger over another, 'as close as peas but no sex, right?' We all laughed then and played backgammon for high stakes until the dawn sun tinged the sky with red streaks out there over Siberia.

The air gains a whiff of brine and the landscape empties. Near to Frieda's, vehicles veer off either side of us, sand blows across our path, giant-winged marsh birds with trailing legs lope into the sky which stretches horizontally, like a widescreen film, where it merges into the sea. Frieda's house stands up like a cake decoration on the icing of sand around it; she's outside waving, as if we might miss her and pass off into the vast basin behind.

'Jenny! Kate! At last. One day you'll get here and find I've just been swept into the sea.'

'Well, if you will live in such a ridiculous place,' says Mum.

'I know, I know,' says Frieda, kicking open her sea-swollen front door. 'But how can I leave the house?'

She takes me through to my perfect room – it became mine after the boys left – with its huge bay window looking out over the sea. Sun-faded curtains and washed-out walls, everything whitened; a few shells scattered around, driftwood, sand between the cracks in the floor-boards. I can curl up on the cushions to look out over the milky green sea, twitching under its water-skin even on the calmest of days. With a pile of books and Star, Frieda's ancient brindled greyhound for warmth and company, I'm ready to go.

'I suppose all you're going to do while you're here is read,' says Frieda, plumping up cushions and shaking off the remains of salty mould.

'I suppose all you two are going to do is talk,' I say.

'You're missing Romany though . . .' she says.

They clatter around the kitchen, her and Mum, exchanging news. Later their voices will quieten and they'll sit down at the table and get serious; about Romany, about me. Mum will agonize over who to fret about most and Frieda will say, 'Ach, you should try having boys.'

She trusts me, Frieda. To be OK, to do OK. I realized that one summer, what it meant; that Mum didn't, still *doesn't*. We were all here – me, Romany, Dad and the boys. A summer holiday a couple of years after Romany came to live with us. She was grumpy – hadn't wanted to leave the city, wanted to go to Glastonbury 92 if she was going anywhere – but Dad blithely herded us all into the car.

'We need some air blowing through this family,' he said and sang loud and flat all the way to Norfolk. Beatles songs, Abba; headbanging to *Sabbath Bloody Sabbath* as if he still had a mane of wavy locks – much to Mum's disapproval, who still felt awkward taking the Lord's name in vain, despite her socialist principles. At Frieda's, Chrissy and Jack were waiting for us with food and music and we all went down to the dunes. Later I lay listening to the sea swooshing outside, my nose and shoulders singed by the sun. Romany near by, feet and fingers flickering, dreaming of dancing perhaps, of disappearing into the sea with a flick of her mermaid's tail.

Someone was in the kitchen. Pacing around. Sniffing. Mum.

Then a low moan and someone else up. Frieda, her slightly asymmetric shuffle, an old injury, worse at night.

'Jenny? Love, you must sleep. Fretting all night won't change a thing.'

Mum spluttered something. I couldn't make out the words, lay still and hardly breathed.

'Jenny, what's done is done. She'll be all right – trust me.'

I waited for Mum to leave, then went into the kitchen where Frieda was staring out at the invisible sea. 'Who's she fretting about, me or Romany?'

'Both of you,' said Frieda. 'Hazard of parenthood.'

'How's that supposed to help, then?'

We sat in the kitchen until dawn, the tide slipping away underneath us. As the soft grey light bloomed the noises around the house changed. The wind freshened and pushed against the windows, a radio came on in an upstairs room and a low wuthering vibrated around us, startling me out of my drift.

'What's that noise?' I said. 'Is it Mum?'

'It's the wind in the rocks under the house,' said Frieda. 'Hardly ever happens, only when the breeze comes from over the land.'

She stared out at the sea, her face like stone in the pale light, but her eyes bright and moist and full of hankering. 'I call it the wist.'

4

It felt like I'd been hankering for ever when Romany came. Her moving in cured me. Before, I was a child – my head full of dogs and princesses and aki one-two-three; reading *The Water Gipsies* in a corner of Dad's office at Braxton's during one of Mum's trips to Greenham Common. Then I hankered and then she came.

'Nice bed,' she said, her eyes still feverish. 'Can I keep it?'

'It's yours,' I said.

'Everything in this house smells so good. There's nothing but stink out on the streets.'

'Where *did* you live?' I said.

'All over.'

'Yes, but *where*?'

One of many stories: her mum and dad couldn't cope, she was too wild for foster parents, rebelled against children's homes' regimes. *It doesn't matter*, was what she really meant, *that was then and this is now*, but Mum was plagued. It was her job, after all, running literacy classes and basic education for the young homeless. She spent hours questioning Romany and then Saturday after Saturday down the council, wading through records.

'How can they have lost track of a child?' she said.

'Happens all the time,' said Romany, 'no one gives a shit.' Mum swelled with indignation; we could see her adopting every street kid she saw, filling our house with orphans. There'd be some lad lounging on the sofa when we got home from school: good clothes, full belly, drunk on Dad's precious single malt – which made him uncharacteristically furious.

'Tell you what, why don't you just open up the attic for them?' he said. 'I've always said we should clear it.' Mum blanched – I think she was actually sick – but stopped inviting work into the house. We could just be a family then, without Romany's past life hanging around to pull at our consciences.

So we went out to the street kids instead. We'd take them clothes and food and cigarettes and Romany would squat down to talk. I was too scared of their brashness and posturing to say very much, but I watched and listened, fascinated. They seemed so brittle, their lives one long ricochet from subway to shop door, heat to cold to hunger, violence to snatched sleep. I worried that underneath the hard shells there was just emptiness.

Once Romany left me in one of the subways between New Street Station and the markets – I'm going with Lise here, she said, just a quick job, bring your flute next time, make a bit of cash . . . I shivered while I waited, impossible to blend in, to crouch down with the other kids, wrap myself in blankets and beg for spare change. Enormous, notched hands landed on my shoulders and I wished I *could* jump out of my skin, but the hooded faces were watching me carefully. My head crept round to meet one clear eye and a milky one, blazing out of a head the colour of a fading bruise, etched with scars like some ancient language all over the hairless skin. 'Hi,' he said. 'I'm Tom. Good to see you down here with us.'

I could let my breath out then. I knew about Tom, he was one of the good guys, although you'd never know from his appearance. He lurched rather than walked, was bald from alopecia and blind in one eye from a bottle smashed in his face. Romany had told me about the first time she'd seen him, he was teetering on a canalside wall, glue bag to his face, the sun shining down bright and brutal. But Tom hung on in. Kicked the glue and found a floor to sleep on; he was sorted, sort of, by the time his hands landed on me. Romany said he'd saved her life once – no question, she'd be a goner without him – and to the younger kids he was god.

When Romany and Ty said they were going travelling, Tom sat in the pub and watched us silently all evening, sipping water as we got drunker and dafter. Eventually we fumbled our way out on to the street; Ty slipped and fell into Tom, his body freezing halfway there but unable to stop. 'Sorry, mate,' he said, from the pavement.

'S'OK,' said Tom. 'Have a good time now, you two.'

'We will,' said Romany. 'Take care of Kate for me.'

'Does that mean I pass?' slurred Ty, looking at Tom, his head lolling to one side, trying to be winning as his words jumbled up in the front of his mouth.

'You've always got Tom,' Romany said before she left. 'No better protection than that.'

At Frieda's the wind blows through a gap in the window frame, the curtains snap and crack like sails. Mum is on the phone to Dad, her voice drops and rises like the seagulls outside my window.

'Kate, time to get up. Your dad says a letter's come from Romany. He's putting it in the post now.'

The day gladdens, spooks from the past a fading memory. Frieda's making bread and I help her with the kneading; yeasty smells float around the kitchen. Mum decides to make biscuits while the oven's hot and it feels like Christmas; we even drink a glass of wine before lunch. Then we go down to the river and crunch over the gravelly beach strung with crinkled ribbons of seaweed. Frieda fills a sack with rubbish: she clears the beach nearly every day and leaves the bags in front of the local council office. Star tears up and down the beach, five-foot strides, flinging himself into the sea after sticks and waves and nothing whatsoever. We all laugh, breathless and freshened, our cheeks burning red. On the swing bridge over the river we stop for a while; Frieda still chattering about her clean-up schemes, Mum hatching an idea for bringing some of the Fresh Start kids down from the city to help. They're excited, this is their ground: activism, change.

'Arms and legs and energy, that's what I need on this beach,' says Frieda. 'We could give the council something to *really* think about.'

'It'd be great for the kids, too. Fresh air. A cause. Half of them have never even seen the sea,' says Mum. For a moment she looks young, energized. Every morning she goes for punishing swims in the sea and then wraps herself elegantly in one of Frieda's African cloths. I think of Dad, balding in the crumbling factory, trying to convince the chary union men he's on their side, doesn't like contract working any more than they do.

'Are you in with us then, Kate?'

'What do you think, darling?' Their faces are eager, like Star with his sticks.

'Shame we don't get a letter off Romany every day,' I say. As soon as the words are out I regret it – the sourness seeping out. 'It's a great idea,' I stutter. 'Of course I'll help.'

'Right then,' says Frieda. 'We'll start planning. Shall we go and get a hot drink inside of us?'

Mum and I throw grateful glances at Frieda and a weak smile at each other. *I'll try not to*, I say, with my look. *Honestly, I will*. But I've ruined their brave spirit, Mum's energy is gone. I doze the afternoon away and dream I'm on the edge of a river with chunks of ice churning under the surface.

Coffee, breakfast. Waiting. Frieda has a cigarette. I wish that I smoke. Bath. Wait.

The postman on his bicycle. A black smudge in the bleakness. My best friend.

Mysore, Karnataka, India

Dear family,

Sorry, sorry, sorry for not writing. I know I promised. Sorry, Kate.

The weeks have just vanished – lame, I know. India gobbles up time. I can't believe we've been here over a month, it's flashed by, a flash with a whole lifetime in it. (Tell me when I stop making sense.)

I'm sitting on the hotel balcony with a group of Hindu pilgrims. They're picking at their fat toes and chattering, glancing slyly. I've had a shalwar kameez made for me, could be mistaken for an Indian, but something's not right and they can't quite work out what. Good. Ty's reading, planning where to go next. That's how it is here – you go places and you read about places and you plan to go places and as soon as you get somewhere you think about moving on again. Always circling – like the eagles above me now, snatching food from the street stalls – never stopping, never settling. I love it.

Where have we been? Well . . . Bombay was like being stranded in the middle of a rave while everyone else was off on one I'd never even heard of. Long-horned cows and beggars on skateboards, hawkers and conmen and 'change money very-cheap-good-price'. Ladies with armfuls of bangles moving like Daleks through the crowds, wrapped in gold and apple-green. Throwing myself in there where I know nothing, am nothing. I love it, I love it, I love it.

Then eight hours on the boat. Sitting on the deck

with the moon arcing over us. It's Bank Holiday for the Indian travellers; they drink and play noisy card games, do puja to the rising sun. I slept and had crystal dreams of people I'd forgotten all about – a boy at Barnardo's, a teacher with hair cut square at her chin. Then I woke to the pale dawn light resting on sleeping bodies and felt like I could have been on my way to the moon.

Ty's going for a walk down the market: whole rows of nothing but bananas – fat-finger-sized lemony ones and giant red ones as big as your arm – and the most amazing smells; this is Sandalwood City, they make the best incense in the world. In the mornings a sweet woody perfume drifts through our window. Stacks of glossy vegetables kept fresh by a boy sprinkling water; cones shaped from spices. We're going up to some monument later, Ty wants to see the buildings. I'll talk to the hawkers and pilgrims and shoeless children who stand and stare unblinking and pick at the wiry blond hair on Ty's arms as if he's a creature from another universe. Ty the Alien.

Kate, I'm writing you a letter, I'm doing it NOW. Don't give up on me.

R xxxxx

5

I wasn't much of a one for going out before Romany came, but she wouldn't have me sitting around, and jiggled with irritation if forced to stay in the house. As soon as she could stand up without her knees buckling she wanted to be out on the streets and I got a lesson in how to be a teenager c/o Romany Jackson.

'Where are we going?' I'd say as she flung clothes around our room.

'Just *out*,' said Romany. 'Here. Put this on.'

Her restlessness dizzied me; dizzied all of us. We hung around parks and shops and the chippy, Romany posing and me skulking in the background. Wind scuttled rubbish around the precinct, rubber slammed on to paving slabs; old men grumbled at their waddling dogs, a solid beat echoing from a flat near by.

'We could be at home,' I said. 'In the warm.'

'You don't get it, do you?' said Romany, knobbling some kid on a skateboard for the word – who? what? how? when? 'You have to get out and about, Kate. Nose to the ground.'

I was happy to be with her, though, and by keeping my mouth shut and my ears and eyes open I learned where she'd come from. A world outside 'home', edged with danger and unpredictability; where who you are rubs up against railings and empty garages and railway tracks – a rough, physical world, one I'd retreated from to books and window seats and wishing. Romany smashed herself into it. Scraping her palms scrambling up walls, running through stream-tunnels under the road, city-sure feet across traffic-choked highways. She loved rain and wind and sun hot enough to melt under; liked to say *Yo!* and slap hands: with the postman, the crossing lady, any number of nameless kids. She wanted to be someone out there, not just another face in the bus queue; more than that, she wanted me to be someone.

'They won't know you exist unless you tell them, Kate,' she'd say. 'Say it loud. Say *I am HERE*.'

I am here. I am here at Frieda's and Romany's in India, no hint of a flinch as it swallows her whole.

Mum worried at first that she wouldn't come back home, but Mount Street was always at the centre of Romany's orbit. A big old house near the Soho Road, a haven with its rambling garden and big old oak trees. One time we'd been out on the streets until late with Tom, looking for some kid who'd gone missing from one of Mum's projects – if anyone could find him it was Tom. I was so disorientated by our wanderings that Romany fetched the *A–Z* and we drew out our route in highlighter pen. Pink arcs stained the pages and we both knew that Mount Street would be at the centre. She said, when she left for India, 'I won't forget where the middle is.'

Our house. I long to be there now instead of here at Frieda's, where everything is bare and exposed, where you only have to blink to imagine one of the waves swelling ominously and crashing through the walls. To be on the streets which are *our* streets, to chat with that crossing lady, those heavy-lidded boys . . .

'Kate? Are you with us today?'

'Be out in a bit.'

'Come now. Come and look,' says Frieda.

I join them on the porch and stare out over the still, watery land. Frieda's gaze is fixed on the long ribbon of road, two black dots buzzing on the horizon. There's a puff of smoke from one of the dots and a distant popping.

'That's them,' says Frieda. 'That's my boys.'

Jack and Chrissy are on tour. Motorbiking fast between friends and family before Chrissy goes to college in Aberdeen and Jack back to work as a ranger in his Northumberland forest.

'Well, not that fast really,' says Chrissy over Frieda's homemade soup. 'We just keep charging about, hoping we look dashing.' Frieda and Mum flutter their eyelashes, pass butter and fill glasses while I roll my eyes. 'It's so good to see you, Kate,' says Chrissy. 'Without you my ego might get seriously out of control.'

'Who else is there to remind us that we're only *men*?' says Jack.

Romany, of course. Her name drifts into the room and lingers over the table; knives clatter on plates, Frieda hacks at a loaf of bread, Mum's eyes burn on me. *Say something. Don't ruin it, Kate.*

'I like the leathers,' I say to Chrissy, '*trousers* too.' I'm not sure if they're Romany's words or mine, but everyone smiles. Frieda squeezes each of her boys in turn. Mum pats my knee.

'So, Kate,' says Jack later, after dinner. 'Come on, spill. You can't hide anything from me.'

He's joshing me, nudging me. A small, jaundiced part of me thinks, what do you care anyway? We're not that close.

'I don't know what all the fuss is about,' I say. His big camel-eyes stare at me, lids moving slowly over the curve of his eyeball.

'Your mum's worried, blames herself . . . for letting you and Romany get so close.'

'Oh, so she could've stopped us, then?'

'You know what your mum's like . . .'

'Yes, I do.' My voice rises. 'She thinks a few more sit-ups will stop me missing my sister.' I can feel Mum cringe in the next room, but there'll also be a glance between her and Frieda. She's getting something out. Can't be a bad thing. And I want to rush in there and scream, *Stop thinking about me. Let me BE.*

'Why don't you come up to the woods with me?' says Jack.

I'm tempted by Jack's forest, could learn where the badgers live, how to pick out buzzards by the breadth of their wing. Lighting a fire at night while the wind presses on the walls outside.

'I might,' I say. 'Got to get back to college now.' I raise my voice for Mum's benefit. 'Can't let my studies slip, can I?'

'What I can't understand,' I say to Tom, back in the city, 'is why anyone would ever think I'd be jumping for joy.'

He's there, sitting on the wall at the end of our street on my first morning home. Still smarting from a row with Mum – *No ifs or buts, Kate* – I nearly go straight past him. He's wearing a porkpie hat with a giant feather sticking out of it, but it's the glint of his eye which snags me.

'Tom . . . Is that you?' He pulls his hat off and sweeps it down to his combat boots. 'You want to get a dog on a bit of string,' I say.

'Done with cities, I am,' he says. 'Only so long you can last out there. But I was passing through and thought I'd catch up. Heard from that sister of yours?'

We head to Feed the Nation for dumplings and I spill out my woes – the worst of which is that no one likes me having them.

'Blast it all out in a letter to Romany,' he says. 'Tell her, *you bitch, you left me.*'

'How can I? The happier she is the more fed up I get. Crap, I know, but there you go.'

'Write it to me, then,' says Tom. 'I can take it.'

We go for a wander. Tom's asking after a girl, Karen. She moved to Brum with him from Telford, their hometown, and there are bad stories going round.

'Your mum'll keep an eye out for her, won't she?' he says.

'She'll try, I'm sure,' I say. 'Talk to her.'

'Everyone says Karen's a lost cause,' says Tom. 'But I don't give up so easy.'

'Neither does Mum.'

Somehow it doesn't feel so bad to talk to Tom about feeling abandoned. With him I don't have to pretend to be brave. We mosey down the canal, throw sticks from bridges; it feels good not to go to college – my choice, for once. I'm miles ahead anyway. Tom makes me laugh with his stories – juggling on the seafront with Coke cans and half-eaten toffee apples, stranding his van in the estuary mud. I tell him Romany's stories – boats and stars and white-frocks-out-of-the-slum; the pure joy of just throwing herself in.

'What about you?' says Tom.

'Oh, you know, the usual.'

A Bounty wrapper twists past my foot and off down the street. My life feels small, solitary; I thought all that was over when Romany came.

'You could go somewhere yourself.'

'I'll stick with my window-seat travels,' I say. 'Romany's the adventurer in our family.'

He comes round to visit before leaving the city. Mum's saved him a good pair of boots donated by one of Dad's old biker mates. 'Purler!' he says. 'My feet are sound until spring now.' I think she was expecting to give *him* advice but instead spends all afternoon listening.

'You have to be trusted,' says Tom, 'and never give up.

And believe that things can be different even if everything you've ever seen screams *disaster*.'

Mum goes all dreamy when he's gone; building visions, solutions in her head. 'If only he could work for me,' she says to Dad, 'we might really get something done.'

'Can't see the council giving him a job,' Dad says. 'Or him wanting one, come to that. He'll do it his own way.'

I set off upstairs to my room. A twinge slithers up my leg and I stop to massage it.

'Oh Michael, he's marvellous, really.' Mum's voice low and breathy. 'To have been through all that and come out so . . . wise. Like Romany, with all her energy, you'd think it'd have been beaten out of them by now. These kids, practically outcasts, we don't even recognize what they know . . . If only . . .'

A sudden scraping of chair legs and Dad pulls open the kitchen door. 'You all right, Kate?' he says.

'Fine,' I say, rubbing my leg harder, but managing only to spread the raw patch further and wider.

Dear Tom,

I'm writing to you poste restante – just like I do to Romany and Ty, never knowing if the letters will be read. You could've moved on; Romany and Ty might bypass the address I write to by hundreds of miles. Scribbling into nowhere, an act of faith. How many lost letters are there in poste restantes all over the world? Dear Johns and I'm sorrys and the dog's dead and wow you won't believe what happened to us . . .

Well, you won't believe what's happened to me . . . Actually, not much. But it was good to see you, to talk. Can't be angry in front of them. Mum would blame herself and Dad feel useless and we'd all go round in some pointless, excruciating family circle. Better to put up and shut up (as she might say . . .)

Travelling, travelling. Everyone seems to be travelling. I met one of the girls Romany used to hang around with at school and she's off to Spain to live up a mountain. No one keeps still – even Mum and Dad get fidgety after a month or so in the house, have to go off somewhere for the weekend only to come back tired and hungover. But then I loved roaming around with Romany.

Another thing, Tom. You said I'll get better, start feeling less lost and low. Maybe. But what if Romany comes down as I slowly move up? Like we're on different ends of a seesaw? Pivoted on a forty-foot wave in the middle of the Indian Ocean?

Come and see us soon. Stay in touch.

With love,

Kate xxxx

Up on my window seat I can pull the curtain over and cut myself off from everything. A cocoon with a view; warm air from the radiator zigzagging up my skirt; cushions, books, breath on the glass. I've already been out to India – checking the guidebooks, the letters. Outside the cats prowl – batting at rocks and stones, lashing out at a leaf or a fly, quick as a lizard's tongue. They skitter across the lawn; tails and fur erect, spooked by something invisible, then stop suddenly and smooth a paw over an ear. I go back to India. Kerala – sliding though the backwaters on a *kettuvallam*, glimpses of Buddhas through vivid green rushes. I drift along in the noon heat, catching a reflection in the water, possibly me, maybe Romany.

'Kate? Kate!' Mum's voice. Disturbed, a little anxious. I swivel round, lurching out of the drifting boat, the cocoon.

'What?'

'That was Ty's mother on the phone,' says Mum. 'She's so peculiar. Not one word of chat in her.'

Ty's mum needs to find him. 'Not urgently,' she said, apparently. 'No, no, nothing like that. If he phones, please let me know.' Me and Mum look at each other thinking *phone*. They didn't budget for phone calls – it would signal disaster to us – but they could, they could fax; even email Dad at work if they were in a big city.

'She said, "Just tell him there's something he needs to know." As if that's the message in itself,' Mum says. 'Come on, let's go down the road and get a coffee. See if we can work out what's going on.'

'Can't we do that here?'

'Don't you fancy a cream cake or something . . . some of those delicious barfis from Ambala's?' she says. 'Come on, love. You know Ty, you've got to help me out here.'

Outside, morning frost still edges the paving slabs. 'So,' says Mum, once we're settled into Greggs. 'What do you know about Ty's family?'

It's sod all really. 'His dad died and his mum sent him away to boarding school. There's an older sister, married with a couple of kids, living abroad. I think he adored his dad, always talked that way.'

'What happened to him?' says Mum.

'He was out rescuing lambs from a snowfall, Ty said, a favour to a sick neighbour. He fell, twisted an ankle, got hypothermia.' Ty remembers standing around the high bed staring at his dad's blackened fingertips. His mother becoming gelid herself at the sight of her husband's frozen body. 'His mum sent him away, shut herself into the house.'

'Ty went to boarding school?' says Mum.

'Quite a strict one, I think,' I say, sucking cream out of a cone of flaking pastry. 'Cross country runs and cold showers, all that stuff. Sounds horrendous to me.'

Mum laughs at my expression and orders more coffee.

'We should do this more often,' she says.

I try to conjure up a picture of Ty's mum. Stern, sturdy; high expectations. Ty told me he always passed his exams at school because it was the one way to keep his mother off his back. He never said much more, just slid into our family like there was a space waiting for him. Dad called him 'son' and Mum bought him socks and T-shirts off the market along with bits for Romany and me. During all the preparations no one mentioned his mum, asked if she minded him leaving, which seems odd now, given his adolescent efforts to keep her sweet. Did he even go up there to visit before they left?

'I don't think he did, you know,' says Dad at tea.

'We somehow forgot about his other family,' I say.

'He did slot in,' says Dad.

'Just like Romany,' I say.

We sit and eat, the light fading outside. Unsettled that the elasticity of our family has another side to it – a darker, excluding side. Mum's distracted – it's a deep social gaffe on her part not to have asked about Ty's family – she slops tea on the table and leaves it there; kicks her shoes off with sudden violence. We eat. No one turns on the light.

As I'm drifting off to sleep I see Ty's face, twitching. He's trying to tell me something but every time he opens his mouth his tic drags his lip upwards, puckering the skin of his cheek and the words get mangled.

Dear Romany,

Just a quickie because Mum's about to go out to the post. Not much doing here – I saw Frieda and Chrissy and Jack. And Tom – he's on the road now. Dad works hard, Mum too and frets for England while she's at it. I can't convince her that I'm all right so you'll just have to take it from me that I am. Imagine if we were both out there, she'd be manic, so you owe me one for staying here.

I wonder what you're up to all the time. A day chatting to other travellers? On a bus rattling through tea plantations; maybe you can swim today, in the sea or a hillside pool. How is it with Ty? His mum phoned the other day saying there's something he needs to know. Did you ever meet her? I want to know if my picture of her is close to the mark. Has he ever talked about his life up there, his mates, his girl-friends? I don't remember him mentioning anyone. All those times we sat gassing about our encounters, he just laughed with us and flattered us by lusting over our lost pubescence. Good times – reinventing our-selves for Ty.

Romany, I don't know what she's written but really, I'm OK.

Sending love,

Kate xxx

6

Did I want an ally so much that I dreamed her up? Six years folds into a few snapshots: her falling through the door, hauling me round the streets, leaving. Our delicious teenage conspiracy, so empowering that I could never have refused.

I turn the snapshots over in my head and come to the one I've got to face. The day Romany met Ty.

OK, I did want to keep him away from her at first. He seemed to genuinely like me – thought I was smart and sharp and funny, all qualities so much better defined in Romany, a clear-focus picture to my dim fuzz. I wanted to be those things so I kept him away from her, told myself she must have secrets too. Ty didn't know she existed and she never asked where I'd been, as if I hardly had a life when she wasn't there.

Me and Ty talked about books, only a few slivers of information – his dead dad, my distant childhood – calved off unintentionally. We shared amazement over people who said *Yeah, it's OK* over some masterpiece that had left us both reeling, both unable to return to Birmingham, England, without it, too, feeling like some fantastical creation. Then moving together past the gurdwara's pearly domes, up the Soho Road through the multinational shoppers, past the jerry-built fairy-light-strung mosque at the top of the hill to look down over the glinting tower blocks of the city, clouds suspended in mirror-finish glass.

Then it happened. Ty and me after a lecture one day, lost in a deep tunnel of conversation and somehow missing his turn-off. Suddenly we were there, outside the house, cats pressing the windows. Romany burst out of the front door shouting, 'No, I don't know when I'll be back!' and then rounded her face to the street and met mine.

'Hey, babe,' she said. 'Who's your mate?'

'Just someone from college,' I said.

Romany abandoned whatever urgent appointment she had and we all went inside. Luckily, Ty never mentioned that I hadn't told him about her.

So we became a threesome. First a singleton, then twins, then triplets. Romany and me needed a bloke who'd listen to us, who'd let us behave badly. A brother, perhaps.

I replay that day in my mind – want to see Romany's face as she leaned across the table. Did she slip a button on her shirt, lean closer while telling tales of princely fathers and misplaced babies? Ty was rapt – we all were.

When they left they were still brother and sister. But it won't last. He's in her world now; what could make him want to resist?

'What are you doing today?' says Mum. 'Are you going out?'

Always on my case despite my unblemished college report. Romany gets bawled out for living it up; I cop it for being conscientious. The post slithers through the letter-box. A few thuds – magazines, junk mail, then a light patter of possibilities.

'One for you,' Mum shouts breezily, too breezy for it to be from India, and there's no second post on a Saturday.

Dear Kate,
You don't know me but I'm a mate of Tom's and have

just picked up his letters. Unfortunately he's gone AWOL – the police round here don't like the look of him so if any travellers' vehicle so much as parks on double yellows it's Tom they're having.

I hope you don't mind me getting in touch but you were writing into nowhere and I'm here with a long winter ahead. Tom you obviously know and he's a top bloke. How did you meet him? Who's Romany?

Anyway, I'm Vaz and I live in a field in rainy Wales. One day I might try and classify types of Welsh rain, like the Eskimos do with snow. It's soft today, a silent mist sinking through the air. The site smells of woodsmoke and soggy leaves and thick, thick mud – the bane of our lives, it's a Zen thing. We have to learn to love mud. Dogs barking, fires hissing and smoking as we try to burn the wet wood.

I like telling you this. It makes me think about what's here. It makes me really *be* here, so ta, Kate. What's it like where you are? I've just got a book out from my bed – it's still warm in there, burrow-warmth, we sleep under six inches of blankets at this time of year, getting ready to hibernate, along with the squirrels and hedgehogs in the wood.

If you're still lost and low I hope this letter might cheer you.

Write again, Kate.

Best, Vaz

Outside, Hutu and Zulu sniff a frozen twig carefully. Hutu springs over the wall and then stops dead as leaves crackle under him. I finger the heavy curtains around my window seat and pull them closer until there is no crack, no gap. Just me here with the whole world outside my window.

'Kate!' A yell, from downstairs.

'Look!' Mum bursts through the door. 'Look,' she says, beatific, holding out a glossy packet. 'This film arrived first thing. I've just come back from the chemist. Photos. There's a letter for you, too.'

Ty said they'd send film back. That way you'll get to see us first, he said, when he found me here on the morning they left, staring at the patterning of the sun on the lawn. The shadow of the fence had moved a good foot since I'd been watching, chunks of my life disappearing in front of my eyes.

'It's a way you can share the trip,' he said. 'So you're not left out.'

'Don't be daft,' I said. 'Anyway, I want *letters*, right. Something to *read*.'

Photos.

Mum spreads them out on the bed. Romany and Ty at Bombay airport, wasted but glittering. Streets so busy you can't see the ground. Packed bodies, a small boy fighting the tide and emerging exultant. Trinket stalls, fruit stalls, baskets of fish. Sea and sky with a semicircle of red sun sliding between. Romany walking on a raised path through paddy fields; both of them eating under a thatch of palm, grinning for the camera.

'She's lost weight,' says Mum.

'She's happy,' I say.

'Don't you think she's thinner?'

'They're glowing, Mum.'

'That T-shirt is hanging off her.'

A burst of irritation in me. I bite back my words – *stop going on about her weight* – knowing that it's just a foil for her real fears. Romany abducted by jungle rebels with machetes clamped in their teeth; joining the sanyasi; mangled in a game of chicken between betel-chewing bus drivers on crumbling mountain roads.

'Look at her face,' I say. 'She's fine.'

Mum sighs and knots her fingers. The faces from the crowded Indian streets flicker through my head. If I close my eyes perhaps I can really be there.

Dear Kate,

Did you get the photos? What do you reckon? Look at people's faces, they're ace, aren't they? I think of town on a rainy Monday and I wonder where all the people inside those bodies have gone.

Well, where are we? On a rock, hurtling through space . . . No – better than that; we're in Madurai, a temple town, packed with pilgrims, incense, incredible vegetarian food. None of that oh-he-must-be-a-weirdo-because-he-doesn't-eat-steak here so Ty is well happy and I pretend that I miss meat. I don't. I don't miss anything except you. I imagine us as mad old ladies travelling in style, poking a finger out of our saris going, 'Ooh, look at that,' and getting chatted up by courtly Indian gentlemen in tea houses on long hot afternoons. We'll do it, one day. Now I've thought of it it's not far off real anyway.

Remember when I first came to Mount Street? All that school timetables bollocks; meals at six o'clock, bedtime. Mum going on about regular sleep and structuring my time. Bedtime was the worst. I'd think, so what? – it's not like I've got to go out and bag a doorway. You've got regular sleep for the rest of your life inside these walls. No bampots with smashed bottles in their fists in 34 Mount Street.

Are you and Mum getting on now? I've told her to keep looking forward, but sometimes the past's as real as now, isn't it? Maybe she should come out here where you can really leave it all behind.

Here we just do what our bodies tell us. I can lie on a bunk all day, listening to the bells and drums and chanting in the street. I can go to the temple where the holy men sit, stiller than statues, time moving around them. Black-stone temples where the gods whisper and you can taste the sacred in the air.

Ty's got his routines; his diary and his reading and his exercises and his list of 'sights'. We're going to the mountains next. Ty wants to climb up above the clouds – that's his adventure, to be out there with just a rucksack and his wits to keep him alive. For me, adventure's in every alley, every street, every temple where the gods' hot breath lifts the hair on the back of my neck.

WRITE

Love to you, R xxxx

'So,' I say to Hutu, who's on my shoulder nudging my neck. 'Are they or aren't they?' I make a list.

Against:
· Romany thinks of him as a brother. Ty is our brother.
· She had a lousy boyfriend record before she even came here, likes to keep sex casual.
· They were never physical with each other, not before they left, anyway.
· Half the reason he's gone is to look out for her. She'd hate that, but it's true.
· Me.
For:
· They're away from everything, anything normal.
· They're sharing rooms, huts, floors. Arithmetic. $1+1=2$.
· The day they met.
· The hill at Greenwich.
· The day they left.

Who could have resisted Romany that day? When she's old she'll look at all the young folk and think, ah, but did you have a day like that? When your feet didn't touch the ground, you were on a cushion, with each step you bounced higher and higher. The sun sparkled over Brum turning grime and grit to gold dust and diamonds, the air full of shiny light, words tumbling out of Romany's mouth in coloured strands. 'Are you getting married, dear?' said an old lady in the multi-storey at Heathrow.

'No,' said Romany, her eyes gleaming in the half-light. 'I'm going travelling.'

And Ty that day. Leaning on a pillar, eyes locked on her. I replay and replay it, knowing this is madness.

'Kate?' Mum nudges the door softly. 'You OK?' I nod, eyes closed. She joins me on the window seat. 'Much new?' she says, fingering the airmail paper, thin as tissue.

'She's fine,' I say. 'Loving it. More than ever, I'd say.'

A tear tracks down my cheek. I feel its trail, wish I could suck it back in.

'Oh, Kate,' says Mum.

Mistake, mistake, *major* mistake to let her see me cry. She won't leave me alone for five minutes now. Campaign, on the phone all evening – Kate needs this, Kate needs that. Here, talk to Frieda, Kate. Jack's coming down before Christmas, won't that be nice for you? Let's go to the cinema – I'll phone for tickets . . .

I retreat to Dad's workshop, which is out of bounds unless you're willing to rub down bits of rusty old metal and listen to his ramblings. He's stitching seat covers for his bike. 'Recycling,' he says, as soon as I'm through the door. 'Think of all the waste metal in this city, factories full of machine tools going to rust. Given the chance my blokes could make *anything* out of that lot.'

'Give them the chance then,' I say.

'Met any benevolent millionaires lately?'

I glance at the photos on the workshop walls. Dad's glamour shots: on his BSA at the head of a march, placard strapped on the headlight – DEFEND WORKERS RIGHTS – hair flowing out from his helmet. 'Polish up the chrome, will you?' he says, handing me a rag.

That's quite a nice job so even Dad must be feeling sorry for me and I feel for him too; that the revolution never happened and he's left battling to save the factory against all odds. 'We produce quality,' he says. 'For a living wage. What the hell's the problem with that?'

I rub the metal until it's shiny and warm. The next job is weeding and clearing brambles, he's not going to let me stay in the shed kicking my heel. He hands me some secateurs. 'Your mother's worried.'

'Spare me the speech, Dad,' I say. An intuition that I'm being outmanoeuvred, but it's too late to change tactics.

'It's not just Romany – there's something else, isn't there?'

'Course not,' I say.

'Is it Ty?'

'Well, I miss him . . .' I stare at the ground; suddenly I can see every pebble, the minuscule buds on bindweed.

'You can talk to me, chick. I won't tell your mum if you don't want me to.'

'I just miss them, that's all. What's so difficult to understand about that?'

Dad jabs the hoe into the soil. He doesn't want to do the fatherly talk any more than I want to hear it, so I start mumbling about coursework and chores. 'Kate,' he says, grabbing my arm. 'Everything changes, you know. If she was here things would still be different. Don't kid yourself on, eh?'

'You finished?'

'Go on, get out of here,' he says.

I go to bed and dream. Never mind tickets and visas and saving up money and long-haul flights – I can go anywhere. I fly over Africa and India and up to Siberia where reindeer fan out and Eskimos light fires on the ice. The world opens up like a children's atlas; whales spouting, schools of dolphins around explorers' ships. Pyramids and kangaroos and the Great Wall of China crenellated up half a continent. People wave from their huts and houses, skyscrapers and streets, and children jump to touch me, as if I'm magic, a talisman, a lucky charm that will last for ever.

7

We made a list of Romany's boyfriends; she swore she hadn't left anyone out and I didn't quibble over the exact definition of 'boyfriend'.

1. Older boy at a Barnardo's when she was twelve. Bought her ice lols outside school until she worked out he was training himself up as a pimp. Bad start. 0/10.

2. Nice kid from up the street. His mother didn't approve so they had to sneak around which Romany's not good at. Sweet, but fumbling. 2/10.

3. Nice kid's not so nice big brother. Disaster. 1/10 (for introduction to other boys).

4. Rob. First 'proper'. They'd once been fostered by the same family so the relationship had a tang of incest which shocked their ex-foster mother into horrified silence. Neither of them liked the old shrew in the first place. Still mates. 4/10.

5. Sonny. Runaway. Wayward even by Romany's standards. She spent the winter before she came to us with him so Mum blames him for nearly killing her. Minus 5.

6/7/8. Boys from school. Thought they were street-wise but utterly outclassed and spellbound by Romany. Ungradable.

9. Sam. Raver. Good laugh for a while. 5/10.

10. Dale. Raver. Either manic or comatose. 3/10.

11. Freddie. Lived on a canal boat with a dog called Rastus. He died when the gas bottles in his cabin leaked overnight. So did the dog. Shouldn't have had the bottles in the cabin, spat Romany, stupid fucking *jerk*, her voice falling into the violent green algae blanketing the canal. 10/10 (and impossible to ever downgrade because dead).

12. Adam. Guitar-playing grungy type. I thought he was gorgeous, but Romany was irked by all the angst and his idea that there was something seriously wrong with his life despite being well-fed/clothed/housed, even drugged. Occupational hazard of being Romany's boyfriend – don't moan unless she thinks you're justified. 2/10 (Romany); 7/10 (me).

13. Robbie. Lovable nutter. 6/10.

Is Ty number 14?

'Kate?' says Mum. 'What are you up to, love?'

'Working.' I pick up *Shakespearean Angles* and stare at it thinking, triangle, rhomboid, parallelogram.

'Put that down for a minute, will you?'

Trapezoid. Oval. Square. She stares at me, I stare at the page. 'Jack's coming tonight,' she says. 'Why don't you take him out? He must get fed up staying in with us oldies all the time . . .'

'I'll cook if you like.'

She sighs; turns abruptly. Part of her wants to shake me, rattle some sense into me, like people do in films, as if a good shoulder-shaking is all anyone needs. Her feet sink into the carpet, her own shoulders droop.

'Maybe a meal out,' I say, my throat bubbling, tainting my voice. 'All of us, hey?' She's on the phone booking a table before I can swallow back my words.

When Jack arrives I'm in the bath – actually I'm in the Himalayas tracking a snow leopard, the peaks above me slicing the purple mountain sky. They must think I'm in my room because their hushed conversation floats up the stairs and slides under the bathroom door.

'Jack! How nice to see you.'

'Hey up, Mrs J.'

'Good journey? Come in, come in.'

'What's all this about our Kate? Mum says you sounded really worried.'

I stop moving, dead still in the water. Out of my reach a tap drips. A paw crunches the hard icing on top of the snow.

'She hasn't been out for over a week, Jack. It's getting worse.'

'Och, you know what she's like. It'll pass.'

'It's not the same this time, really . . . She did say she'll come out tonight though.'

'There you go then.'

I spread water across my stomach and watch it pool in my bellybutton. There's no way I'll get out of this meal now, best to brave it out this time, a mark in my favour: 'I went for dinner with you and Jack, didn't I?' I make an effort getting ready because that always goes down well, and I brush up quite nicely, they always tell me.

'Katie, you look wonderful,' says Mum. 'New top? I'm so glad we're all going out. There's nothing quite like a nice meal in a nice restaurant, don't you think?' She's gushing, and we all shift around waiting for her to finish.

'Couldn't you find a clean shirt?' she says to Dad.

We get out of the house on Mum's gaiety wave but I'm sagging already, pulled by the undertow – that I'll enjoy myself, we'll have a successful, fun-filled, family bonding experience. Pukevomit, as Romany would say. Mum witters on about the Soho Road as if I've never seen it before, but falls silent as we move into Chinatown, shafts of light cutting across the street, which is strung with tinsel decorations, twisting in the wind.

In the restaurant we meet up with Griz and Carla, old friends of Dad's, who still live in the disintegrating communal house that Dad once stayed in. Mum is sympathetic about the latest damp problems, the endless stream of other tenants who play drums all night, nick food and won't have their cats neutered.

'You were so lucky to get Mount Street done up,' says Carla. 'We should have gone for urban renewal.'

'The others wouldn't have it, would they?' says Griz. 'Didn't want the rent going up.'

The men take over, ordering food, talking about Jack's projects for introducing rare trees into his forest. I feel queasy so I imagine I'm being read a story, picture seed-shoots pushing through the crumbly forest floor. Mum is smiling, quick eye-flicks over to me and whispers to Carla. I bet she'd quite like to feed me, spoon me puréed mouthfuls until I burp.

'. . . but the *best* thing,' says Jack, 'is that I think we've got Scottish wild cats. They really would be something worth coming to see.'

'Oh, Kate, yes, you must go,' says Mum.

The wine snakes down my innards and out into my bloodstream. I think of pictures I've seen in books, lynx-tufted ears and ringed tails, and tell them about the snow leopard, up in the mountains where Romany's going. My stomach calms and I find that my plate is empty. Mum beams as if I've won the Nobel Prize or something and I can hear what they're thinking; it echoes back to me from the restaurant fishtank.

See, she's OK.

Can you blame me for being worried?

Jack squeezes my leg. 'I don't know what they're making

such a fuss about,' he whispers, but Mum's radar is on full sensitivity.

'But, Jack,' she says, unable to resist this chance to talk about me, even though I'm sitting right opposite her. For a second I'm sympathetic, I know what it's like when everyone's bored of your subject. 'You should have seen her last week.'

My going-out smile is slipping.

'Shssh, Jenny,' says Dad.

A jaundiced smile, plunging towards my stomach.

'Why are you all pretending it's not happening?' says Mum, her voice pitching upwards. 'Kate won't go out. She hasn't since Romany left. Doesn't anyone else think that's a problem?'

The slipping, souring smile hits my undigested prawn curry. I scramble from the table. Their necks crane after me before they fall back to muttering.

I'm OK in the toilets. Functional: puke, swill out mouth, wipe myself down. Then I'm outside in a corridor and there are fishtanks everywhere. Huge bass nudge up against the glass, curl their tails and flip themselves round, their swimming length only twice their body length. I want to smash the glass, watch the water and the fish and the seaweedy gravel pour out on to the floor and the fish have a last, long flap. This is bad; worse than ever. Outside the city rumbles; traffic, trains flashing through concrete tunnels beneath me and then out into the night. I can't move, curl myself into my lap.

'Kate? God, Kate, what's happened?'

It's Jack, his arms curve around me. I look up. The fish are settled between fronds, sleeping maybe. 'I'm OK,' I say. 'Just lost it for a second. Honestly, I'm fine.'

Jack nods, seriously. He knows what I'm saying. *Don't tell them. Don't tell her.*

*

Dear Vaz,
You said you wanted me to write to you again so here goes . . .

Dear Vaz,
As we haven't actually met yet I thought I'd tell you a few things about me . . .

Another ripped sheet of paper, scattered flakes over Romany's bed. Where is she? I've lost track, this time lapse between letters – between us – is impossible. Dad's sorted his email at work now, but they'll only be able to use it in the cities and my guess is that she's way out, in Kerala, watching the silted waters move slowly around her. Or up in the mountains, the Cardamom Hills where the air is fresh as mint.

Where are you, Romany? Are you in your bed? A bed with two bodies in it, a limb or two slipping out from under the covers, mosquito bait?

Romany and Ty are in love. I knew before I even opened the letter.

Dearest family,
Hey, I know I should have written before, soz everyone. Time really does go so quick – it feels like watching a cartoon strip of your own life. There's me, Romany, in a queue at a roadside stall. Me again, body-surfing, in there with the gritty waves. Me with Ty, sipping coffee bought from waiters with jewelled fans and crests on their heads; rubbing grubby marks from my cheeks; buying oils in the market to calm down my hair.

Facts. Pin them down and nail them. We're in Madras, getting ready to go north. Ty wants some mountain adventure and I want him. Yes, Kate, it's

59

happened. Number 14. We're inside a bright shiny bubble, bumping gently into people and places, grinning like idiots.

Ty's trying to grab the pen but I won't give it up. Now I've started I want to write and write about me and him and us and India. I suppose we got closer than I realized, he's so calm, so laid back – just what you need out here. Everyone treated us as a couple anyway, and one day he slipped his hand over mine in a café and love seemed the easiest thing in the world. You feel like you've loved them for ever but you know you haven't, that one day – one second – it must have changed.

Now I feel like I loved him on that hill in Greenwich, even then. Did I, Kate? You were with us.

I broke off from reading. Saw myself crumpling the paper into a tight, illegible ball, but knew I couldn't because it wasn't even mine; this letter, or this news. Mum had just come in from her run, pink and flushed, and was frying eggs, the sizzling sharp in my ears.

'Have you finished yet?' she said. 'Are they OK?'

'They're fine,' I said, amazed that my voice sounded normal. 'In fact they're madly in love.'

The frying pan clattered to the floor, yolk leaking across the lino; the cats patted and pounced on the slippery whites.

'What?' said Mum. 'Oh, my goodness.' And she grabbed the letter, nearly missing the chair as she sank down.

I escaped to my room, but there's no evading this news. Ty and Romany inside their bubble of love – colliding gently with palm trees and market traders and rickshaw wallahs and bright birds high in the trees – cradled by the pliant sides. My window is cold, hard. Outside, the year's first snowflakes fall on to the frozen earth.

Dear Vaz,

It's snowing here today and I thought about you in your field, your bender sagging under the weight. The snow subdues the city; for a few minutes it's quiet and blank. Have you seen Tom? If you see him, please ask him to write to me.

You asked me who Romany is. Well, she's my sister, my soul mate, but she's in India and in love with my friend Ty. That's why I was lost, lonely, and now it's all got ten times worse. I promised her this wouldn't happen. I want her to have her adventure guilt free, I do. But it curdles me inside – I have to fight to stop the sourness leaking. But it does, it is, in this letter to you . . .

I've been trying to write something for ages; my room is full of scraps of paper, verbal dandruff. A snowscene inside to match the falling flakes outside my window. Out there a squirrel leaps from tree to tree, cheeks stuffed with food, a pair of jays bat through the trees. What's around you? What do you see, Vaz? Write and tell me what it all looks like to you.

Your friend,
Kate Jackson.

I don't read the rest of her letter till nightfall. Trying to bend my head around this fact, that Ty is hers, now. I can't work out who this Ty is, though – her Ty goes on early morning treks and slips back into bed still cold from the high air. Mine reads books and agrees that Mum's endless exercising is suspect. I don't even recognize his figure in the photos. That Ty is skinny and brown and only wears lunghis; the Ty I know is pale from sitting around in libraries, flicking through books with inky fingers. But that

61

Ty's gone now. I've lost him to India, to Romany, to love.

Romany's told him everything. The bullying foster parents and lackadaisical children's homes – she's opened her book, told him what she's lost; how she's trying to live with that, to live *well*. I recognize the conversations because we had them, when she first came. The things that no one else knew, once.

Voices rise up the stairs, through the floorboards, from outside in the workshop and I know I can't escape. Even Dad is watching me, vigilant as a nesting bird.

'What do you want?' I shout.

'We're going out. All of us. It's Jack's last night.'

I have to pull myself together – literally, piece by piece. Brush my hair, paste on a smile.

'We're getting rid of you then?' I say to Jack, downstairs. He grins at me. Dad does too. *See*, they say, *she's OK*.

'Yep,' Jack says. 'That's enough of the city for me for a couple of years. You'll be coming up to see me though.'

'Yeah, sure.' I say. 'In the spring?'

'Anytime.'

'Well, that's settled then.' Mum's beam fills the kitchen.

'Anyone for a drink?' says Dad.

'Yes, please,' I say. 'I just feel like a glass of wine.' I don't. But if Dad has a couple he won't want to drive.

We don't mention Romany and it's a relief. Jack talks of his wood; voles and otters and barn owls, feathers shined white by the moon.

'Nice life, kicking about the woods,' says Dad.

'You'd be bored in a few hours,' says Mum.

'Kate wouldn't though,' says Dad.

'No. Kate will like it.'

That night I fall asleep quickly, but just before I do Jack's grey eyes flash under my eyelids and turn wildcat yellow.

8

We're kind to each other over Christmas, a holiday truce. They rang, on Christmas Day, but the contrast between their chatter and our guarded questions made me wish that they hadn't bothered; sent me to my window seat, Mum for a run and Dad to bed with indigestion. Then, out of the blue, a letter from Ty. He wants something from me. *I know I can trust you, Kate.* He doesn't actually say *don't tell Romany* – couldn't be accused of that. He doesn't explain himself either; just writes, *There's someone I know in prison and I need you to be his friend. A contact with the outside world.* That's a laugh. Me, keeping a prisoner in touch with the 'real' world; me, who'd rather stay behind the covers of a good book. I suppose I could always send the guy something to read, if that's allowed. *They might let you send him some books*, Ty continues. I'll do it. He knows I will.

The rest of the letter is a trajectory across India by train. On my map I trace the railway line from Madras to Calcutta; thirty-six hours through tea and rice plantations, mountain ridges and jungle; night then day then night until they arrive at dawn, the city lagged by thick fog. Playing cards, drinking contraband whiskey as the train rattles and hoots its way past village after sleeping village, talking up a storm. You've never heard such talk, says Ty, from Marx to Maharishi; crowds gathering in the corridor to debate divinity, the symbolism of the mountains, of Shiva's head, his hair the great rivers flowing down to the plains of India. Nodding out, woken by an earnest face, gently shaking. 'Sorry, sir, but I think you are confused over true nature of *moksha*. Would you care for a cigarette?'

The train stops in the dead of night, a walk to the carriage door for fresh air where a small boy is brewing chai on a fire at the side of the tracks. Every night the train stops here. Every night the boy collects sticks and boils a kettle of tea, one rupee each, twenty scalding spicy cups. Perhaps an uncle is the train driver; owes the family a favour. Whatever, it's a living. His teeth and the whites of his eyes gleam in the firelight. He adds cinnamon, sugar, swirls the tea around his pot – best chai for a hundred miles. There isn't any road to this place; the boy's livelihood a chance act of geography, a gift from the gods. In summer he sells oranges, bananas, but tea is the basic, the staple. He's got his reality sorted; overnight travellers will always be thirsty.

And into Bengal. I can see the tracks washed by sheets of silver water, the train riding magically on top, chased by a wave which splashes the window where Romany's sleeping head is resting. We were on land, Ty says, but could see only water and a few floating thatches – homes on stilts – and boys flipping like dolphins from open canoes. Then at last the train swallowed into Howrah station, home to thousands, a giant Victorian night shelter with the great black trains rearing to a halt in the middle of breakfast.

Then Ty's request, an aside, *psst*. I reach for my book on Calcutta and join the throngs crossing the Hoogley Bridge amid the shrieks and patter of the city shaking off sleep.

I order books from the library on prisons, even catch a bus past Winson Green, dead air leaking into the surrounding streets. Mum is ecstatic that I'm leaving the house without being dragged. I waffle something about an exhibition, which she swallows like a hungry baby. But I'm intrigued by this hint of Ty's past, popping up on my shores like a message in a bottle. I'm careful to plan my journey, give myself plenty of time, make sure I won't be out in the dark. When the bus climbs back up into Handsworth I gulp at the fresher air: made it.

At home I make up a parcel for Adrian. The prison address is somewhere in Shropshire and I get a sudden flash of stilled hillsides, a squat, anonymous building with a lonely boy locked away inside. I feel a shiver of recognition, enough to propel me down the post office to post the parcel myself.

The next day a postcard arrives of the Hoogley Bridge. Mist steams up from the black water and curls around the latticed ironwork of the bridge. On the back Romany has written, *To my sister, my doppelgänger, and our bridges past and future, with all my love, Romany xxxx*

'That's very sweet,' says Mum. She's swelling slightly around the temples and chest; pride in her girl, who can be so kind, so thoughtful.

'A bit gushing for Romany,' says Dad. He's wearing an old fisherman's jumper over his pyjamas, goes straight into the garden dressed like this most weekends. Our immaculate, church-going neighbours who came over from St Kitts in the fifties never got used to Dad's fraying example of an Englishman. They approve of Mum though – she manages to be elegant in trackie bottoms and redeems all of us by minding their house and never forgetting a birthday.

'You'll get one next, saying what wonderful parents you are.'

Mum casts me a quick, anxious glance; Dad cuffs me gently around the ear. Sunbeams fall through the tall sycamores on to the kitchen table and the Hoogley Bridge gets pinned up in its place on the underarm of Asia. A message, a nod to our connection, the one she swore would never break. *Cross over*, she's saying, *cross over and join in*.

Easy to say when you're never the wallflower.

Adrian writes back straight away; gushing. Thanks for the books, thank you so much for writing, yes, yes please write back. Urgency in the slanted scribble, I feel it tug, along with a prickle of irritation with Ty for giving me no way of finding out about Adrian except for asking him straight out, which feels crude, blundering: *What are you inside for anyway?* Instead, I ask about prison, what would he like me to send him? *Yourself*, he'll say, bolted into his cell, warders outside rattling clusters of keys. The thought of entrapment again enough to drive me down the shops to buy a postcard for Romany.

Mum is waiting at the gate when I get back. 'You didn't say you were going out.'

'I only went to the shop.'

'I didn't know where you were.'

She looks deflated. As if a part of her, one lung perhaps, is slowly losing air.

'You're always on at me to get out more.'

'Yes . . . but . . . I thought something had happened to you.' She's pulling at an earlobe, glancing back at the house, the blacked-out attic window.

'Like what, exactly?' I'm pushing her, I know. But I resent this, the implication that I'm incapable, prone to sudden attacks of lunacy; that one minute she's begging me to go out and then she panics when I do.

Her head sinks.

'Tell you what, when you've decided what you want, let me know,' I say.

*

They're in Calcutta – the City of Joy. Bengali poetry and Marxist politics and Victorian architecture; cricket on the Maiden among the dwindled flocks of displaced goatherds. Tiffin at the stock market, human rickshaws, backstreet government ganja shops. Rickshaw drivers running barefoot through the city, dodging between lorries and taxis and men pulling carts – plump ladies to the sari shop, pinafored schoolgirls delivered safely home. Their skin-cracked feet poke through weatherworn hoods at night.

Romany's postcard says there's an iron staircase in Sudder Street, left behind when a building collapsed. The rickshaw drivers' chai stall underneath it, a small fire lit in an alcove; the spiral winds into the sky – they call it the Stairway to Heaven, pin their dreams on rising there step by step.

Down the road from here is a taxi drivers' garage with a tea van and pile of thumbed-through sports pages, boys squatting outside with buckets of foamy water. What are their dreams? I wonder. And for one blissful moment I, too, swell with pride for my sister, out there, living her dream.

The postman; four letters. All for me.

One from Vaz, sealed with blotches of candle wax.

One from Adrian, neatly printed. Prison number in the left-hand corner.

One from Jack, updating me on the wildcats.

And one from Romany. From Calcutta.

Three blokes and my sister. Even Dad looks a bit miffed over breakfast.

'Romany's got her act together at last,' says Dad. 'Who are all those others from?'

'Jack,' I say. 'And just some other people.'

I tap my nose. Dad raises his eyebrows. Mum rustles the paper and musters a weak smile. Nice try, Mother.

Dear Kate,
Thanks for your letter. It did snow here, only for half

an hour and it's thanks to you that I noticed. I was reading in my bender and realized that the rain outside had quietened, the air was more chilled and I thought *snow* . . . poked my head out and there it was, soft and cold. So thanks for that. No one on site believed me – Nah, man, they said. You've been dreaming.

Apart from that it's done nothing but rain. We've moved uphill twice already this winter, but still have to put planks between the benders and vans – the vehicles are bogged till spring. Sometimes it feels like the whole of Wales is going under.

I don't know what to say about you losing your sister. But if you've had that closeness once you can have it again. Don't be lonely, Kate.

Your friend,
Vaz

Rain needles at my window. I'm working at home today and Mum is, too, downstairs, fingers tapping out a stream of letters and reports and pleas for funding, frowning over how best to word them. We just *need* this money, OK? Hutu and Zulu pick their way around the garden, lifting and shaking paws; birds land on the lawn and sink up to their feathers. I think of Vaz huddled around his stove and Adrian inside his cell. He'll have lost touch with weather, with colour and light, wet and dry. We're not meant to live like that, but we do, don't we? We adapt.

Dad puts his wellies on to go and check the workshop. Two inches of water – he mouths up to me – two inches! We're going to have to buy sandbags, check out the cellar. He looks quite excited; man against the elements. Even here where the earth is subdued with tarmac and brick and concrete.

Adrian's letter includes a visiting order. That'd give mum

a jolt, if I suddenly went off to Shropshire. But I – Kate, the lady detective – need to find out more: there has to be a clue, in his letter or something Ty's said. *I knew Ty wouldn't forget about me*, says Adrian. So, Ty used to visit, feels obliged. I find the right books, *Sherlock Holmes*, *V.I. Warshawski*; imagine myself at a desk, behind frosted glass, a nameplate on the door.

By lunchtime I've got a plan. One: stay friends with Adrian, he has to trust me. Two: find out about prison life – I've had a brainwave on that one: Frieda. She was locked up for a few months once; arrested at Greenham Common. Mum went to visit, came back with her skin drawn tight across her cheeks. Three: investigate Ty.

Mum's head slides around the door. Her eyes land on Romany's unopened letter.

'Here,' I say, 'thought you might like to open it.'

'Oh no. I couldn't do that. It's for you.'

'I'll read it out loud then,' I say.

Below us Dad sloshes around the garden checking his wattle-fencing and sorry solar panels. The sky is clearing, ice blue in the distance, but we are warm and dry; the radiator pulses below us. It reminds both of us – I can tell by Mum's wistful eyes – of when I was little and we'd curl up here with storybooks. As soon as I could read I'd insist that I tell the story; I'd read to her of talking cats and frog-princes and wicked witches. My girlish voice chirping out *Once Upon A Time*, then stumbling over 'rectory' or 'whisper' or 'famished'. Catching the drift of the story and adding bits of my own; Mum leaning back on the cushions saying, 'I don't remember it ending like that, love.' I had an aversion to happy endings – would throw the royal family, princess and all, into the pit with the snakes; let the Ice Queen freeze everyone into statues with heads of icy hair.

I can do the same now with Romany's letter. She's giving me permission. But I just start reading.

Dear Kate,

First thing at Modern Lodge, Sudder Street, Calcutta. I'm up on the roof drinking chai with the porter, who warms his hands on the glass. We talk about families. He's blessed with boys but hints that his baby daughter moves him most. That's what it's like here, strangers open up to you. A man poorer than the scurfiest tramp that ever stalked the Soho Road. He's wearing sandals left behind by a tourist, the soles too thin for western feet. But he smiles with me in the smoky damp of Calcutta and gives thanks for his daughter and his chai.

I love it here. Not all twitchy excitement like Bombay or the lazy-haze of Goa, but deeply, clearly. Queen Victoria and Mother Teresa had it right, coming here, nuns from Ireland or Spain still do, they never leave; spend their whole lives with the street people of Calcutta. Ty's off visiting monuments and churches and temples but I've hardly left the street – I don't need to. He comes back dusty and weary and we fight to tell our stories first, hot with the life of this place.

Yes, we're still crazy about each other, but it's better if anything. It's OK to be apart now, say ta-ra. Every day like an all-you-can-eat buffet to pick and choose from, knowing the table will be full again tomorrow. I pinch myself every morning. What could be better than this?

Gypsies live on Sudder Street. The children are out already, playing with bits of wire and string; chanting Bengali rhymes and chasing each other up the street. I can see the recess in the wall near the stairway where the dope dealer lives – he has a picture of Shiva and a cloth-wrapped chillum for a pillow. Hawkers, rickshaw wallahs, business ladies running bookstalls, barbers with cut-throat razors, street kids screeching under a tap which rarely works. A grave Anglo-Indian gentleman takes chai and watches everything, grabs kids as they dash past, inspecting their burns and cuts, their claggy eyes and sticky-out ribs. 'When did you last eat?' he says, passing his rice to a boy. 'Go to Miss Arman's and get some drops for your eyes. Tell her I sent you. Go on. Go!' He pushes the boy roughly; all his anger and love in that shove. Tears fall out of my eyes – my tap turned on now. 'Excuse me, miss, but do not cry for us,' he says, sitting up straight, adjusting his collar. 'I'm not,' I say. And I tell him about life on the streets in England, being chased from kitchens where they throw away food, swept up by the council men who clear the streets of more than rubbish. He listens. When I've finished he pours me tea and considers his answer. 'Yes,' he says, eventually. 'But that is England, not my Bharat.'

Bharat is India. India is here. I'm here and you're in Birmingham, but we'll always be joined, Kate; a cord twists between us no matter how far I go. Ty thinks of you, too. 'Do you think Kate's OK?' he says. 'I hope she's OK without us.'

Anyway. The sun's up, the city's noise building, honks and shouts and the twang of a guitar from a nearby roof. The Japanese hippies are up – they all look like Yoko Ono, even the blokes. Ty's up – time for breakfast.

Until later,
Romany xxxxx

Mum's head is on my shoulder. It's even darker outside – clouds mustering.

'I didn't say anything,' Mum says. 'I was going to but I didn't.'

She clutches my hand. 'Honestly, Kate, I don't know where he's got that from . . . because you are OK, aren't you, darling?' She pats my thigh, hand and eyes lingering there.

They've got a cheek, the lot of them. A flare of anger which isn't Romany's or Ty's or even mum's. It's mine.

A corner of Adrian's letter is poking from under my piles of books and papers. For a second I swear it glows, greenish, then fades to paper white as the trees' skeletons fade into the night and a rattle of hail crashes on to the window.

9

Romany's been in prison. Well, not exactly; police cells, tea and a blanket, social workers for breakfast. 'Remember that time I was in London and they locked me up for begging outside Buck House,' she'd say, as if I'd been there with her. 'The old bill weren't too bad, considering. There was me, skinny and starving, no place to go and they've got that fuck-off great mansion.'

I wish I'd asked her more about it. Did she wake up in the night thinking, shit, I want out?

There were nights like that, but not in prison. And it wasn't one of the stories she told to shock, to make sure no one would forget Romany Jackson. She had to tell me – Sonny, her scary ex-boyfriend had appeared at the school gates and tried to follow us home.

Romany stiffened at the sight of him.

'He mustn't know where we live,' said Romany. 'He mustn't find out about the house.'

There was no shaking him off, so she had to go and talk to him. I watched from a distance, his finger jabbing the air around her head, his body moving backwards and for-wards. Romany stood firm – I sensed a quiver deep down inside her, but he missed it and in the end he turned and left; scowling, throwing glances over his shoulder like spit.

We cut down an alley, along the canal towpath. Didn't hit a proper road again until we were nearly home.

'He's not following us, is he?' I said.

'Nah,' she said. 'I've sent him packing. He won't be back.'

But I always worried about Sonny, especially after she told me about being locked in that house. Alone for four days and four nights, wrenching at the boarded-up window. Terror; that was the memory which had made her quiver. Sonny lost his nous, she said, which is as bad as it gets when all you've got to live on are your wits. Even the worst alkies and junkies still keep some instinct, she said, a nose for the way out. But Sonny owed money to the wrong people and when his time was up they took her. Four days, she spat; he left me there for four days. In this country *anyone* can get money quicker than that.

I think about writing to Romany to ask what it was like inside. But she'd talk to Ty and he'd know why I was asking. There's a secret underneath this love of theirs and to uncover it I need to be cautious – devious even. I don't need tactics with Frieda though; just ring her up and tell her I'm studying the women's protest movement and off she goes.

'How marvellous,' she says. 'When I was at school all they taught us was kings and queens, and even then they didn't say which ones went mad or took opium or slept with the servants.'

I get a potted history, then a string of anecdotes, snatches of song and wistful rememberings before we get anywhere near her prison experiences.

'God, we tried hard to corrupt those American soldiers,' she says. 'They must've been giving them bromide for breakfast, dinner and tea.'

'Maybe they just didn't fancy you, Frieda,' I say, and she roars for a good minute or so.

'Good point,' she says. 'All those wet cagoules and smoky dreadlocks, hardly standard erotica I suppose. Your

74

mother was the only one who managed to look glamorous, God knows how.'

I ask about the suffragettes on hunger strike in prison and slowly wind the conversation around to what it was like inside.

'It wasn't too bad for me,' she says. 'All the Greenham women were on the same corridor and we just kept singing. The sound of those voices rising up through the prison . . .' She'll be staring out of the window, at the vast spread of sea and land around her.

'Is the wind blowing tonight?' I say. 'The wist?'

Frieda is quiet for a moment. 'How odd you should ask that,' she says. 'I first heard that sound in prison. I was woken in the night; gurgling pipes, grunts, groans, scratching that might have been rats. And something else – a distant whine, low and strangely pitched, seeping through walls and floors and locked doors.'

The telephone line crackles. A clock ticks behind me, the soft thud of a cat dropping off a chair. I can hear Star's tail brushing the wooden floor over at Frieda's; she must be fussing him, muzzle nuzzling up underneath her hand.

'And that's the same noise that you hear now?' I say. 'Under the house, when the wind blows off the land?'

'Yes,' says Frieda.

'Doesn't it bother you?'

'It reminds me,' says Frieda. 'No harm in that.'

She never found out who was keening. A mother separated from her children, perhaps. Or maybe a murderer's lament of regret, of longing to change the unchangeable. The sound of loss. 'A noise that's in all of us,' says Frieda, 'even if you don't want to hear it.'

'So you go and live on top of it,' I say. 'I call that masochistic.'

Frieda laughs. 'I call it realistic, Katie dear. Just so you don't get taken by surprise.'

We chat a bit more. She invites me to come and stay. 'I will,' I say.

'You do that,' says Frieda. 'And good luck with the project.'

'Huh?'

'See you soon, Kate,' says Frieda. 'Take care now.'

I tell Mum that I've been invited to Frieda's and her eyes lift, unforced. 'Now I hate to nag,' she says, 'but it's high time you went into college. And please, no more of that nonsense about reading weeks.'

'I've been out,' I say, watching for her reactions, muscle movements under her skin.

'Yes,' she says. 'But not to *college*.'

'But I can work here.' I'm whining – we both hate it; wish we could communicate without these fractured sounds.

'Kate, I'm just not having all this again.'

She hates her voice like this, too – harsh, hectoring. But we both understand – that despite our truce over Romany's letter I've got to go into college.

Actually, I'd already decided to go. There's someone from Ty's hometown there, I'd know his face. Out of the window the trees puff and billow, traffic grinds for miles around and I brace myself to deal with all that slipperiness and greasiness and rush. Keep focused. Find Ty's friend, pacify Mum. If that's not enough, think about waking in the night knowing you *can't* get out. That should do it; get me to college and back.

I'm resolved. I lie in bed and picture resolve as an iron bar, the next rung on a ladder, my fingers curled around it, then fall into sleep thinking of Frieda at Greenham, sitting round the fire singing as soldiers pace the perimeter fence, rifles clicking on their bullet belts.

I was born a big strong woman
And you just can't take my dreams away.

Morning. Outside. The mist clings to the frost on the ground. Rush hour; exhaust fumes turning the fog yellow. Headlamps blurred then suddenly blinding, buses lumbering, icy patches on the pavement, overflowing drains, people stumbling, shoving, pulling up their collars, hands up in their armpits. I try to imagine a similar street in Calcutta, but can't conjure it up amid the chill. For that I need to be on my window seat, my magic carpet, with the radiator beneath me warming my imagination. Jesus, Mother. What you put me through.

At college it's a little better. I spend a few hours in the library and then head to the office to hand in work, pick up essays and nod and smile as the secretaries chat at me. I make an appointment with my tutor for later, then sit in the bar with a stack of Bengali poetry to hide behind. It's Friday; everyone's supposed to come in for tutorials. The bar is mobbed with lookalike blokes in logo-ed sweat-shirts and baggy combats, I check every face – Detective Kate is nothing if not thorough – but nothing. So, a different tack, the college admin department; I'll think of some reason to ask. But first I need to pacify my tutor.

'Kate! How nice to see you.'

'Hi. Did you get the work I handed in because if everything's all right I'm in a bit of a rush.'

'Yes. Your work is fine. We haven't seen you for ages though, are you OK?'

'I'm fine,' I say. Back off, I'm thinking. Off my land.

'Are you sure?' He doesn't know how to handle me. Good.

'I'm fine.' I nod at my essays. 'Shall we?' I say.

'Oh yes,' says the woman in the English department office, 'I remember Ty. Went off travelling – such restless souls, you youngsters. My daughter's just the same, postcards from Malaysia and the Philippines and no plans to come back. If we get any grandchildren at all they'll probably be born in Tibet.'

'He's travelling with my sister actually.'

'Well, you know how it is then.'

She doesn't remember his friend so well, but tracks down an address. 'Richard Aston, that's him. Comes from the same area as Ty, I try to keep the records up to date. You wouldn't believe how many parents ring me about their children; not writing, not phoning. It's terrible. I tell them all to give their other kids pagers when they leave home. Richard went on to study journalism apparently. So *his* parents can look forward to reports from a war zone.'

'Is your daughter enjoying her travels?' I say, out of politeness more than anything, but it seems to touch a nerve.

'That's the oddest thing,' she says. 'Half the time it seems like she's struggling; if she came home she'd soon get a job, get herself started. But she doesn't seem to want that.'

'No,' I say. 'Neither does Romany.'

Mount Street. The corner house three doors down with the rounded tower – Rapunzel lives there, me and Romany thought, or a wise recluse, protecting us with prayers in foreign languages – then our house, there behind the still-frosted trees. Romany knew immediately that this house is special – no one has died or been murdered or lived a diminished, melancholy life here. Mum says that's why they moved in, even though it was ramshackle, on a busy road in a run-down area.

I've only come from college – a bus ride and couple of road crossings, but feel as if I've trekked over the tundra, dropped down crevasses and hauled myself back up solo, fist-by-fist up the rope. But I've done it. She owes me.

'Hi, sweetie, good day?'

'Not bad. Tons more work to do.'

'See anyone you know?'

'Yeah, a couple of people.' My tutor anyway.

'That's nice.'

'How about you?'

Mum's head jolts; she moves it further round as if she's heard an unexpected noise, but I'm not fooled. I know she's surprised at me asking. 'Good. Really good actually. Lots of work on the literacy initiative. I've got to do a presentation to potential sponsors. We could really get something done this time if only we had more money. It's so frustrating to have to go cap in hand time and time again but . . .' She's felt my concentration shift. 'Anyway, you know the story. Here – second post.'

Second post. I hadn't even thought about it. Too distracted by investigations, journeying.

Dear Kate,

God, how I wish you were here or that I was there or that we could both be in both places at once. We make these choices without knowing where they'll lead, don't we?

Still in Calcutta. Still in Sudder Street. Still in love. Is it OK for me to write this? I need to see you to know for sure. Remember us at school – sticking fingers down our throats when yet another girl went starry-eyed? Well, that's me right now; starry-eyed, starry-faced. Everyone on Sudder Street calls me *Shurjo bon* – the sunny girl – street barbers, camped-out villagers, beggars, posh ladies taking tea at the Tollygunge. It does so much good, this love. Ty does me so much good.

So, I can't brush this off – *yeah, we get on OK, he's an OK geezer* – I want to share it. Ty really listens to me, Kate. How can I not love him when he listens too?

79

I'm not blind though. India is full of struggling couples from the West: weary and ratty and confused. They stare at us and the silence between them seeps into any gap, any crack. I see it, want to stretch out this time when nothing can touch us. Ty's grown into his skin here; on and on about trekking up roadless valleys, digging snow-holes up above the clouds. He has this calmness around him – tourists ask about trains and black market exchange rates and the Indians treat him like a holy man. I just want to eat him all up, a greedy kid who's found a house made of sweets.

We can be who we like out here. You step on that plane and out of your life. It makes me leap inside that it's possible, that I've had the chance. A new country and a new life. A miracle, a magical thing. You understand what that means, Kate, don't you. No question mark. It's there for you too.

Love,
R xxx

10

'So where are they, then?' says Dad after work one day. 'It's like they got to Calcutta and hit a great big stop sign.'

The map of India is on the wall, lengths of string straddling the continent. It's alive for me; the hills bulge up in relief and snowy plateaus are icy to the touch. 'Ty's talking about trekking,' I say. 'Wants to do the full hero bit, come back missing a toe or two.'

'Like Romany,' says Mum.

'Well, I can't see *her* going up any mountains,' says Dad. 'Remember when we went to Scotland? Had to prise her out of the car to get on that horse.'

'Bribe her, you mean.'

'She's not the wild country type by any stretch.'

That horse ride was the only time in my life when I've travelled faster than Romany. Her horse had its own agenda while mine trotted obediently. Romany sulked and grumbled while I cantered across the moor; the easy lollop of movement awakening my senses, purpling the heather and frosting the tumbling brooks.

'Get yours to run,' I shouted back at Romany.

'What the hell for?' she screeched. 'I'll be sleeping on my belly for a week as it is.'

Fingers of sunshine dropped over the ridge above me and wavered over the landscape. Yellow gorse turned to drops of gold, heather to opal fields and the brooks to streams of liquid silver. For a second we all forgot everything – even Romany her sore arse – and pulled up short to stretch the moment.

'Maybe she'll stay in the city while he goes off,' I say.

'I don't like the sound of that,' says Mum.

I stare at the map. One cartoon camel becomes a train, baring their teeth and flicking their outrageous eyelashes; brown dolphins leap out of the Ganges-which-is-Shiva's-hair. Mum and Dad are bickering quietly about work – she's taking on too much; no, *he* is, he's never here, that's the problem. I drift. The Taj Mahal, a mausoleum to perfect love, frozen in time for ever. Could I ever stir such longing? I think. All very well for *her* to say it's there for me too. Where? I banish the thought and let the image of the Taj float out of the map like it does over the sleepy Yamuna River.

The phone rings. Mum looks up from her papers, snaps a file shut and stalks off to answer it. I should lay the table, I think, but I don't – back to the map instead: prayer flags in the Himalayas, tigers prowling the foothills. Dad turns over the page of his newspaper, glances at the oven door – baked potatoes just about done, we can smell their crisp skins rubbed with butter and salt. We realize together.

'Something's happened.' Dad's on his way into the hall. I follow. Mum's on the bottom step of the stairs, fingers threaded into her hair.

'What is it, love?' says Dad.

'Not Romany . . .' I say.

Mum lifts her head, drops it down again. She's paler than the air. She moves back into the kitchen, steadying herself on the wall.

'Jenny, what is it?' says Dad. 'That bloody place'll finish you off one of these days.' She stares into the blackness of the window. I'm thinking: What? Who?

'Someone's died,' she says.

'Who?' I say. A coarse grey hair springs from Dad's head, caught in a swirl of heat from the stove. I look at Mum's back, her heels worn down, her ankle twisting to one side.

'Kate,' she says, talking to the blackness. 'Katie, Tom's dead.' Her ankle slips and she collapses sideways. I grip on to the table but it doesn't stop me lurching too, all of us violently jolted. No, I think. *No no no.*

In the oven, baked potatoes turn to charcoal.

*

Dear Vaz,
I've got something to tell you.

You'd think by now we'd have found ways of doing this; ground preparation, rituals. All we manage, though, is: I think you'd better sit down.

Are you sitting down, Vaz? Because Tom is dead.

He was found in a stairwell by a prostitute and her punter. 'The poor lass,' my mum kept sobbing, 'imagine finding a dead body.' A blow to his head, his legs slashed up, slumped by the rubbish chute with the dirty nappies and food-smeared wrappers. What's that all about, Vaz? I mean, what could Tom have done to deserve that?

Romany would say, 'Anything, nothing.' But what did his killer think, leaving him there bleeding? Did he think at all?

I guess Tom strayed into something, refused to leave it be. And for that someone took away his life.

Romany's favourite Tom story – he'd joined some road protesters squatting a condemned house and the bulldozers were due. They had a party out in the street, the demolition ball thwacking down the terrace behind them. Tom in his stripy clown trousers – the joker, the fool; the one who's allowed to cross boundaries. He'd painted a target, concentric circles, on the back of his shirt, with a suckered arrow on the bull's-eye. They made a cake for an old lady who'd lived in the street all her life, candles and everything; Tom making her laugh while metal blasted through her emptied home.

There's nothing else to say. Except how to go on?

Yours in sorrow,

Kate.

'I'm going vegetarian,' I say, the next day at breakfast; meat looks too much like flesh, like blood. Mum snatches my bacon sandwich, pulls it apart, chucks the bacon in the bin and hands me back the bread, before slamming out of the house. I don't eat it. The house is cold, ice creeping through it in the night.

'I'll write to Romany,' says Dad.

The post comes and there's another VO from Adrian – please come, he says. You've no idea how much a friendly face can do for a bloke in here. But I can't be bothered with him now; he's safely locked up, well out of it. The mystery over Ty seems trivial. Mum is out there trying to find out what happened to Tom – the police called one of her colleagues. Maybe she'll arrange the funeral, phone a woman in Telford who once had a son called Tom. Or ask the police to do it, a knock on the door and a WPC saying, 'I think you'd better sit down . . .'

Dad comes up to my room looking grey. He climbs onto the window seat with me, puts a blanket around our shoulders.

'Nasty cold snap,' he says. 'Your mother shouldn't be out.' He hugs me until it hurts, my fingers digging into his thigh and curling inwards.

Later, Frieda arrives. She practically spoon-feeds the three of us, sits up all night with Mum while I lie brutally conscious, stroking the cats, jealous of their peaceful sleep.

Frieda stays a week, sends Dad back to work, puts me in charge of cooking and cleaning: it's Mum she's most worried about. My role as the family problem eclipsed by Mum's terrible insomnia, her sudden frailty, her indifference to what's going on. What I would have given for that a month ago.

Romany said that. You always get what you want. Trouble is you can't choose when.

Or how.

Tom is dead.

*

Mum and Dad first met at a dance. I've always liked the story, Romany did too. We used to replay it – her as a youthful Dad spinning me around the bedroom dance floor. Everyone wants their parents to have a true love story, I suppose; we were thrilled and a little awed by the thought of it. Mum, twenty; a dedicated nurse, living at home and caring for her invalid ex-Services, ex-clergy father. Dad, a wild-haired student portering at the hospital; glimpses of her in the corridor, lingering as long as he dared on her ward. A Christmas dance was his chance to make a move – we made up a routine to tell the story. *At the Christmas dance, he took his chance; while the records spun, her heart was won.* And, fuelled by the half bottle of Scotch he'd sunk while practising charming looks in the mirror, he gathered enough courage to coax her away from her friends, take her eyes off the doctors and actually look at him. There was a moment – a gulp in their chests, Dad said – and they moved out to dance, barely touching the floor.

'Gulp,' said Romany, as we collapsed in hysterics. 'Gulp, gulp.'

Mum thought their engagement would cause problems. Her father believed in good works, duty; and here was

Dad, billowing with outrage at injustice and poverty, his conversation peppered with slogans, walking into their plain little house as Grandad folded his fingers over his Bible. 'Be respectful,' she said. 'And don't break anything.' So Dad sat drinking tea, cup rattling on saucer, expecting it to leap out of his hands and ruin his chance of happiness.

Actually Grandad quite liked him. 'Glad you've found a man who wants to *do* something about the world,' he said, apparently. 'He'd better tidy himself up for the wedding, though.' Mum said if she'd known it was going to be that easy she'd have got herself a boyfriend years ago. She was already pregnant with me – conceived at a socialist study weekend, the story goes, which made Romany howl. More like a socialist sex weekend, she said. Grandad performed the ceremony, too. They bought the house in Mount Street for next to nothing – it was 1976 and no one wanted to invest in Handsworth; there were council grants to do it up. Dad got a job at Braxton's on the condition that he cut his hair. Then I was born – a perfect baby – and they sat in the sunny kitchen stunned by their good fortune in contrast to the damp, dark squats of their friends.

Romany and me used to pester them about their marriage. Picking at the seams to see if there was some simple piece of magic we could expose and steal.

'You're born cynics, the pair of you,' Dad said. 'Who'd have thought disillusionment could come so young.'

Mum's eyes brimmed. She refused to be cynical; said it was lazy, defeatist. She believed in change and progress. What was the point otherwise? There had to be a point, even if she wasn't so sure about God any more. Inconceivable that it's all random. So Tom's slashed-up body in a stairwell – the boy who pushed boundaries, inspired change *and* protected her daughters – there had to be a point to that as well. 'Huh? A point to that?' we all say. Even Frieda can't find one. No wonder my mum's depressed.

Romany and I decided the dance was the point. That first dance, their feet tapping out neat circles and their bodies leaning back; a twirling figure-of-eight joined in the middle by their crossed hands.

But Romany doesn't know about Tom.

Mum stays in her room watching puddles form outside – the frost has gone but the ground is sodden, nowhere for the water to run. The funeral is later today. No one is coming from Telford. He died for them years ago – someone even said that – and that got me right in the guts because if there was one thing that Tom never did it was give up on a person.

'Mum . . .' I say, approaching tentatively – like she used to with me, scared I would snap, or withdraw, curl up like a snail into my shell. 'Mum . . .'

She turns, scarily grey, her skin like ash. 'Yes, love,' she says mechanically.

'Tom had his dances, you know.'

'It's not enough, Kate. Nowhere fucking near.'

A letter arrives from Romany – heartbreakingly joyous – and we can hardly bear to read it. Processions of papier-mâché gods, gargoyle-eyed, elephant-nosed; Mahakali with her girdle of severed arms. The heat, the early morning markets, milky dawns and days when the haze never lifts. Ty striding around the roof of the lodge quoting the *Ramayana* – India's landscape carved by that love story. And down on the streets men sell their kidneys and offer rice to insatiable gods. It's crossroads international here, Romany says, people turn up from Japan and Australia and Nepal and Burma and they all end up on our roof clutching cups of chai, exhausted and thrilled and disturbed. Yet there're plenty who arrived years back, for a short visit; now they eat curd for breakfast and sometimes buy a month-old English newspaper. Dutch guys and

English girls, as much part of the street furniture as the pavement barbers and legless beggars.

Mum starts. 'You don't think that could happen to Romany, do you?' she says. There's an airless moment, the second hand on the clock clicks but doesn't move.

'What? Getting stuck in Calcutta?' says Dad.

'Of course,' says Mum. She wrenches the fridge door open and a milk bottle topples out, splatters across the floor. 'What the hell else did you think I meant?'

A beam of sunlight hits the garden lawn, the grass translucent green for a second. Then it's gone, blotted by a cloud; impossible to imagine the brightness was just there.

Frieda stays with us until the funeral; gets us into the long dark car behind the other long dark car where Tom is. We've all refused to wear black – he never liked the colour, was with Romany on that one. I think of her in the street in Calcutta, mixed in with the acid greens, yellows, the kids with shiny bangles and sparkly dresses, and I am suddenly doubled up with grief, like a punch in the stomach.

'I can't do it,' I mouth to Frieda. 'If he'd gone, if he'd gone with her . . .'

'Shussh,' says Frieda. 'Nothing to be done about that now.'

Mum and Dad's heads twitch when this shocking fact reaches them. Dad is crying and I wish hard that Mum would, too. I worry about the wording on the gravestone we've chosen: *Tom Coley, 21 June 1973–31 January 1997. Rest in Peace*. That this is all that's left of him, and it's nowhere near enough, not even with the dances.

The church is one I used to go to with school; harvest festivals, Christmas carols. We couldn't think of anywhere else; even Mum hasn't been to church in years and Grandad never had a parish of his own. The vicar greets us at the lychgate. There's a pub over the road where Romany and I used to go; a few shifting figures are hanging around in the doorway. They come over and we clutch each other's hands.

'We tried to get the word around,' says a girl with a base-ball cap hiding half of her face. We exchange condolences clumsily, the words heavy on our tongues, then move into the church, squeezing water from the soggy graveside verges with the weight of our bodies.

In my head I'm writing to Romany. *Mum's so sad, why has this hit her so hard? We're all so used to her coping.* But I know, really. Tom's death is the trigger. I stare at the tapestry-stitched kneelers, the vicar's voice washes past my ears, light falls through stained glass – St Francis, birds resting on his outstretched arms. We're all awkward here: my family, Tom's street friends, the social workers and bureaucrats who failed him. I wish I was brave enough to say something about his life and who he was, but that's Romany's job and she's in Calcutta, in love. I try not to feel it too hard, too much, in case it all hits her in the face in the middle of her journey, as she's strolling down the sunny side of the street halfway across the world. Perhaps it already has.

Afterwards we all want liquor. Hard liquor, hard and fast. I swig brandy. More of Tom's friends come in the pub wearing borrowed jackets, shoes, hats which they take off and twist in their hands; the busker Crow; others, their faces taut with shock. Dad puts some money behind the bar and the landlord lets us all stay. Rumours buzz around the bar but no one really knows how it happened: he'd been out of town, kept his movements to himself. I think he might have liked that; independent, no need for company, not pulled to stay in one place. Free at last.

'He's free at last,' I say, lolling in my chair. Brandy slops out of my glass and I watch it soak into the fabric on my leg.

11

Richard Aston takes a moment to recognize me. 'Er, hi,' he says. 'You're Ty's friend, aren't you?'

'Yeah . . . Kate – sorry about turning up like this, but I really need to talk to you.'

'Has something happened to Ty?'

'No. Nothing like that.'

'Come in. Kettle's just boiled.'

I'm here because Dad made it clear the morning after the funeral that I had to get out of that door and leave my mother in peace. I'm numb, my movements jerky and un-coordinated, but moving's no worse than staying in, now. We can't find out what happened to Tom – there are no answers – but I can try and clear up one mystery, as if that might help, somehow.

The flat is in a tower block in Highgate; sparse and studentish: scraps of carpet not quite covering the lino, piles of books, and a mattress in the corner. The view is great, so high up above the streets that sounds are dimmed and people look tiny and angular.

'Good, isn't it?' says Richard, seeing me staring out of the window at the roads dipping and curving below. 'Are you OK?'

'What? Oh yes. Thanks.'

'Why don't you tell me about Ty?' he says.

'He's asked me to befriend someone called Adrian,' I say,

watching his face for changes. 'He's in prison somewhere in Shropshire.'

'Prison?'

'That's what I thought,' I say.

I tell him the whole story. Ty and Romany going travelling, the letters, the phone call from Ty's mum, the love-bubble, then the sly request from Ty to me.

'That's when I realized we don't know much about him,' I say.

'Hasn't your sister said anything?'

'No. Everything out there's strange, I guess it's quite easy to hide bits of yourself. And Romany . . . she's so made up to have a bloke who cares about her that I doubt she's even noticed. He seems genuine, doesn't he?'

Richard doesn't know Ty that well, they're from different villages, but he knows the area, the shape of the land where Ty grew up. 'I miss it when I'm here,' he says. 'Me and Ty both did – the moors, forests and empty spaces. On a sunny day it's the best place on earth: light and sea and hills rolling off into the distance.'

'Do you know the story of Ty's dad?' I say.

'Yes. I remember him running up and down the touchline at football matches, clapping his gloves together. *Go on, Ty, go.*'

'Ty used to play football?' For some reason I'm surprised.

'All the boys did. Sunday mornings – bloody freezing it was.'

'Was there anyone called Adrian?'

'Could've been. It was a big school, kids from miles around travelled in.'

'Was there anyone else he was close to?'

'I don't know. After his dad died he hung out down at the coast. My grandad always said he couldn't face the hills any more. I went to another college to do my A levels; hadn't seen him for a couple of years until we both came here.'

91

Dead end.

'You'll have to go up there,' says Richard. 'That's what us journos are told – chase your story.'

'It's the truth I want, not a story.'

I kind of knew this – that I'd have to go and find Ty's mum to discover what's really going on – and I do have an invite to Jack's, but the thought of travelling all that way . . . no. Not yet.

The only thing that's moving in our house right now is the water level in the cellar – from the thaw, Dad says. Mum is mechanical, her mouth tight. Dad's quiet; even the cats creep about, mewing silently. No news from Romany or Ty – they might not even know about Tom, although Dad sent his letter straight to the hotel in Sudder Street. I write letters and read without interruption – bliss, before Tom died. But now it's strange and lonely.

I try to reach Romany by talking to her charcoal eyes. *Romany, how can I tell you that Tom's dead?* I can't write it down, my pen won't make those shapes, but it's ages before it dawns on me that this might not be to do with Tom. I never find it hard to talk to Romany, even in my meanest moments I'd rather have her than him. Our connection's been tested, sure, but not broken, not up till now anyway. I look in the mirror, try to see her face – at a chai stall or slicing a watermelon for the street kids, but nothing. She's not there. *Shit.*

Dad's staring at sheets of paper, scalp visible through his hair. 'Dad?' I say. 'Do you think Romany and Ty are still in Calcutta? You did send her your email address, didn't you?'

'They'd have let us know if they were moving, chick.'

'I keep trying to write but can't find the words.'

'Sometimes there just aren't any words.' He takes my hands, rubs my wrists with his thumbs.

'I wish I could see her.'

'We all do.'

And we sit; a quiet, sad tableau. Mum upstairs with the cats, her face runnelled by tears. Us curled together taking small comfort in the warmth of bodies, waiting for something to shift, dreading that this time might be the time that it doesn't.

Morning. A letter. Postmarked Pembrokeshire. Vaz: Tom's friend Vaz who lives in a field far away from the city, not a rotten stairwell in sight.

Dear Kate,

Thanks for letting me know about Tom. I'm sorry I missed the funeral. I went away and by the time I got back it was too late. Everyone here is grieving; we've lost one of our own.

I remember the first time I saw him, on a site somewhere in Wiltshire, all city clout, a crowd of kids round him like some modern-day Fagin. I hadn't long left home myself – my brother joined the convoy in the eighties, so it was always an option for me. I never dealt much with cities, but Tom, he could hold his own on a sink estate or up to his arse in mud – and snatch some magic out of it, too. Most people move in their own worlds, little fish in little ponds, but Tom was different, he was a big fish wherever he went. And now someone's cut him down.

I can't manage much more – can't find the words, you know how it is. But please still write to me Kate, Wales feels even lonelier now.

Take care of yourself.

Love,

Vaz.

*

93

'That's about right,' says Dad, when I show him the letter. He's just come up from the cellar, the chill follows him into the kitchen. 'Are you staying in today?'

'Yes.'

'Stick your nose down the cellar a couple of times, will you? Phone me if the water's still rising. It's an inch up on last night and now it's started to rain as well.'

'OK.'

'Don't forget, Kate.'

'I won't.'

I do, though. I go up to my room and start to write to Romany again, thinking what she'll do when she hears about Tom. Will the news bring her back home? Contract the elastic that stretches between us and propel her back here? I try to read but can't concentrate, lean my head on the cold glass of the window, press my nose and hands against it, squashing my flesh flat.

The doorbell rings and I ignore it at first, then realize with a jolt that it could be the second post and rush down. The postman is standing on the doorstep, writing a note. He passes me a letter.

'Can you sign for it?' he says, holding out his sheet of stickers and signatures. The letter is from India. Dad's kind handwriting to Romany Jackson, Modern Lodge, Sudder Street, Calcutta, India. I turn it over. On the back in neat, square letters: RETURN TO SENDER. R JACKSON CHECKED OUT – DESTINATION UNKNOWN.

There are stamps and squiggles and signatures all over the envelope. I turn it over and over in my hands. The postman's sheet appears under my nose.

'You have to sign for it, love,' he says. Rain splashes off him as he turns to leave. There's a sudden crack, high up in the house. I twist to look upwards, at the attic, but my leg cracks too, throwing me at the postman's sodden jacket. He pulls me towards the gate as beams creak and floorboards groan – like the whole house is about to come down on top of us. Then a rumble; lights go out, Hutu hares out of the door and up a tree, water roars down the stairs and out past us to join the river running down the street.

'Looks to me like you've got a flood on your hands,' says the postman.

Part 2

Romany

'Men go out into the void spaces of the world for various reasons.'
Sir Ernest Shackleton, *The Heart of the Antarctic*

12

I stir in my sleep and find Ty twitching next to me. We're sleeping on charpoys – wooden frames with rope laced across – and can't help rolling into each other; the rope stretches in the night so we wake with our hips and shoulders grazing the floor. I lie for a moment, watching him. There's a humming noise, *nee nee nee*, like batteries running down – mosquitoes – and I swat around my head, the little sods still about at dawn. We're right next to the river; this room's flooded for half the year and the walls are still damp so I suppose there're bound to be mozzies.

But I swat at nothing. The humming comes from between Ty's teeth. His eyes jump open and he bolts upright.

'What's the matter?' I say.

'Can't feel anything in my hand.' He's out of bed, tramping round the room, shaking his arms and legs.

'Bad dream?' I say and Ty stops, blows on his fingertips as if this might bring them back to life.

'This is all a bloody nightmare,' he says.

I can't be doing with that so I go outside. Whatever's happened we're still here, in the holy city, the sacred

Ganges flowing a few feet away from this terrace. My first dawn in Varanasi; people are moving down from the old town above us to bathe, pray, collect holy water in brass pots like they've done for thousands of years and will do for thousands more, hoping – believing – that this will protect them from fate. What else can you do? 'Shit happens,' I always said to Kate and she'd say, 'Tell me about it.' Here it's a way of life, part of the *dharma*, the wheel of existence. Your house is flooded, your crops ruined, your daughter lazy and your son a thug. So? A bad marriage, a sick child, a ruined business, a car accident. Pray; do your duty, grieve, soothe, but don't torment yourself with asking *why?*

A car accident.

When we left Calcutta – elbowing my way to the front of the Ladies queue, pleading for tickets – I wanted Ty to comfort me. On the train, rattling through the night across the continent, cool air through the glassless windows, I hoped he'd pull me into him and say, *It's OK, sweetheart, don't let it get to you.* But he just sat and twitched, grimaced, flung his clay chai cup onto the railway tracks where it shattered into the orange peel, gravel, puke and oily rubbish. We arrived here in the pitch dark; the cycle-rickshaw popping over the cobbles and turfing us out at the lodge, where an old woman guided us to our room. She pointed at the charpoy and left; I didn't want to let go of her hand.

Ty squints at me from the blackness of our room. There's something in his look – accusation, defence – which I'm not used to. I want to say it: 'What the *hell* have I done?' As if he'll suddenly crack. 'God, sorry Romany, it's just that . . .' and spill it all out; what's bothering him, all sorted and clear and ready to fall into my forgiving lap.

His flip-flops slap on the terrace. He stares at the river.

'What's up?' I say.

'Nothing.'

'Bullshit.'

'Leave it, Romany.'

'No,' I say. 'I won't.'

Ty drags his eyes away from the water and pulls on the T-shirt he's had slung over his shoulder. 'You should,' he says, before stalking off up the terrace and disappearing into the maze of alleys above the lodge.

Only two days ago we were strolling down Chowringhee, fingers linked, raising our arms for groups of schoolgirls, swerving to miss carts stacked with Gold Flake cigarettes, pan, chaat, mirrors and trinkets. Rickshaw wallahs lit their beedies from smouldering rope hanging from the corners of each cart, street boys snatched quick glances in the mirrors and smoothed down their hair. We stopped at the post office where the scribes and translators work. A postcard of a bridge over the cut at home had arrived from Kate; it made me want to tell the story of our meeting, our faces, *I could be you* – Ty's heard it a hundred times before, of course, but he still smiled. Then. Not sure if he would now.

What I need is Kate here. Now.

It's definitely the accident that's changed him. *Shit*, I think. *Shit shit shit* – aiming the words at the floor. A few more seconds in bed that morning and we'd have missed it; one more cup of chai under the Stairway to Heaven and it might have gone and fouled up someone else's life. If only we'd sidetracked into the market to buy dates and mangoes; let a sari salesman draw us into his harem of silks and then back out into the street where the accident's already history. Ty had talked about a trip out that day, to Diamond Harbour where the Hoogley turns south and flows to the sea. But we didn't go. There's plenty of time, we said, let's just stroll around again today, let it all just happen.

101

'. . . Er, er . . . hello.'

There's someone standing next to me. I wonder if he saw me, spitting *shit shit shit* into the dust.

'Hi,' I say.

'Fit to shit,' he blurts. 'Shit to flit.'

I look up. Western – English maybe, or Scandinavian, they always sound more English than us. Shoulders writhing, like a fish got caught in the net of his skin; his feet shifting and hopping as if he's got no shoes and the hot terrace slabs are burning him. A long neck, head wobbling, eyes trying to catch and hold mine.

'Yes. Shit,' I say. 'It happens. Too right.'

'Shitswearing,' he says. 'Wearingshit.'

'If you say so.'

'FuckmotherFUCK,' he says, and suddenly calms. 'Have you been to see the ghats yet?' he says. 'You must, whatever's gone on. I'm Dom. Dominic.'

'Romany.'

'Apologies for my outburst. It happens.'

'You're not wrong there.'

'So what's up with you?' He takes my arm. 'Come on. Walk. It's easier to talk when you're walking. We'll go along the ghats. I expect that's where your boyfriend's gone anyway.'

We step down to the Ganges, navigating from ghat to ghat. Dom moves smoothly now, over the crumbling brick-work of buildings long since slipped into the river, past carvings of cows and through narrow alleys blocked by water buffalo, herded by a squawking barefoot boy with a stick. I scurry to keep up with him, chipping chunks of flesh off my toes, hot blood sticking my feet to my flip-flops.

'Shit,' says Dom, when he sees them, and for a moment I think he might spasm again, brace myself for the torrent of words and the gawps from the pilgrims heading to Panchganga Ghat. A vein throbs in his neck, then wiggles down his throat, a quick shudder and he's with me again. 'Come on, you may as well wash those feet in the Ganges,' he says.

We find a space on the riverbank and sit watching boys dive from rickety platforms; women in saris wade out into the river, gold and green trains floating behind them. The children scrub and giggle and splash, the adults do puja and trickle holy water over their foreheads. My feet are in the water and, as the Ganges eats at the dried blood and washes it away, my story stutters out.

'My boyfriend and me . . . we were in Calcutta and . . . it's the first time we've really argued.'

'What happened?' says Dom.

'There was this accident. One of those mad city junctions; buses, cows, *tuk-tuks* piling in from all over the show. We were trying to cross the road and this beggar on a skateboard's at our feet, pulling at Ty's trousers. Something drops off a bike in the road – sugar cane I think – and the beggar dashes over to grab it, his big flat hands pushing the road from underneath him. This car's heading straight for him, three or four fat Hindi ladies chattering away inside. They swerve at the last minute, straight into a school kid with his nose in a book. Dead; just like that. He was right next to Ty: me, Ty, him. The life thumped out of him, a dribble of blood from his ear, gone.'

'And you argued about that?' says Dom. He touches me a couple of times, on the nose, the chin, and then tucks his hands away.

'We were frozen, a dead boy and these women tumbling out of the car. They were kissing his cheeks, wailing, beating their breasts. They'd made me laugh before it happened, all bustle and brightness and scandal – then they changed, sank to the ground, winded. I said to Ty, "Poor women" – and he turned on me. "What the fuck do you mean, poor women?" he said. "That boy is dead."'

I watch the Ganges wash my feet and remember the flint in Ty's voice. I'd protested – I didn't mean it like that – but Ty just pulled me away. *We're going*, he said. *We're out of here now*. Back to Sudder Street, throwing our stuff into rucksacks, over the Howrah Bridge to the station and out of there. No checking the post office for letters. No farewells to the rickshaw wallahs or homeless boys who fetched us oranges and cups of chai. Not even a backwards glance at Sudder Street, where I could have stayed for ever.

Dom and I are sitting so still a dog sniffs us. Packs of them live down here; gruesome tales of uncremated legs stolen from the burning ghats, pups swimming out to bloated bodies. Rowing boats drift past, their oars tapping the river's slick surface; behind us the sweep of temples, palaces and mosques crowds forward, leaning towards the holy water. Sandstone buildings climb out of the river and glint in the sun, and in front of us a white-clothed man breaks the surface of the water, clambers onto the pillar of an old temple, folds his legs beneath him to meditate. I stare at this magical place, hoping its spell might shift the shock that we – even we – end up scowling nastily at each other over cold chapatti.

'It's upset him then,' says Dom. 'The accident.'

'He won't talk about it. I was upset too, but there's more to it with him. He says I should leave it. "Just leave it, Romany," he says. Drives me mad when people do that.'

'If that's what he wants, then maybe you should.'

We walk up some steps, skirt round the edge of a castle, corners bulging with rounded towers. Dom points out landmarks – the Golden Temple and the Manikarnika Ghat, the most sacred in Varanasi. The ghats are crowded with flower sellers and pan wallahs, barbers with cut-throat razors, yogis in impossible tangles, their backs as straight as new shoots.

I'm scanning for Ty. It matters where he is now. When we

were in Calcutta he went off all the time, I never knew where, but we were happy then and everything was fine. Now there's a gap it nags at me. Dom stops to chat to another traveller; they fall into conversation, settling down to roll cigarettes and exchange news. I long for that – that easy chat with someone I trust – and look out over the river, to the flat salt pans on the far bank and think of Kate, and how far away she is from this, and the life I'm living now.

Another twinge inside, another gap. I twitch like Dom, like Ty.

I'm dozing in our room when he bursts in. For a moment I can't focus, a dream of being pulled, being torn, which enlarges into a memory of Mum and Dad at Mount Street standing on the upstairs landing, arguing.

'Romany, who the hell is that guy out there? He's just given me a mouthful even your street pals couldn't come up with.'

I sit up, the heat knocks me down again. 'Where've you been all day?'

'And then I called out to you and he starts going, "Romany Romany Romany, Rrr."'

'I've been looking for you. All day.'

'He's still at it now.'

'Why d'you have to walk off like that?'

'Why do you have to make friends with the local nutter?'

'He's not a nutter.'

'Looks like one to me.'

'Well, he's NOT.' I'm up now, right in Ty's face. We're yelling at each other, nose to nose. All around us the pilgrims' city is settling down to cook and eat and sleep. Wiping sticky fingers and folding sari cloths and hushing children, and I'm screaming at Ty. Snarling, baring our teeth. I can see down his throat. He snatches himself away.

'. . . Nutter stutter nutter stutter NOT a nutter NOT a flutter.' The words break through our silence.

'Who is he, Romany?'

I fumble for my baccy in the darkness. There's no electric in this room; we buy candles or sit outside in starlight, moonlight reflected in the Ganges.

'His name's Dom. He's OK. He has these kind of fits,' I say.

From outside: 'Who-is-he who-is-he who-is-he who-is-he.'

'And he repeats things. It stops after a while. Then he's just normal.' I pass Ty a cig, start rolling one for myself. 'God, I hate that word.'

Ty kicks the door open. Smoke curls out. Across the river a few small fires have been lit and again I think of Kate. I *must* write and tell her we've moved, about the accident, about Ty. The words won't come though, I tried earlier on. Can't explain things to her; haven't the faintest what's happening myself.

Ty is staring blankly out at the water. 'I was in town,' he says. 'Round the alleys of the old city. Got lost a few times, it's a bloody maze. You'll love it.'

I sit down, my blood still wired.

'There was this cremation on the burning ghat. Huge crowds. They put the body on top of this massive pyre and set it alight. Clouds of incense and smoke everywhere but you could see the body shape burning, turned over like a piece of meat by these guys with long sticks.'

I feel my heart beat again – he went for a wander, that's all. It's only now I realize that I thought he might have left.

'My dad got cremated,' says Ty. 'We never saw it, though. The coffin just disappeared behind a curtain. But it's the same thing that happened to him.'

I wrap my arms around him from behind, rest my head on his shoulder. His arm slides back around my waist and we stare at the river, smoke drifting above the perfectly round reflected moon.

'Full moon madness,' I say.

'Something like that,' says Ty.

'Tell me about your dad.'

Ty shrugs. 'He was just Dad. Tall, wiry, smelled of Old Spice. Good at mending things. If he had a few drinks he'd sing sea shanties – his dad was a sailor. I didn't really know him as a person.'

'Who does? Dads should be dads.'

The two-tiered bridge over the Ganges emerges out of the evening haze. Trains and trucks and cars, bringing more and more pilgrims and travellers here, to seek absolution in the holiest river in the world.

We wake at dawn, arms still wrapped around each other, except Ty has turned towards me now, his breath on my face. Yesterday seems like a bad dream, like we were pissed-up or something. There were mornings like this back on the streets in Brum; semi-conscious, trying to piece together what the hell had happened. The day fractured, like a smashed mirror, slivers of it frighteningly clear – half a sentence; a swift, vicious kick – but most of it wiped. I shudder at the memory. Here in India the homeless still have a life, a visibility at least; they pray to the same gods as the rich, cook out on the street, wash their clothes and string them up over alleyways.

Can you imagine it, Kate? Me lighting a fire for a brew in the middle of Digbeth or up the Soho Road, spreading wet T-shirts over someone's wall to dry? Tom used to do it. Back from the countryside with his tin pans and matches wrapped in plastic bags, find some bricks and kindling, start a fire. Warming up 5p tins of beans and toasting stale bread, his tea-stained mug tied to his coat. 'Proper tramp I am now,' he said. 'There's loads of places to sleep if you can handle being alone – sheds, garages, outbuildings. Got my kettle and my matches, people don't mind giving if they only see you twice a year.'

He was happy with his fire and his brew. When we first met him everyone called him the Buddha because of his bald head, even though he was raging then. Gnasher – that was his other nickname, because he growled and snapped, even at people he liked. But there was still something different about him from every other fuck-up on the street, even then, before he cleaned up and got serene. I hope Kate's still in touch with him; we'd be mental to lose someone like Tom.

'Rupee for them . . .' says Ty. His eyes are open, so close to mine that our lashes brush. 'Ten rupees.'

'I was thinking of Tom.'

'Kate'll stay in touch with him,' says Ty.

Yesterday's fractures are sinking from the surface, and we let them go, smoothed by our skins' soft friction. The heat of the day builds, the rope from the charpoy cuts into us as we sink into each other. I want to kiss him so long that our lips blister together. Like the yogis who hold an arm in the air for ten years at a time, or bury themselves up to their necks in packed sand. We'll stay this way for ever, untouchable.

'Romany, sweetheart, I can't breathe,' Ty gasps.

I fall backwards, laughing. Ty comes with me.

'I love you,' he says, tattooing the words on to the skin under my breast with tiny nips of his teeth.

*

Dear Kate,
Hi babe, soz for not writing for a while, we've had a bit of a weird time . . .

Dear Kate,
Finally got out of Calcutta but not quite how we'd have wanted.

Dear Mum, Dad and Kate,
How are things at home? I ramble on so much about me that I thought I'd just try and picture you in this letter.

'It's no good,' I say to Ty. 'I can't do it.'
'Leave it then.'
'I've got to let them know I'm OK.'
'Just write a postcard. *Moved to Varanasi but heading for the mountains, write to us in Kathmandu.*'
'We off to Nepal, then?'
'The sooner the better.'
We're in a café eating cardamom curd for breakfast, although it's way past noon and two of the waiter boys are already curled up under the counter for a quick ten minutes' kip. I ask for a banana and one of them is shaken awake and sent out to fetch some.
'You going to tell her about the accident?' says Ty.
'Do you think I should?'
'I'm not sure she'll want to hear that,' he says.
'Why did it get to you so much, Ty?'
He shrugs. 'I'm OK now. Come on, let's go.'
We should talk, I think, but don't say it. I hate the gap, but mithering's worse. I won't be one of those women who's always pleading *talk to me* . . .
'Come on, Romany,' says Ty.
We step outside, into the narrow alleyway stained with red blotches of pan. Traders have laid out jewellery on pieces of cloth. Dom is squatting down talking to one of them.
'Hi,' he says. 'On your way to the ghats?'

'Yes,' I say. 'This is Ty.'

'We met.'

'See you down there then,' I say.

'Yeah. If Christa's there tell her I'll be along in a bit.'

The street is murder to walk on; cracked cobbles and slippery clay, flights of steps, edges worn by monsoon floods and thousands of pilgrims' feet. A streak of red pan from an invisible body in a dark doorway shoots out in front of me.

'Who's Christa?' says Ty.

'Some girl who's having her hair shaved off down at the ghats,' I say. 'Dom seems to know everyone.'

'An English girl?'

'Australian, I think. She's got yellow hair right down her back and wants it all cut off. Ritual cleansing or whatever, like the Indians do before they bathe in the Ganges.'

'Wow.'

The walking gets easier, we're down by the river now, out of the narrow alleys and the risk of being trampled by water buffalo ploughing towards the water, pinning us to the walls with their bristly flanks. Dom catches us up and we exchange travels – where we've been, where we're going; we got stuck in Bengal, he's finding it hard to get out of Uttar Pradesh.

'I'll get the itch to move on soon enough,' he says. 'But I've never felt calmer than I do here.'

His shoulders twitch slightly, he stumbles over nothing, and I wonder if he might start spewing out gibberish again. We're on the steps of the Dasaswamedh Ghat, pilgrims milling all around us. Wet saris and shaved heads, splashing and prayers and the cries of vendors selling rice and flowers to throw into the holy water.

'I want to get to the mountains,' says Ty.

'Yeah man,' says Dom. 'You look like the mountain type.'

110

He does. It's amazing, the transformation from the swotty bloke who Kate brought home, trailing around after us in clubs but never leaving until we did; tottering up the road hanging on to him, one of us either side. When we first got here, to India, it was me who was excited. On the plane staring down at light spilling across the Arabian Desert, miles and miles of empty land and sea, and I thought I *never* have to go back if I don't want to. But it's Ty who's completely broken free, never seems to think of England, never writes to anyone, not even Kate any more. The shadow of a statue of Mahakali drops over him and when he moves away I hardly recognize the face that's still sore from my kisses.

There're loads of Westerners down at the ghats, loads of them everywhere, across the city, the continent, right across the planet, I guess. Always talking of moving, where they'll go next. Thailand! Burma! China! Sri Lanka! Gotta go there, man, can't miss out on that. Ty got into it straight away; talks of sneaking into Tibet under a pile of yak skins, knows what to buy in Nepal to sell in India, can live off bananas and lentils and ganja growing wild in the ditches. Easy to see him walking down a dusty red road in Morocco, following a valley to the Altiplano. I'm a good traveller too; can cope with being hungry, too hot, too cold, too tired to think. But could I do it without Mount Street – solid and safe, untouched by monsoons or landslides; fairy lights at Christmas and daffs in the spring? I badgered Ty for months, all the time I was saving my money – let's go, let's go – and he'd say, 'Why, Romany? What's out there that you want so much?' The questions stopped once we got here.

'Is that her?' says Ty. His skin is golden in this light, the light of Varanasi. Around us pilgrims clasp their hands in prayer, perch cross-legged under fraying raffia umbrellas. We catch a flash of blond waves, wind-rippled sand down

Christa's back. 'She's not going to get it all cut off, is she?' says Ty.

'Her and her mate went to an ashram in Rishikesh and the guru told them they'd never reach enlightenment without humility.' Golden hairs glint, nagging for attention.

'She's mad,' I say.

'Isn't that why we come here though?' says Ty. 'Opening ourselves up to different ways to live? I admire her, a pretty girl like that. All her life she's been judged by that hair.'

'She doesn't know what she's doing.'

I sit down on the steps. A few feet away from me a woman is bathing, the stippled pattern on her sari matches the mehndi on her arms and hands, the wet cloth slicked to her skin. A crowd gathers around Christa; her friend sits close by. After a ritual genuflection the barber wipes his cut-throat and starts to shave, hanks of yellow waves like a rag-doll's hair, black at the roots. Everyone stops to stare – the Brahmins with threads around their chests, the beggar boys, the women emerging from the water. Christa starts to shake slightly, says something – nervous words – and her friend squeezes her hand. The hair is all around her now; kids push between people's legs and steal a few long, golden strings. Her friend is chattering – nonsense, I can tell from here – to soothe her as all that weight is lifted from her scalp. As the last few strands are sliced off, Dom's shoulders start to twist, his feet to dance. He's staring at the girl – unrecognizable now – and at the shock on the face of her friend, who recoils very slightly, a tiny movement, but everyone sees it. It's out there, she can't ever take that look back.

'Shit,' says Dom. 'Shit quit git BOLLOCKS.'

Christa holds her bald head in her hands and starts to cry.

'That's what Kate did when she lost all her hair,' I say.

13

About six months after I fell over the step at Mount Street, Kate had to have an operation, some old scar tissue tidied up. She was back home, doing fine. I nursed her myself, liked fussing round her; good to be the capable one after being so knackered myself. That's when I learned how to work a house: washing machine, central heating, micro- wave, video. While Michael and Jenny were out and Kate slept, I fiddled with dials, poked around in cupboards pulling out candle stubs, scribbled recipes, instructions for broken hairdryers. In a box in a drawer Jenny kept her mother's embroidered hankies and newspaper clippings of her dad marrying and burying; Michael had a stash of posh-looking wine under the airing cupboard – we never drank any of those bottles, not in all the time I was there. I'd never been trusted alone in a house before – not one of my foster parents ever gave me a key – and then suddenly I was there, caring for Kate, a tenner from Michael, 'In case there's anything you need.'

Kate was fine. The nurse had been to change her dress- ings. She'd had her painkillers, the cats purred, the radio murmured as she dozed. I stroked back some hair from her face – a few strands came away in my fingers – and carried on with exploring. I couldn't get enough of that house: old armchairs worn by elbows and feet, crumbs and pennies under every cushion. Marks on the kitchen wall as Kate grew, inch by inch. Drawers full of receipts, plastic bags, ancient, solidified toffees. An umbrella tree in the hall which turned the corner when it hit the ceiling, nudging spiders' webs with its tiny, new-leaf hands. I loved the solid walls, the worn stair carpet, the sideboard with no drawer handles, the smells: sandalwood soap, shepherd's pie, Jenny's precious Chanel No. 5 which Kate and me would sniff, share a dab on our joined wrists, like boys do with blood.

I'd never even had my own room before – only bunk beds in a shared dorm, or the corner of a strange house where I knew I wouldn't be staying. They always took me back, hand clamped on my wrist – Kate was the only reason I trusted Michael and Jenny not to do the same. But at Mount Street no one bothered when they found me half-way through a box of Kate's old music books, or pulling out bags of tinsel from the back of a wardrobe. They had nothing to hide, it seemed. No one slapped my fingers if they found me reading old letters, told me not to touch, to keep away from what wasn't mine. Late one night Jenny found me rifling through a box of family photographs. She was in her nightie, after a drink of water, but sat down on the stairs with me instead, let the strap slide off her shoulder as she leafed through. Pictures: her mum and dad's wedding, her as a little girl – Kate's the spit of her – and even one of Granny Platt, shored up by pillows, her skin yellowed and waxy. 'That was near the end,' said Jenny, pulling her strap back and patting my legs. 'It's a gift, you know, your body. Remember that, Romany.'

The one place I hadn't explored was the attic, so I fetched the ladder from Michael's workshop, climbed up and pushed open the hatch. A light switch and a working bulb – the glow cast a wan light over the room. A bed, a bedside table, a lamp, a chest of drawers. A child's bed with a frilly-edged duvet and crocheted blanket on top. And stuck to the side of the chest, photographs. Kate climbing a tree, Kate jumping over homemade stiles in the garden, pretending to be a horse. Kate on the beach as a toddler, sturdy little legs chasing the waves, no knickers and an Arran jumper. Kate in a swimming costume holding a trophy, Michael and Jenny crouched either side of her, beaming, a hand on each of her shoulders.

'Romany?' Kate, from downstairs.

I scrambled out of there, a vivid snapshot of that perfect child's bedroom the last thing I saw before my head dropped down from the attic, from its foreign shores, too much even for me.

Later that night, Jenny and Michael hissed at each other on the landing, right there under the hatch. Like she had a nose for it, could tell it had been disturbed. 'I want to go up there, just to check,' she said.

'Love, you know what it does to you.'

'And you think it's not doing that anyway?'

'Jenny, it has to go.'

'Just leave it, Michael.'

Kate's hair fell out the next day. She was sitting by the bath and I was lathering, had bought new orange-scented shampoo – revitalizing, it said on the bottle.

'Here you are,' I said. 'We could both do with revitalizing. You do mine next, OK?'

'OK.'

'Get that hospital smell off you.'

'Better than Eau de Alleyway,' said Kate.

I cuffed her, flicked shampoo off the ends of my fingers. Black hairs twisted round my palms, strands of it stuck on Kate's shoulders and breasts. I took the showerhead and started to rinse the foam from her scalp with jets of water. I was singing some daft song – *when this old world keeps getting you down* – pushing back her hair with my hand to see if it squeaked clean. A hank gave way. When I looked

115

down the bath was thick with coils of Kate's black hair and her bald head was quivering on top of the hands which hid her face.

*

'How come her hair fell out then?' says Ty.

We're still on the steps of the Dasaswamedh Ghat, Dom too, plaiting a clump of Christa's hair while listening to Kate's story. Christa vanished, didn't even bathe in the Ganges after her ritual shave. The barber distressed that she hadn't – that was the whole point, she would be renewed now, like after a fast. 'I do plenty women,' he cried, as Christa's friend led her away, draping a scarf over the baldness. 'It is not so unusual.'

'Her hair'll grow back,' I say. 'Kate's did.'

'Why did it fall out?' says Ty.

I shrug. 'The anaesthetic. Shock. It dies under the skin apparently.'

'That's what they said about my brother – physical shock,' says Dom. 'Crashed his bike into a lamppost and was out for five days. Never had any hair after that.'

'Poor Kate,' says Ty. 'Have you written to her yet?'

'Have you?'

'Did her face change?' says Dom.

'Not as much as that Christa's,' I say.

'I've never seen anything so weird,' says Ty. 'It wasn't just her face; her whole body was softer with that hair. Like that was all anyone ever saw. But underneath it she had these black eyebrows and big shoulders and sadness.'

'Everyone at their lodge has been talking about it for days,' says Dom. 'She joked about it, called it the shearing. "Like the sheep back home, get rid of all the daggy bits." Said she wanted her true self to show through, on and on about it to anyone who'd listen. "People treat me like a bimbo," she said, "a bit silly, a good laugh, a grafter who never makes a fuss." She wanted to be seen as more serious, more spiritual, I guess. But even when she was talking she was acting the little girl. Playing all these tricks, brushing into the blokes, widening her eyes at stories she'd have heard a hundred times. I don't think she even realized.'

'Silly cow,' I say. 'Stoking up all that drama. If she's so keen to lose herself she's only got to hang on a bit. Life'll catch up with her soon enough.'

'She was trying to *make* it happen though,' says Ty.

'Silly fucking cow.'

The sun is hot on our backs. People come and go around us, in and out of the water, praying and meditating, dunking themselves and drying quickly in the sun. An energetic masseur is kneading someone's shoulders, working the flesh down his arms to the ends of his fingers with deep grunts, as if the skin itself won't budge. Then he flings his hands open, fingers splayed wide, stretching them across over the river towards the arid side of the Ganges.

'I dig out the bad energies,' he tells us, when he's finished. 'Like this . . .' He grunts, pummels. 'Then they go, *pffft*, across there to the stony ground. Or into the water to be eaten by turtles.'

'Turtles?' says Ty.

The man leans closer, his skin glistens. 'The ones in the river that feed off dead flesh. They eat bad spirits too.'

Ty squats next to him and watches. The sun inches higher and I draw my scarf over my head and shoulders for protection, like the Indian women do.

I lose Ty for a couple of days to the masseur. He's up before dawn and down to the ghats to practise yogic breathing, says he can feel the *chi*, the life force, flowing around his body. He seems taller, and the muscles stand out from his bones in small, hard slabs; even his floppy blond wings of hair have gone, shaved off 'because of the heat'. If he was in England people would nudge each other, say he's got a mad gleam in his eyes, that he's out there. It used to be me with the mad gleam, pulling at him, hassling. *Come on, let's go, let's just go, bollocks to the rest of it.*

And me that pushed us over into love, too. In Bombay, in Goa, lying on a sweaty bed, right in his face, saying, *You do love me. You do.* A twitch, then a smile. *Of course I do. Of course.* Moving through India hardly touching the ground, dancing through temples, along beaches, up into the pine-cool mountains. All the way to Calcutta like that, joined by tangled feet and hands, always touching, leaning into him, sliding under his body.

But Ty's strange here; Dom says everyone is. That strangeness is in the air and the water, in the cobblestones and dust, and that's why he's here, a place with enough movement to calm even his tic for travel, and a charge in the air which sends blond Westerners to the ghats, minor aristocrats to give up their worldly goods.

'You know people who've done that?' I ask Dom. We're writing letters, paper curling in the heat.

'There're white guys in the mountains who've joined the sadhus. Given away everything but a begging bowl and a chillum. Some disappear completely. You'll meet mothers wearing placards, photographs of their bearded sons, last seen two or three years ago, searching the mountains valley by valley. But the mountains are too big. If you want to get lost you can. It's what we're all doing, I guess. Getting lost for a while.'

'And they can live? People give them money?'

'India is generous,' says Dom.

Dear Kate,
This is a selfish letter; I'm writing it because I want one back. I'm sorry we've been AWOL for a while –

too caught up in the here and now. In some ways it's like living on the streets – everything's in the present, anything can happen, a chance meeting and off you spin. We think about food and shelter and money, dwarfed by this landscape of great rivers and plains, ancient buildings, epic journeys, spiritual quests. Where do you start? I could just write lists and lists of things we've seen and people we've met, but what would that mean? It does bother me that it might mean nothing at all.

Ditto Ty. Being caught up. Being involved. Worried that it means nothing at all.

It's like the alien game – remember; us bored in the car, saying 'We're aliens, right' and getting in a muddle trying to explain tides or motorways or starfish to the little green men back home. On the bus round the Bull Ring laughing over what the aliens would make of the crazy traffic. I know you've read about this place, that there's a map on the kitchen wall with pins and string but it's still secondhand. Like school – 'In medieval times everyone was tied to the land' – we try to imagine that, but don't really know what it means. 'In India the spiritual permeates every aspect of life.' Does that mean anything to you, Kate?

I'm sorry if this makes you feel even further away. I wish you were here, I really do. We should have found a way for you to come, too. I want to know about everything: Mum and Dad, Frieda and her boys, Tom and the shop doorway crew. Did you say he was travelling, too? Gypsies, the lot of us. Can't keep still, pulled around by the wind and the moon and our blind urges. It's like I'm being carried along by one of India's invisible rivers and there's no getting off until she lets me. There's this guy here called Dom who has

119

these spasms, starts swearing and jerking, stops just as suddenly. Travelling's like that, spinning from place to place and then we blink and think *wow, so this is Varanasi* . . .

We're off to the mountains. Kathmandu first. Write to me there. Tell me what's happening – I want to know everything that's gone on; who's in and out of the house, what you're reading, listening to, talking to . . .

Missing you, babe,
R xx

14

Dawn. Varanasi bus station. Exhaust smoke and honking horns, the signs on the buses are all in Hindi script. Ty buys a bunch of bananas for the journey – brain food, he says – he's calm and a little distant but pulls me out of the way of a creaking rickshaw and touches my cheek, tentatively, as if he's forgotten what my skin feels like. Dom has come to see us off and it's him that finds the right bus, double-checks with the driver and passengers. He's twitchier than ever – so easy to get it wrong, he keeps saying, so easy – clicking his tongue and tapping me and Ty on the shoulders, little jabs at our stomachs.

'As long as it's going north, I don't care,' says Ty.

'Well, I bloody do,' I say. 'Kate will write to Kathmandu.'

'No Kathmandu,' says a man sitting next to Ty. He has a little boat-shaped hat on, patterned with orange and blue zigzags, very dapper. 'No this bus.'

'Shit,' shouts Dom, from outside the window. His shoulders begin to writhe. 'Shitfuckshit.'

'Where's it going, then?' I say. My feet are jammed between a wicker basket full of manky chickens and an enormous lorry tyre split right through to the mesh.

'BollocksbollocksWANK,' says Dom. Half the bus station stop to stare at him; even the little beggar kids know English swear words.

'Sunauli,' says the dapper Nepali. I recognize his look

121

now, from a photo or TV; I saw a group of them busking in Bath once. 'On the border. You must change buses there, oh yes. Maybe you wish to stay at my brother's lodge for the night?' He hands me a card. The bus is revving, Dom twists and hops outside. Ty takes my hand.

'It's OK,' I mouth, through the window, to Dom's fare-well dance. 'It's OK, mate.'

It's the last I see of Varanasi, Dom twisting in a swirl of dust. I crane my neck to wave, but he's fading into the crowds: street hawkers with baskets of sugar cane, racks of cycle rickshaws with green and red painted saddles, blue-tongued cows, pilgrims. A traffic policeman wearing a stiff white cap and cuffs stands on a podium in the middle of a road junction blowing his whistle. His arm-waving has as much effect on the mass of cars, bikes, rickshaws, buffalo, donkeys, kids, beggars and priests as Dom's Tourettic tornado as he blurs into calm.

The bus journey from hell. Ty and I are jammed into a corner, elbows and knees poking each other's faces, half an inch of foam between us and the hard wooden bench, windows rattling in their frames as the bus lurches over rutted roads for ten hours. Ty meditates. He says I should too, that it suspends time, so we'll arrive refreshed and enlightened in Sunauli. He looks as ragged as I feel though – glass grinding against metal, the high-pitched hum of the accelerator, the jolts, shouts, the driver jamming the brakes so hard that the back of the bus flips up.

The road is thick with people walking barefoot, baskets on their heads, kids strapped on their backs. I wonder where they're going, where there *is* to go in this huge basin south of the Himalaya. Water, says Ty. Or food, or work. That's why they're moving. The basin is scooped deeper every year by floods from the mountains, no trees to hold water in the soil, to steady the landscape's changes. The dapper Nepali eats his way through the journey; sweets, fruit, cones of sugared nuts, then finally a massive wodge of pan slipped into the side of his mouth. By the time we stagger off the bus his mouth is a red hole and his eyes are swivelling wildly in their sockets. The border town is pitch black – the Nepali wriggles between Ty and me and takes a hand each – but the air is fresh. I feel the chill from the mountains, from the abode of the snow curved above us.

'Wicked,' says Ty.

The Nepali's brother's lodge is full of European trekkers. They're sprawled around the downstairs room, drying socks, rolling joints, spreading out maps on the table. They even have some wine – God knows where from – and we have our first drink since the whiskey on the train to Calcutta. I feel a throb at the back of my neck straight away, reliving our excitement.

'Remember Calcutta?' I say to Ty. 'Howrah and the bridge and Sudder Street?'

'You stayed there?' says one of the trekkers. 'God, I could hardly breathe in that place.'

'Yeah, the air is bad there,' says Ty, taking a gulp of wine. 'Any chance of looking at your maps?'

Is that all he can say? That the air's bad in Calcutta? I sit apart from them – the boys, no other women here – as they talk to Ty of glaciers and crevasses and air so clean that it cuts up your lungs. He fingers the purple-edged maps and asks question after question; food, fuel, porters, equipment. I wish we could talk alone, just us two and this half a cup of wine; draw ourselves together with 'I remember that'. Moments of harmony and understanding that seem long gone now, leaving me hugging my knees and rocking like some lovelorn teenager. For a moment I think tears might spill out of my eyes, splash into the wine, roll around on the dusty floor. I can't believe this is me – if Kate was mooning about like this I'd have to have a word. *What's your problem? He's still here, you're together, you love each other. You're doing the things you dreamed of. He's just excited about the mountains, what's wrong with that?* I know all this. I know Ty loves me, but something is gone already, and tonight the loss is crushing. 'No more,' me and Kate said, 'we won't lose any more.' But I left her behind, stepped so easily away, and now there's nothing to hold me up except Ty.

There has to be a way through this; keep moving, keep going, I'll stumble across one like I did back in Brum – I can taste the place tonight, memories piling in through the gaps between me and Ty. The secret routes that flow like rivers round my city; blocked by a railway, snubbed by a row of terraces, winding the back way through alleys and snickets where cats and foxes tread. I followed Kate and Jenny back to Mount Street – right back then, the very first time Jenny knobbled me behind the burger van. 'Home?' I said. 'What's that got to do with me?' Something like that, anyway; tough, 'ask me if I give a shit' words, wrenching my shoulders away from them, from their tender eyes and soft hands. In the children's home would-be foster parents came in to view us kids and afterwards we'd sneak out, over the back fence and out to their address, to look at their houses and cars and dogs and children; could we ever fit in there? So I knew how to do it, followed Jenny to work and Kate to school. Squatting on the roof of the garages watching Michael in his workshop scribbling calculations on scraps of paper. I knew all their visitors, their routines, saw Kate on her window seat reading, a capsule of light floating above the dark gardens like a spaceship.

That was all before Sonny, mind.

Casing them out – forewarned is forearmed. Into the garden on a Saturday night to watch them eat, windows misting so I'd have to climb for a view. Scanning their faces on a Monday morning, when everyone's foul-tempered and begging's a dead loss. It makes no difference when you're on the streets; Mondays, Tuesdays, another day is just one more to get through. To eat and sleep and try to keep clean, like being a baby, except there's no one there to look out for you.

Except Tom, of course. Tom was my inspiration – Mum and Kate's too, later – real, living proof that a person can turn themselves round, that it's really possible to pick yourself up, shake yourself down. When I first met him he had glue cans up his sleeves; scratched survival out of tat and rubbish. Tom never begged. We talked about Kate, the house. 'They say I can live there,' I said. 'That's your chance,' said Tom, 'grab hold of it, girl.'

In Sunauli, on the border of India and Nepal at the foot of the Himalayas, the memories flow in, clear and sharp as the peaks above me. I'm lying in a bunk above the downstairs room, where the trekkers and Ty are still talking. There's a skylight just by my face, a window to the stars. They're moving, popping and bursting and whizzing across the midnight-blue sky. Multicoloured: emerald, turquoise, white-gold. Awesome. I gasp out loud – 'have you seen the stars?' – and am out of my bed and through the room and outside. Ty follows and stares, glad to touch me, to pull me towards him. Stars explode all around us; the sky bigger than we could ever imagine. The trekkers look upwards and then at me, suddenly interested in this sulky girl – was she nearly crying earlier? – who's brought them outside to the sky, the stars floating out there. They lurch around in the dark, briefly aware that the ground beneath their feet is always spinning.

I wake early, cold. I'm curled around Ty's back with my arm trapped under his shoulder but I don't want to move; it feels good to be squeezed together like this, on the narrow bunk, noses poking above the blanket, catching the chill. Ty hitches himself deeper into the warmest part of the bed. I stroke his back, rest my palm on his ribs and feel his lungs rising and sinking. He murmurs – something about air, fresh air – and arches back into me. I slip my hand over his hip and between his legs, his breath catches and his dick stiffens: just what I need to feel, to hear. He rolls round to face me, groaning; I clamp my hand over his mouth – we're in one of ten or so bunks recessed into the walls, will wake the trekkers. Within seconds he's inside me, and we lie, counting silently – one, two, three – feeling each other, knowing that our bodies can't stay still, that they'll have to move soon. The tension and friction between us is growing, and for a moment I think I might yell, ecstatically, and fling myself around – crashing into the flimsy wall, splintering wood and ripping sheets. Ty bends his head to kiss my nipple and we're gone, thrashing deliciously, shuddering together, fusing for a brief blissful moment and then we're panting, grinning and trying not to laugh. A body shifts in the next bunk along and we go under the blankets together.

'Good day for the mountains,' says one of the trekkers, at breakfast. 'You look refreshed.'

'It's those bus journeys, man, they take it out of you.'

'I slept for two days when I first got here,' says the German, the one who had all the maps. I'm sure his is the bunk next to ours.

'Yeah, I was wasted last night,' I say. So tired I got paranoid, panic seeping out, from wherever it lives, deep inside me somewhere. I see myself sitting here, brooding, scowling probably, kicking my legs against the bunk as I stared at the German thinking *dickhead* for no real reason. Tom used to chide me for that: you're too quick to judge, Romany.

Now we're chatting over chapatti, coconut curd and chai

from a shop next to the lodge; we can hear the slapping of dough through the wall, smell the spices from the vat of foaming chai as it's stirred and thickened. Ty has jammed the door open and a breeze blows through the room, ventilation, and everyone is excited for us, our first time in the Himalayas, the mountains rucked up behind this lodge. Range after range, up and down, up and down but always climbing, right up to the pinnacle, the highest point on this earth. The sacred mountain, Sagamartha.

'You gonna do the Everest trek then?'

'Nah, go Annapurna. Everest's like the M1, man. All bog roll and Coke cans.'

'If you go rafting you can get to valleys where there're no roads at all.'

'A bit different from Brum, hey,' says Ty, shuffling his chair close to mine and putting his arm round my shoulder.

'It's all a bit different from Brum,' I say.

'We're OK though, aren't we?' he says. I nod without thinking, my body answering him. 'Come on then, angel,' he says. 'We've got a bus to catch.'

The bus is cramped – even more cramped than the Indian one; Nepalis are smaller and so are their buses. Ty and I feel like aliens, both of us taller than the rest of the passengers by a good head and Ty so fair. Before long we're out in the stony foothills, no sight of the glimmering mile-high slabs of ice and rock for hours yet. The road loops upwards, hugging contours; ten miles by road and all the time we can see the pass over to the next valley – only a mile away as the crow flies. When the bus driver stops for a herd of goats, Ty slides out of the window and up on to the roof.

'Come on,' he says. 'There's loads of room up here.' He hauls our packs up and we wedge them between packages and crates. I stretch out my legs, shaking out the pins and needles. There're a few others up here – dodgy-looking

127

blokes with scarves wrapped around their heads. One with a cutlass hanging from his belt. They crowd around nosily as Ty and I pull jumpers and scarves out of our packs, one lunges for Ty's Swiss Army knife but he's too quick, slips the knife in his pocket and offers them biscuits, swiftly building a place for us and securing our stuff. The bus grinds forward and Ty and I huddle close, no gaps for the sharp mountain wind to push through.

'You OK?' he says.

'Fine.'

'Yesterday was shit, wasn't it?'

'You can say that again.'

'This is fantastic, though. It's going to be great here, I can feel it, it's like we've come through something, don't you think . . .'

I say nothing, stare ahead of us. We're nearly at the top of a pass now, the bus is straining and lurching, engine screaming under the strain.

'I'm sorry about Calcutta,' says Ty. 'I love you, Romany.'

'I love you too,' I say, as the bus levels itself at the top of the pass and we get our first view of the fire-tinged peaks, which float like icebergs in the far distance, high above the hazy valleys, halfway to heaven.

15

Two weeks later we're living in a lone hillside shack, north-east of Pokhara. Ty's trying to teach me yoga.

'Come on, Romany, fill your lungs from the bottom, that's it, now slowly out, *push* the air . . .'

'God, I must be enlightened by now.'

'Hang on till the sun comes up behind Machhapuchare. Feel the calm, it's there, you just need to get in touch with it.'

'That's not calm, that's *hunger*. I tell you, half the ascetics on the continent think they're reaching God when really they're just malnourished.'

'Shush. Here it comes. Back straight, now *breathe*.'

I close my eyes to concentrate and when I open them again the ball of fire rising behind the mountain is spreading colour on to the pre-dawn silver of the meadow. The fishtail of Machhapuchhare slices up through the sun's rays and sends glistening lasers to her surrounding valleys – mountains are female, like ships and aeroplanes – then turns translucent for a moment, the giant thorn of rock and ice flooded with light. Ty and I are transfixed, our backs straight and our breathing deep and steady. Miles below us a morning breeze stirs the pools along the river and the standing buffalo wake up, swish their tails, snort, start tearing at the tough grasses. Our meadow is alpine – tiny blue and purple flowers on woody stalks – a shelf of

129

grassy abundance above the villages, a resting place for travellers before the mountains proper, which bank up sharply all around us.

'*Namaste*.' A boy has joined us, maybe a man, it's hard to tell. Even old people in Nepal are wiry and fit, up and down the slopes all their lives, breathing the sweet, thin air.

'It's holy, the mountain,' he says, squatting down and staring with us, at the valley and the mountains which guard it. 'No one has ever climbed it; only a fool would try, and the mountains are not kind to fools. Pure, and un-touched. This is a wonderful thing, no?'

'Yes,' we both say.

'Do you live near here?' I ask.

Ty unfolds his legs and stands up, nodding his head and joining his hands in respect to the man-boy. A genuine gesture and the man-boy responds in kind.

'Yes, I was born in the house by the big rock,' he says, pointing to the other side of the valley. 'I still live there, with my family.'

'Would you like some tea?' says Ty. 'Join us for breakfast.'

'Thank you.' He nods at Ty, turns to me. 'And you, where were you born? Where is your home?'

'Oh, I'm a bit of a nomad, me.'

He nods again, and we stare at the mountain. If you said that in England people would think you were having a laugh – *What's her point?* But here nomads are nothing special; packing up your home and moving on isn't subversive. And what else can I say? That I am, or was, homeless? The word's always pissed me off anyway – homeless – like it's somehow your fault, you lost a perfectly decent home because you're a dosser, from bad stock.

When I first moved into Mount Street, Jenny was determined to find out my history; needed someone to rage at – 'Do you know what nearly happened? How could you let her go?' Storming down corridors, bursting into

130

meetings, powered by anger and protectiveness, her need to make things right. We tried to tell her – things *are* right now, but it wasn't enough; she had to know why it happened, why I ended up on the streets, an underage runaway, prey to every lunatic out there.

'Some of my best mates are nutters,' I said.

'Don't make it worse, Romany.'

I can still spot an outcast at a hundred yards, even here in Asia. Learned early the wisdom of the wild; that skinheads can be saints. Before Kate, before Mount Street, mothers would shield their sons' eyes from me, hoping to distract them from the pull of a street girl with Sunday morning football, holidays on the Costa Brava. I always knew if I could have them. Waking up on some old drunk's floor, curled in a corner like a dog, looking round the room: newspapers for carpet, water cut off so the taps just judder. Fifty pence off the floor and a twist of baccy and you're out of the door, clocking the open window in the outside bog in case you're that desperate one day. What chance has a mummy's boy against that?

'All those blokes,' Kate used to say. 'Chewed up and spat out by Romany Jackson.'

'I was just Romany then.'

'What *is* your second name?'

'*Their* name? Don't use it. No way.'

'There must've been reasons.'

'To abandon their only child?'

'Don't let it eat you up any more. It stops here, OK?'

And it did. Kate and Michael and Jenny; Frieda and the boys; going to school and using my brain; the house with its good smells, its full fridge, space for just me. But most of all Kate – she's what stopped bad feeling bleeding into the rifts inside of me. Every time I smudged those walls with my fingers, brushed cat hairs off my jeans, saw my face in hers, I felt disaster being stalled.

131

'My home's in Birmingham,' I say to the Nepali. Smoke rises from our shack. Ty has the fire going already, he's a genius with it, can conjure flickerings from the dampest wood, nurture them patiently into flames. 'A big city in the middle of England. The house is like this . . .' I draw with my finger on his palm. Three floors, a front door, windows and the gable end.

'A palace,' he says.

'Yes. It has switches. Click, like this.' I press on his hand. 'The lights come on. Taps like this for water.' I twist my wrist. 'And heat straight away.'

The Nepali is smiling. 'Magic,' he says.

'Cupboards full of food, and books in every room – my sister, she reads all the time – and a big bath where you can lie all day like the Queen of Egypt.'

'The Queen of Egypt likes a bath?' says the Nepali. His eyes sparkle as the light spreads more colour across the meadow, the valley, the water. Only the peaks remain untouched, pure white, cutting jagged lines in the deep blue of the sky.

'I would've thought so, wouldn't you?'

'Yes,' he says. 'You are a princess, to have lived in this palace all your life?'

'Not all my life. I'm adopted.'

Ty brings us tea and porridge. He squats down to eat, like the Nepali. They talk about trekking routes, resting places, fuel. Ty fetches his hiking boots from our hut – carried all the way from England and unworn until now; they look plastic-new compared to the Nepali's frayed pumps. There are nuggets of dried mud in the notches of the soles – from Northumberland, says Ty, from the hills behind my mother's house. The Nepali fingers this earth from halfway across the world and then scatters it around the meadow.

'Your home is not the city?' says the Nepali.

Ty's brow flickers. 'No,' he says. 'I guess I'm a country boy at heart. It can be harsh, where I come from. My father died in a blizzard.'

'Blizzard?' says the Nepali.

Ty scans the mountain peaks around us. To the east there are high clouds, half-moon shapes suspended face down in the clear blue, signs of a storm. The mountain peaks below them are lost in a blur of wind and ice. Ty points at them. 'That's a blizzard,' he says.

'Ah,' says the Nepali.

For the next few weeks Ty is engrossed in preparations; physical and material. Punishing exercises and endless kit-checking – just what is needed to survive up there? The Nepali – Kishore – visits frequently, to eat, chat, pass the time of day. We learn of his potato patch, his ancestral village over the pass, his wife and children – he points them out as they make their way down a path on the opposite side of the valley, bundles of sticks on their backs. They have an adopted daughter, too, a relative of some sort. Kishore says she's *baulaha* – touched – she was sick as a baby and her parents sent her over the pass with some traders in the depths of winter. They knocked on his door, threw the baby into his arms, then vanished down the valley. Miraculously, she survived – Kishore says the holy mountain protected her – but she's always been wild. He doesn't like her going to the village because the men tease her, the children steal her bangles, the women try to oil and comb her hair, which is matted like a holy man's.

'What does she do all day then?' I say, though I'm a fine one to talk, having spent the last fortnight staring at the clouds above the eastern ridge, dreaming. When else will I get the chance? I ask myself. Anyway, I'm waiting for the post to be forwarded from Kathmandu.

133

Ty packs and unpacks his rucksack, wraps matches in plastic bags, hoards lumps of sugar and salt, decides which book to take – only one and he says he'll rip out the pages as he reads to shed weight. He meditates too, and it's as if he's detaching himself, link by link, from anything that isn't *now*. He wants me to join him on his long practice hauls up the hills – you have to get used to the weight, Romany – but I'd rather walk lazily, in the woods or by the stream, unencumbered.

'There she is,' says Kishore. He points down to the buffalo. They're wallowing at the edge of a pool, their broad, flat backs perfect perches for egrets and barefoot girls; she splashes from one to another as the buffalo twitch their tails at her ankles. 'She spends most of the day with the buffalo.'

'They don't seem to mind,' I say.

'No,' says Kishore. 'They are good creatures.'

Ty practises climbing moves on a patch of sheer rock behind our hut. His hand inches upwards, feeling for a crevice, a nodule of rock to cling to, while his foot swings up towards a slippery bulge.

'I'm going to the village,' I say. 'I thought I'd take the short cut, the way Kishore goes. Want me to fetch anything?'

Ty drops off the rock, landing lightly in the sandy soil. He is red from exertion, glowing, strong. It's hard to recognize him, especially with his shorn head. I try to imagine him behind a stack of books, pushing a lock away as he reads, but there's nothing left of that boy now.

'Have a look for some secondhand rope. We'll need good stuff, mind, if it's going to be any use.'

'Why don't you come with me?'

'I'm on a roll here . . . It's really coming together, you know, the breathing, all the training I've been doing.'

'OK.' I turn to leave and he's by my side.

'I'll come as far as the woods with you,' he says.

The paths are all single file so I can't see him as I walk. 'Do I look the same,' I say, 'as when we left England?'

'You're thinner.'

'Some days I hardly recognize you.'

'Don't be daft.'

'It's true.'

'I'm fitter. Using my body. Can't imagine just sitting around looking in books for answers now. Being up here, well . . . I don't know. It's like the mountains are calling me. Hindus and Buddhists go off on journeys all the time – to change themselves, not just bag another peak for their slide show. They're encouraged to.'

'Only if they've discharged their responsibilities in life.'

'Well, yeah, but . . . I really understand how you can clear your mind by testing your body. It's like I forgot about my body back there.'

'Not everyone has the luxury.'

We're at the edge of the woods. The trees are broad-leaved and the sunlight breaks through in shafts, spot-lighting the path as it winds down to the village. Ty takes my hand and squeezes it. I squeeze back and try to slip away, but he grabs my wrist.

'You don't seem very keen on this trek, Romany.'

'Do you blame me? Weeks and weeks of sore shoulders and blistered feet? I lived like that for years, remember.'

'That's not what it's about. You should be getting pre-pared. It won't be easy out there.'

'So why are you so keen to go?'

'I'm going to do this, Romany.'

As I step off into the rustling woods – Ty's hand on my back, a little rub and a pat – it hits me for the first time that there must be a reason why he's so keen to go. And it looks like that reason has sod all to do with me.

*

When I first met Ty I thought he knew my history – from Kate, she would've told him, about the children's homes, living on the streets, the meeting on the bridge, our pact. I took it for granted that he knew the stories, our teenage conspiracies: nicking money from Dad's pockets while he snoozed under the *Evening Mail*; my night circuits in and out of the house, stuffing a rolled-up blanket under the duvet. He loved those conversations, leaned forward smiling. 'Maybe it's because his sister's so much older,' I said to Kate. 'We made ourselves sisters,' I said to him once. 'We wanted it enough.'

But when we got to Bombay it turned out he didn't know much at all. So we sat in that broiling box room in Colaba, slowly adjusting to the frenzy we could hear a few feet away, and I told him. I didn't think it'd take long: there are only a few facts. Born at the QE – like Kate – in and out of care from four onwards; fostered out at six, eight, ten, and the last time at twelve.

'I wonder why none of them adopted you?' Ty said, an innocent enough question, but it opened up something in me, a place left well alone, only Kate ever went there.

'I don't know,' I said. 'I guess I looked pretty good as orphans go – no obvious defects – but it was never long before their disappointment showed and then they'd turf me out just like my mum and dad.' Tears rolled down my cheeks, but Ty just pulled me close, held my hand later, as we picked our way down Colaba Causeway, laughing at the chaos caused by a cow with flowers on her horns stopping in the middle of the road for lunch.

He wasn't scared of the damage in me.

So Ty must be damaged too.

I sit down in the woods above the village and say her name out loud – Kate – because I need to reach her right now. Kate, Kate, what did Ty tell us about his past? Nothing came out, even after I'd told him everything. I've had blokes who'd vie with me over crap-childhood stories, like that old sketch – 'hole in't road, hole in't road, we used to *dream* about hole in't road . . .' Freddie, my gentle boatman, would say it sometimes: 'Romany, sweet, think about the kids who grow up starving, never satisfied from the day they're born.'

I guess I thought there was nothing to tell.

And I can't reach Kate. Can't even see Mount Street clearly any more.

A bird calls in the trees above me, to its mate, maybe. It sounds like the foghorns you can hear at Frieda's sometimes; low, mournful hoots to guide the ships home. That, and the memories, and the exquisite fountain of branches and leaves above me are overwhelming – my heart is thudding fast, emotional chemicals flooding my chest. I have to put my head between my knees, concentrate on breathing, deep and low, steady now . . . steady.

A crack, someone treading on a stick. Deliberately, it must be. I look up. It's the girl – Kishore's adopted daughter, Nyala, the wild one. She looks at me with curious, concerned eyes, then sits down beside me and nudges me, shoulder to shoulder, a sisterly gesture.

'Foster homes,' I say. 'You were lucky. We used to *dream* of foster homes.' And she smiles, although she can't understand a word I'm saying. Kishore says she doesn't speak much. She points at me and then down the path towards the village. I nod. She thumps her hand on her chest and then at the path again.

'You're coming?' I say.

She mimes us walking into the village together and I nod; it's an hour at least down into Kotmuni and she's easy company. Why not? My first trip away from the hut for a month – we've been buying food through Kishore – and I'll walk in with the orphaned, adopted, mad girl. Kate will smile when I tell her.

There's no post for me. The shopkeeper says the van should be here soon, give or take a few days. I'm half tempted to catch the bus to Pokhara or even Kathmandu, stay overnight, but I'd have to go and tell Ty first and by the time I get back up to our plateau a week won't seem so long to wait. I'm nodding to myself as these thoughts pass through my head and the girl next to me nods too, with an expression on her face that I find inexplicably reassuring. Kate must've written; our letters will get back in sync.

I'll read her old letters for now – they're tied up in a bundle at the bottom of my rucksack; she always dabs them with perfume to see if the scent will last the journey. A trail of Chanel No. 5 all the way back to Mount Street. I've got to finish my letters first anyway, to Mum and Dad, a long one to Kate about the accident in Calcutta, Dom and the head shaving, our nightmare journey north through the foothills and our resting place above the valley, Ty's preparations. I know what she'll do: go to the window seat and imagine herself here, there, everywhere we've been. She'll prise apart every sentence, work out where my head is from odd, throwaway phrases, unfinished paragraphs. There's no way I can bullshit to her, so I'll save those lines for Mum and Dad. *Don't worry, I'm fine. Safer here than in Handsworth any day of the week.*

We go to the market, the girl trogs along behind me – behaving herself – casting low glances at her potential tormentors; laundry women, stall holders, groups of kids with hair as wild as hers chasing tin-can footballs. The looks are grimly familiar from my days on the streets – they don't trust her, finger the coins tucked into their waistcoats – so I pull her forward, loop my arm through hers. Here it's me who has the power – my hard currency, my passport and endless free time – so I enjoy the shopping. It's amazing how being away from shops for a while makes a stall of bits – rubbish really, plastic bottles and scraps of fabric –

look like a treasure trove. I haggle for potatoes, rice, fruit, some dried trekkers' food and fancy that the girl at my side somehow helps; she shuffles her bare foot towards me when I'm close to a good price.

There are stalls heaped with old trekking gear: frayed ropes, soleless boots, crampons with broken teeth – a sense of the Wild West about the place; people stocking up before arduous journeys, staggering in weary and relieved after weeks of travelling on foot. We take on these journeys for fun, exhilaration, to test our mettle – maybe even to escape. But Nepalis spend their lives up and down these mountains. Monks walk down to India on pilgrimages; old women trudge over passes five thousand feet high, baskets of sticks on their backs.

Nyala tugs on my shirt and pulls me down an alley to a stall half hidden in the shadows, a blanket spread out and covered with religious knick-knacks. Buddhas carved from stones, hand-held prayer wheels, strings of the flags which flutter over every pass in honour of the gods who let us travel there. And other, stranger objects: bones, shrivelled skin, tiny skulls strung into necklaces – at first glance they could be flowers or beads. Nyala picks up a skull, and turns it round in her hands, gibbering to the empty eyes.

'What's she saying?' I ask the stall holder, who's shrunken into a hooded robe, each hand tucked into the opposite sleeve. I don't understand his reply, but he presses the skull into Nyala's hand and shoos us away. We head for the woods, she bounds ahead of me and slips behind a tree, emerging just as I get there, like a wood nymph sliding out of the silvery bark.

Back at the hut Ty has company. Climbers just back from their trek, exhausted but buzzing, their damp clothes spread over rocks. They've been away for a month – on another planet, they say, of ice and rock, way above the clouds – and are hungry for news, contact, fresh food and conversation. Ty told them I went to the village for post and they rush towards me. 'Is it here yet? There'll be letters from home for me, for sure.'

'It's being sent from Kathmandu this week,' I say.

'I'll have to get to a phone,' says the tallest one. He is jaunty but gaunt, blurting out apocalyptic tales of falls into crevasses, waiting out storms on six-inch ledges while chunks of avalanche graze his frozen eyelashes. 'I told my mum if she didn't hear from me in a month I'd probably be dead.'

'What d'you want to say that for?' I say.

'I thought it was a joke before I went up there.'

I make a fire and cook potatoes and dhal. The trekkers eat, then sprawl out, sleep coming easily in the afternoon sun. Ty pores over their maps. He walks over to his meditation spot, facing the mountain, the great fishtail of Machhapuchare. In some ways he's already gone, I think. Into this world of rock and ice and pureness, where your body needs every mouthful you give it. Where there's nothing to save you but yourself.

'You OK?' says Ty. I've been drifting off; my type of meditation, staring at the clouds, the rippled reflections of mountaintops in the river.

'I met the mad girl on the way to the village. Nyala she's called.'

'Is she mad?'

'I like her.'

'Those lads have been on an amazing trek. Right up high, off the main routes, over glaciers and everything.'

'And that's where you want to go?'

'We'd need to be prepared. How about trying some climbing moves together?'

I look at Ty's shiny practice rock. I don't want to hang off it from my fingernails. Let alone another piece like it thousands of feet up, snow glinting red-gold and slippery all around me.

'Romany, you can't go if you're not ready. It's too dangerous.'

Isn't that the point? I think, but I say, 'There's so much we can do from here; keep the hut, go off for a few days . . .'

There's a lump rising in my throat that I mustn't keep down. I have to tell him that I want to stay here in our hut, still for a while, only time and space and the clouds moving. That I'm worried about being so far away from Kate and the house, might lose it, might already have . . .

'That's what you want then,' says Ty. 'At least I know that much.'

'You should write to your mum before we go anywhere.'

'Why?'

'She'll be worried, Ty. She must miss you.'

Ty straightens his back, his face pulled, as if a piece of invisible string is attached to his cheek. He breathes the tic away. 'Romany, I really don't think my mother would give a shit if she never saw me again,' he says.

16

The next morning I slip out before dawn and walk up to the col, to look over the top. It's cold; I'm underdressed, unprepared. It's black behind me and blacker before me, Ty's headtorch flickers up the path. The cold makes it hard to breathe and the path is frighteningly steep, a tremor and I'd be off, gone. Patches of snow grow around me, islands in the blackness. Higher up, the snow is sculpted by wind into fantastical shapes – waves with foaming white horses; the inside of a giant's ear, a giant as big as Machhapuchare itself. I hold my hand out to touch a crystallized ridge of snow and it vaporizes – *pfft*, gone. I stumble and find myself walking backwards downhill, pulled down to the hut where Ty is beginning to stir. I warm my hands before sliding down next to him, tasting his breath and his skin like it's rationed.

'Something happened to her that none of us can reach,' says Kishore.

We're sitting in the morning sun while Kishore talks of Nyala. Ty is sorting out his rucksack, a daily ritual now: check stove, compass, map. I'm trying to take in Kishore's tale of the swaddled, thrown baby, the toddler who slept with the goats and played alone in the woods, the wary girl who draws strange pictures on the rocks and frightens the villagers.

'She can teach us something,' says Kishore. 'Be sure of that.'

Ty sharpens his knife on a rock, distant from the conversation, from me. He's contained, focused, has been ever since he saw those highest peaks, although sometimes in the night he clutches me and stutters my name – *Romany, Romany, Romany.*

'She sees things that others don't,' says Kishore. 'Her pictures are alive for her, as alive as you or me. One day she came home and drew out a journey back to our ancestral village, convinced she'd just been there. But she was only over on the pasture with the goats. I was watching her while I darned my trousers.'

I look across to the other meadow on the opposite side of the valley. There are goats there now, a boy tending them.

'It was still morning when she came down,' says Kishore. 'She'd had to beat the goats to get them moving. "They're still hungry," I said. "They've had no time to eat." She stared at the sun and at me, a needle still in my hand, and a look crossed her face, something didn't fit . . .' Kishore shrugs. 'The gods must know what they're doing. She's always been a happy child, despite her strangeness.'

'A journey back to her home . . .' I say. 'What could that mean?'

'She draws her pictures,' says Kishore. 'That's all we can know of it.'

'She's all right though, isn't she?' says Ty, as if that's the end of the matter. Even Kishore seems surprised at his abruptness. Ty hitches his rucksack on to his back, pulling on the straps, shifting about to spread the weight across his shoulders. 'Romany, we need to talk, because I'm ready to get off now,' he says.

Despite the weeks of preparation, his decision seems sudden. 'I'm waiting,' I say. 'Till the post comes from home.'

'Romany, you're the one who wanted to get away from home in the first place.'

'These aren't the fucking Lickey Hills, you know.'

'I'm leaving tomorrow; at dawn,' he says.

That's it then. If I'm not ready he'll leave without me.

'Don't you care about anything except mountains? Something might've happened to Kate.'

'Like what? Anyway, you're always saying that the last thing Kate needs is people worrying about her. Now, are you coming with me or not?'

I try to stay angry with him, but in less than an hour I'm down from my sulking spot, a dropping-splattered ledge I've seen Nyala use, squatting while she stares in puzzlement at the sky. Kishore has gone back to his side of the valley and Ty is waiting for me.

'Romany, honey, don't let's part like this,' he says. 'This trek is something I need to do. You can come too, if you want. Please believe that I want to be with you.'

Oddly enough, I do. I've been sitting on the ledge thinking of how I'd have reacted back in Brum, if a boyfriend announced he was leaving whether I liked it or not. That it was something he had to do. Bullshit, I'd have said. You don't *have* to do anything. What kind of a twat do you take me for? And I'd have been out the door, on a bender for three or four days, throwing Mum into a panic and Kate into league with me. 'If he phones tell him you don't know where I am,' I'd say to Kate. 'That you're worried.' And Kate would say, 'I will be worried if you keep on pouring vodka down your neck like that.'

But this is nothing to do with Ty loving me – he does, I've seen it, felt it – so maybe it's not to do with me at all and I should just let him go. I was always wanting those boys to *prove* that they loved me, to track me down and burst through the door saying, 'Romany, I was wrong, it's *you* I

144

want . . .' and I'd say, 'Tough, you've had your fucking chances.'

'Come on, sweet, let's go out,' says Ty. 'For a meal. There's a new place opened up in the valley, Kishore says. You could wear your jewel.' Ty bought me an opal in Varanasi; had it set by a jeweller in Kathmandu.

'I look like a banshee,' I say. My face is puffy, hair slowly matting into locks like Nyala's. 'I need to wash my hair.'

'Let me do it for you.'

So we go to the stream where pure, freezing water gallops over the rocks in streaks of silver and blue. There's a pool where the water is greener and warmer, perfectly placed by nature and the gods to catch sunlight. We take all our clothes and beat them clean against the rocks, watch the colour run out of the cheap cotton and tip over the edge of the pool, purple and red swirls joining the silver and blue. Ty gives me a massage, breathing in and out, in and out, our bodies synchronizing, our heartbeats calming; then tips icy water from the stream over me and I scream from shock and delight. We smoke some best Nepali black, naked apart from the scarf that Ty wraps around the base of the chillum, which then wraps itself around Ty as he stands on a rock in the stream. *Ali boom Shiva*, he goes, glancing the chillum off his forehead and he's lost to me for a moment in a cloud of smoke and spray, as more water crashes down from the heights. Then we lie on the bank, cushioned by spongy moss, pools of water settling in our tummy buttons, inside the curves of our ears and the pit of Ty's throat, like it does in dips and hollows of the landscape.

The restaurant is a couple of hours' walk from our hut. In the daytime it's a meditation space; people sit around on cushions and hum. At night they bring out candles and tables and serve schnitzels and buffalo steak for the

European punters. The glass pyramid roof is supposed to channel light and energy; Ty reckons even Himalayan light couldn't wake this lot out of their stoned daze, not that we can talk, careering down the hill dolled up and light-headed for our farewell dinner. I feel jittery; Ty and I touch each other all the time – faces, hands, bumping shoulders, tripping on the raffia matting into his lap. It's like a long-delayed date, a brief encounter at an airport, planes waiting, engines running, to take us off in different directions.

The place is full of noisy trekkers; we're invited to join some, but me and Ty are in a bubble tonight: just us. I'm proud of myself that I'm not holding him back, that I won't let the hurt in me ruin our last evening, and I tell him so. *Aren't I good*, I'm saying, tipping my head, leaning forward so the candlelight flickers over my half-hidden breasts. *Look at me*.

'You look beautiful,' says Ty. 'I must be mad to leave you.'

'Insane,' I say.

'What are you going to do while I'm away?'

'Have my own adventure.'

'If you need anything, ask Kishore.'

'I'll be fine.' My hand strays to the chain around my neck, to my jewel. Our food comes – we're having chips, toasted sandwiches and salad; English food, outrageously expensive compared to local fare but a proper treat after months of dhal and rice. There'll be nothing like this in the mountains.

'I'd never been to a restaurant before I moved in with Kate,' I say.

'She told me you had three starters and two puddings once.'

'I made them take me places that I'd begged food from when I was homeless; doesn't taste much different, I can tell you. But it was great to be on the inside for once.'

146

'And in Nepal we get excited over a plate of chips.'

After the meal we walk along the river. A small boat is tied to a tree stump and Ty lifts me into it, leaving his boots on the stump to show that we haven't gone for good.

'I hope they don't get nicked,' I say. 'You're going to need them tomorrow.'

'Maybe I won't go then,' says Ty. We have a paddle each, and are dipping them into the water, Injun-style.

'Don't play games, Ty. You've thought about nothing else for weeks.'

'We might wake up and find everything's different.'

'Are you telling me you don't want to go up there?'

We both look up. The midnight-blue sky is cut by thousands of stars, and pricked all around by the shining, moon-bright, snowy peaks. Our boat spins slowly round in a circle, the full panorama, and stops with the bow pointing straight at the pass above our hut.

'I'll get myself sorted up there,' says Ty. 'I promise.'

'You'd better,' I say.

Ty's boots are still on the stump; he's careful to tie the boat well and holds my hand as we walk slowly home. Suddenly I've become precious; he sits me down, lights a fire, wraps a blanket round my shoulders. We drink butter tea and Ty goes through the stores with me, even though we sorted them together, the candles, oil, rice and flour that Kishore bought. He sits behind me, kissing my neck and whispering; not words, just flutters of his lips on my skin. The last thing I remember as I drift off to sleep is the smell of his neck, imprinted into me now, chocolate and plain soap, a touch of musk and pine. My Ty. Mine.

I dream that I've unpacked his rucksack and that everything he needs to survive is there, laid in a row. I start repacking but nothing fits. I've done something wrong, but no matter how many times I try I can't work out what it is.

*

In the morning we're subdued. I make breakfast before the sun is up and stir extra honey into his porridge; he's going to need his strength. Ty paces around outside, hitching his rucksack on and off, fussing with the straps, the weight, a last-minute repair on a pocket. Dawn begins to glow behind the fishtail mountain and it's time for Ty to trap.

'Shall I walk up with you for a bit?' I say. His face is twitching, invisible strings pulled by an invisible puppet-master. Pulling him away from me.

'No,' he says. 'Let's say goodbye here.'

'Bye then.'

'I love you.'

'More than ever right now,' I say.

Ty's face twists – he wants to protest, no, no, it's not like that – but he can't deny the truth: that he'll walk up that path flooded with bittersweet tension, torn between staying and going. Like me at the airport looking at Kate, wanting her backing. 'Go,' she said to me. 'But write. Every day.'

'Go on,' I say to Ty. 'Go now. Go because you can.'

17

The Last Chance Saloon
aka Frieda's House
Norfolk

Dear Romany,
I'm sending this to Kathmandu, crossing fingers that
it'll reach you before you disappear into the mountains. We got your card from Varanasi, eventually;
loads has happened here and we don't know what you
know. Three or four letters have gone missing, all sent
to Calcutta, but you left so suddenly.

What happened, Romany?

Me and Mum are staying at Frieda's at the
moment, Dad with Griz and Carla while he tries to
sort Mount Street out. It was terrible, that flood from
the attic; none of us can bear to see the house so
wrecked but Dad goes over for the post, so we got
your letter at last. They think water froze around the
cold-water tank, and when the thaw came it brought
half the ceiling down. God, Mum's face when she saw
this hole in the attic floor – she just about fainted on
the spot. She hasn't got over Tom yet. Sometimes I
wonder if she ever will.

You see . . . Sit down if you're not already. Take a
deep breath. You see, Tom is dead, Romany. You
didn't know, did you? I hope Ty's there with you, that

you haven't gone off to the post office on your own, because it gets worse – he was killed; murdered. God knows what happened. Mum spent weeks badgering people to find out more, but drew a blank. Some fight, some argument. Maybe Tom stood up for someone, like he always did. A blow on the head can kill you, a drunken punch. It could have been anything. Anything can kill anyone at any time – we know that. But why did it have to be Tom?

Only the good die young, they say. Well, I want to be old and bad, then. I want us to be old and bad together . . .

I broke off from reading. My hand crumpled the paper, arm swung backwards to throw it away, into the gutter to be squashed by a *tuk-tuk*, shat on by a mule. Destroy this news. Mash it up. Now, above me, slicing through the china-blue sky, is an aeroplane. I jump up and wave at it, *wait wait*, my fingers can nearly reach it. But it's gone. The white trail across the sky fades. I hold on to the ground outside the hut and smash my arms and legs into the earth.

Nyala told me there was a letter. As Ty's silhouette shrank up the pass, she was on her way across the meadow. She drew the shape of a truck on my hand, mimed mail bags being unloaded, and pulled me down to the village. By the time I got to the shop my letter was waiting for me on the counter. JACKSON, R, POSTE RESTANTE, KATHMANDU, NEPAL. PLEASE FORWARD IF NECESSARY. PLEASE HOLD. THANK YOU. Kate's writing. I went outside and sat on the step to read it. I swooned, I think; stumbled back up to the hut thinking foot-in-front-of-foot, foot-in-front-of-foot. The next thing I remember I was back up here, Nyala squatting in front of me with a cup of water.

She's in the woods watching me now, as I batter myself into the ground.

. . . I don't know if I should go into this now – don't know anything much any more. Me and Mum and Frieda sit here in a daze, the wind whistling under us, even now, two months on. Mum especially – it's really knocked her for six.

I need to tell you something else. Before all this happened, Tom and the house, Ty wrote asking me to contact a friend of his who's in prison. I should've said, I know, but you were on such a high, and I didn't want to be the one that brought you down. I haven't managed to find out anything much about him yet except that Ty knew him up north. He's locked up for burglary and fraud, petty stuff. Maybe Ty feels responsible in some way, I don't know, but I'm going up to Northumberland soon to stay with Jack so I might at least go and look at the house where he grew up. It's weird how we know nothing about him before he came to Birmingham? But maybe you do by now.

I'm sorry, Romany. This is all too much, I know. Write soon to Frieda's; write to Mum. We need to hear from you. I know how you'll be feeling now the world's without Tom. More vicious, less safe. That knowledge there, like grit under your skin. And if we're not careful the grit will stir, grind out more holes. And you know this, my sister, that the only way to deal with the holes inside ourselves is to be together.
Love always,
Kate xxx

A cold wind slithers down from the pass above me. Kishore has joined Nyala here. They wrap a blanket around my shoulders and feed me soup.

'Shall I fetch him?' says Kishore. 'He's only been gone half a day. Nepali feet are fast. You know where he was going over the other side?'

I shake my head. I can't speak. The only words I want to say – *Tom is dead* – are stuck in my windpipe. I can't breathe unless I say them but they're jammed, sideways, at the back of my throat. Nyala is miming – *breathe, slowly* – and I try to follow the rise and fall of her chest. I grab on to both of them – the meadow is lurching, one twitch of the earth and we could all be dashed on to the rocks. The mountain peaks crowd in over us; I see the sky through a shrinking hole. Wind snatches the paper, the letter, out from my limp fingers, Kishore goes after it but I wave it away. I hang on to Nyala's arm as the jagged ridges above move closer together, giant stone jaws closing, blizzard-teeth, and I'm trapped here, alone, thousands of miles from my home; the empty house which has just come crashing down all over my family.

Fever crawls through me. I manage to give my passport and money to Kishore, saying, *Take what you need to take care of me*, and to scribble a note to Mum and Kate at Frieda's, which Nyala carefully folds into her blouse. I think a doctor comes – there are some pills anyway, for dysentery, Kishore says – but all I really remember is hours cramped over the pit which is our toilet; Nyala brings a plank so I don't have to squat. She keeps me clean, leads me back to bed. Then I lie on my sleeping bag and cry like a whipped dog.

My head is with Tom – snatches, fragments. Trying to find a shape for his life that makes sense. Under this fever my street front – *yeah man, shit happens* – shrivels and I feel like Jenny, outraged, doors slammed in my face as I yell, *Why?* Selfish cow – why was I so wrapped up in travelling before I left? He was on the road, yes, picking mushrooms, recycling tat, stealing milk from cows' udders. But he kept coming back to the city, couldn't leave well alone.

A thought slops around the back of my brain. That winter, before I went to Kate's. I was with Sonny, squatting a derelict house with a load of other runaways, food dye in our hair to try and fool the police. There was a junkie girl there – Karen – the first time I'd seen all that close to. She'd butchered herself – her body a mess of bust veins and septic sores – and she scratched, all day; what was left of her skin coming off in chunks. I hadn't seen Tom for a while. He couldn't stand Sonny; told me to my face he was waiting for the spell between us to break. Then he turned up one day with a kid he'd found half frozen under the bandstand in Handsworth Park. Called as he came up the path, 'Romany, get a brew on, fetch some blankets' – my head out of the upstairs window.

'Tommy, nice one. I thought you'd forgotten all about me,' I said.

'As if, Romany. Is your dodgy boyfriend in?'

'You can talk . . .'

'Is he in?'

'Nah.'

'Get down here and open up then. This kid's been sleeping outside for three nights.'

'Karen's in the front room. Be lucky if she can make it to the door, mind . . .' I bounced down the stairs and pulled off the plank that locked our front door.

'Who's Karen?' said Tom.

'Smackhead. She was here when we came. She's a mess. But lovely when she's stoned. There's a sweet heart in there somewhere.'

Tom pushed on the door to the front room. Karen was slumped on the sofa, scratching. She managed a bleary flicker before launching into a long, paranoid ramble to nobody.

153

'I know,' said Tom. 'I know that sweet heart.'

She was his love. They were both from Telford, Shrews-bury, some place like that. Ran away together when they were still kids – I was driven out, Tom said, no space for anyone my colour in a small town like that; she came with me. He spent hours with her over the following few weeks – I don't think anyone had sat down and talked to her for years. Got hold of some methadone, took her off to rehab, stayed with her as much as he could, but it was useless. Smack was the only life she knew, the only life she could handle. I saw her around and about that winter and I'd think *poor Tom*, but I had my own problems.

Sonny was on the run from the army and a bunch of kneecapping drug dealers. I knew I had to split – Kate's face hovered, stuck around the edges of my mind like distant light – but I couldn't make the final break, caught up in this fierceness between me and Sonny; we'd kiss in the middle of town, two urchins snogging in the museum doorway while crusties and their dogs took baths in the fountain outside. Forcing the world to see us. The ties weren't just to him but against everyone who'd ever wronged us, who pretended they needed fifty pence more than we did, whose fear turned to anger if Sonny went too near.

Tom would have gone back for Karen, I think; couldn't break away. A hopeless case just like him – like me, some would have said. And I didn't give in and go to Kate until the last possible moment. Tom said that to me: 'Either go to them or end up dead out here.'

Isn't it better that I stayed alive? Instead of dying on the street, in a stairwell like Tom?

My fever lasts ten days and I come out of it weak as a baby. Kishore and Nyala – especially her – are patient, loving. Nyala sits by my sleeping mat and draws pictures in the dirt floor: skulls, flattened clouds, stick-men with oversized heads. I need to communicate with her, this girl who stayed with me as I sweated and puked and shat stinking water for hours. I hold her hand, touch her face; too feeble to do much else. As I get stronger I comb and plait her hair, wash us both in a sachet of soap I find at the bottom of my rucksack. We take the reeking bedding up to the pool to wash. I can only watch her, and be grateful for the water between my toes, the sun on my face. She's pleased to see me better, draws devils and demons in the sand and then crosses them out, flings her hands towards the sky – yes, I think, that's what a fever is, like being possessed – and I nod and mime, pouring water out of a cup, *all gone, all gone*. She points at me – *you* – then writes on my hand and flaps her arms like a bird. *Your letter is gone*. Then she walks around the pool, shoulders back, adjusting the straps on her imaginary pack and twitching. *Ty is gone*. She doesn't need to act the next question. *Now you? What will you do?*

I mime being pulled in two directions; hold out my shaking, weak hands. She nods sympathetically. I could just get on the bus to Kathmandu – I'd be there in a day, a flight out in a week or so, catapulted back to Brum, the piece of elastic that stretches between me and the city suddenly contracting and *bang!* I'm home. But I promised Ty I'd wait for him; can't just abandon him as if everything we've had out here was nothing, slice him out of my life. There's no house to go to in Brum anyway, and this thought sends me dizzy, I feel the heat draining out of my face. Nyala takes my arm and leads me back down to the hut. I collapse into feverish dreams where the devil squeezes into the void inside me and no amount of sweating and thrashing can get him out.

Dear Kate,
You'll have had my note by now, I hope it wasn't too

155

rambling. I fell into a fever but I'm getting better now, no need to worry. I want to come home but Ty's off in the mountains and I'm up on a hillside waiting for him. It feels like I've been riding along on a tidal wave this whole trip and now I'm suddenly dumped here, on my own; memories that were held in the wave raining down on me, pinning me flat to the rocks. Tommy's dead, Ty's gone and I'm floored – can't seem to break through to the next minute and move on. I'm sorry, Kate, I hope you can understand. I'll be back as soon as I can.

Can't the house be fixed? It always seemed so solid to me. I think of you out at Frieda's, battered by storms, Mount Street empty and soaked and it makes everything go rickety. How's Mum? It's hard to think of her so down. We always made out she was kind of naïve, her and Frieda – their slogans and protests and bloody petitions – but the thought of Mum cynical like the rest of the world, it's horrible. Remember when they came back from their Greenham reunion, singing all night, out on the beach with a fire and those old drums of Jack's? Mum and Frieda at the sea's edge like two old warriors, crunching back up the beach with new plans to tell us, defiant as everyone needs them to be.

I can't bear to write about Tom, but tell me where he rests so I can think of him there. I hope it's some-where pretty, with flowers and foxes and birds in the trees. And yes, you're right about Ty – there's plenty he's not told us. He says he's gone to the mountains to sort his head out, that being up there will do it. More questions – did you go to see this bloke in prison? Have you seen Ty's mum, his house?

I know this letter isn't enough. I'm sorry. I should be on my way to you now. I will, as soon as I can.

156

Maybe if you think hard you can send me the strength
to move.

    R xx

Food, says Nyala, placing a bowl of dhal bhat in front of
me. *Eat*.

She's not actually saying anything and I don't have to
voice my reply either. *I'm not hungry. It makes me sick.* I
haven't spoken since I heard about Tom; not one word,
though they whirl around my head. I must ramble at night;
sometimes I bolt upright, mad-eyed, and dig my nails into
Nyala's arm. Two girls on the mountainside, who don't
speak, whose hair is knotted, who talk to creatures no one
else can see. There are tales up here of faeries and spirits
that live in the rocks, the trees, in a wildcat or a baby.
That's Kishore's explanation for how Nyala is: a spirit
slipped into her as she was thrown from the trader's arms,
her soul snatched in those few footloose seconds. That's
why she loses time and draws strange pictures and can't
speak, and also why she must be cared for. She's a holy
thing, 'in a different place'.

'It is not so sad,' Kishore says, seeing my face. 'There are
always people like this, a little strange. Maybe we need
them.' But I'm not sad for Nyala but for Tom and for the
feeling that my soul too has been snatched. A demon –
waiting for years for me to plummet like this – has
dropped like a kestrel out of the sky and grabbed it.

Eat, says Nyala with her eyes. She's sitting on the edge of
my bedroll, dipping chapatti into dhal. A flicker of sun
through the wooden shutter and she could be Kate, when I
first went to Mount Street after that winter on the run with
Sonny, dipping bread into soup and holding it out to me.
'Here,' she said. 'You've got to eat.'

'Get my strength up,' I said feebly, taking a mouthful to
please her.

157

*

Kate liked looking after me. Folding clean sheets and towels; sorting the tray of bandages, dressings, drugs, swabs, sachets of sterile water and tubes of cream. A deep scratch on my leg had ulcerated and wouldn't heal; left a scoop the size of an egg in my calf. The cure was a foam dressing which had to be mixed from two powders and then poured into the wound where it gelled; fingers of liquid foam sneaking into unseen fissures in my skin and soaking up dead, infected cells. Kate had to prise the foam out twice a day, wash it and put it back in, but not before we checked the wound for crystals of new flesh, slowly granulating from the inside out. Every few days the foam was too big to go back in and we had to mix a new one, keeping the spiky-shell shapes on the windowsill as trophies, reducing in size until I was healed, skin sliding over the lesion in the night.

The first thing we did when I could get up was go to the photo booth in Woolies, all our pocket money into the slot, picture after picture of us copying each other's faces until we muddled even ourselves. I couldn't get my head around this idea of free money – money for just being me. Michael and Jenny were brilliant about it, from day one they gave us exactly the same. If Kate had new shoes then I could choose some; if I begged for an album she could have a book.

'They're so even-handed,' I said to Kate. 'All I ever got told was, "Who said it was going to be *fair*?" Teachers and foster mums and everyone who's ever been near a kids' home.'

'They can't buy me stuff and not you,' said Kate, nodding at the posters in the kitchen: FAIR TRADE, DON'T DUMP YOUR NUKES ON US, old FREE NELSON MANDELA ones, his face young and fierce. 'It's what they believe in.'

'Both of them?'

'Dad's a bit more realistic. Sometimes I think Mum wants to make it up to everyone who's ever been wronged.'

'Me, at the moment then,' I said.

'Yes.'

I stared at the photos. Frozen moments: tongues sticking out, cheeks pressed together. Then the last picture of the last strip – two girls staring at the camera, hands joined and held up between faces with identical unplanned expressions: chins out, eyes accusing.

'She can't make it up though, can she?' I said to Kate. 'Not that she shouldn't try, but . . .'

'No,' said Kate, 'she can't. But we can.'

'Deal.'

18

Dear Romany,

Hello, my darling. Hello, hello. Now I know where you are I've put a pin in the map north of Pokhara. Went to the library and got all the glossy books on Nepal out, so now I'm surrounded by slabs of blue rock, carved mani stones and rainbow prayer flags. High meadows and wooded valleys; families with huge baskets on their backs strung out single-file along paths, ice shimmering high above them. Describe it for me, Romany, so I can be there, too.

Things you'll want to know. Tom's buried at St Mary's. Where Mum and Dad were married and where I used to go with Juniors for harvest festivals and Christmas carols. I was the Angel Gabriel in that church. We didn't know what else to do – Tom was dead and I didn't feel I could take his ashes off on my own; maybe if you'd been here we could have, but at the time the Church was there – someone, something with a way to deal with death. He's buried right down at the end, where the graveyard stretches back into the beech trees, where we used to smoke dope and spook each other with ghost stories. But we couldn't really get scared, could we? Because we were together, we had each other.

Come home, Romany. We need you.

The house is in a state. Dad's doing his best – drags Griz over there at weekends, but to tell you the truth they're glad of the excuse to get the Led Zep albums out and pretend they've still got hair. Mum and Dad can't even agree on what needs doing, and Mum won't go back there until it's how she wants it. Carla phoned and told me she went round and found the living room full of empty cans and them in the pub playing air guitar along to 'Parisian Walkways'. 'Don't tell your mum,' she said. 'Not just yet.'

It's OK here, though. The emptiness is seductive – no traffic or hoardings, no distractions from the flat lines of sea and sky. After you left I found it hard to go out; felt too exposed, too alone. It's better here: everyone in the village knows me now and at least I *can* go out unlike poor Tom. There's the beach and Star. The cats are here, following us down to the dunes, bursting through the marram grass to swipe at Star's tail. They curl up with me as I look out at the sea and read – climbing epics at the moment, *Touching the Void*. Do you think that's what Ty's after? The books are full of those sorts of questions – Why climb such mountains? Why seek out danger? 'Because it's there' of course, the famous phrase. But I think Joe Simpson's title gets closer; we want to reach something special, something beyond ourselves. 'It may be that we shall touch the Happy Isles,' Tennyson says, and Ulysses refuses his happy ending in favour of one last voyage. And, anyway, staying at home's not any safer, is it?

Mum's ill. Not lying in bed with tubes and drugs and dressings – that would be easier; there'd be a doctor to talk to, nurses with charts, a glimmer of progress – but deflated, close to cowed. She moves slowly. 'Your mum's always loved being strong,' says

161

Frieda. 'She knows what a gift it is, what a miracle.' Did you know that Mum nursed her mum as well as her dad through long illnesses? Granny Platt never came through it – she broke her hip and lost her spark and her life just sort of drained away. Frieda says that's when the running and the gym and the swimming started, Mum would settle Granny into some sort of comfort, feeding her tea through a toddler cup and then she'd be off out on the streets to pound it all out. I want to drag her down to the sea, yell, 'Come on, Mum,' like she did with me, for years. But she's well past the point where shouting's any use. 'Softly softly,' says Frieda. 'She's got to heal.'

I look at a Nepali hillside in my book and imagine you standing there. If I squint I can see you jumping up and waving at me, both arms reaching for the sky, but then you're jerked backwards, an invisible string hooked under your armpits. You look around, uncertain. Family plague – we're all uncertain at the moment. Dad visits, hovers around us. He doesn't know what to do or say. Frieda tells him to wait, to let Mum sit out her sadness. Send him a letter, Romany. I know he'd be glad of it.

I'm writing this on the train to Northumberland. So when you're reading it – now – I could be outside Ty's house, his childhood home. I want to talk to his mum, ask her about Adrian. I've written but he won't say much, except that Ty was a good friend. He wants me to visit him, says he'll tell me more if I do. After Tom died I got really angry with Adrian, thinking, lucky bastard, you're better off locked up. But he's not safe really – Frieda put me straight on that, the violence inside prisons. But freedom being so scary that you're better off inside? I shouldn't be thinking like that, Romany, not even for a minute. And I'm sorry I didn't say anything to you about Adrian; events just took over, like I guess they did with you when you first got to India.

Vaz wants me to visit him too – Tom's mate who lives in a tipi in Wales. They all want me to come to them. Instead I'm on my way north, on a journey of my own.

Write.

Love,

Kate xx

'My sister,' I say, to Nyala and Kishore.

Kishore translates for Nyala, *didibahini*, and she looks at me and nods. She even tries to say it, 'Sssst.'

'Yes, my sister, it's from my sister in England.' For a second I really believe that she'll speak as well, miraculously. My voice is back and I want her to talk, too.

'Sssst,' she says.

'You will go home?' says Kishore.

'Yes . . . No. I don't know. How long . . . I mean, when do you think he'll be back?'

'The trek is three or four weeks, but your man, he talked of climbing some peaks. He may have to wait, for weather, acclimatization. Out there weeks can just pass – *phut*.' He slices his hand through the air.

I look up at the col where I last saw Ty; spend hours staring at the old map he left behind trying to conjure up his landscape. Our journeys have split; his higher, mine stalled, sliding backwards even. Nyala skips around me, sniffs the air like the goats do. She's covered the broken rocks around the hut with her drawings, curls and scrolls and odd, alien-shaped heads. I like to think these drawings might protect me. In Nepal the landscape is never still, Kishore says – on the highest pass there'll be mani stones and prayer flags to thank the gods for safe passage. Every boulder has a tale to tell and the streams bring down stories from the places humans can't live. Nyala belongs to this; she talks to the trees and listens to the rocks, makes marks everywhere – swirls of mud in a puddle, her footprints in the first of the snow that creeps towards the meadows.

'Caring for you has been good for her,' says Kishore. 'I worried that we might lose her completely after that day she brought the goats down early. She seemed confused – would press her cheeks against the trees, taste water from the streams, puzzled by pebbles and air. Nyala may never leave this valley, but sometimes I think she's seen more than any of us, things the rest of us miss.'

'She's been an angel to me.'

'My wife says she can watch the younger children, now. It will help us.'

'Good.'

My hand strays to the scar on my calf, the skin thin and glassy. Being ill has made me aware of my body, the map of scars – tiny, invisible ones, like the set of half moons on my forearm, from the dug-in nails of the brute who was after Sonny. Burns on my hands and wrists from being careless or drunk with fires and candles. A fence spike straight into my thigh. Scrages and scrapes on knees and elbows; a split right between my eyes from falling out of a tree, a spurt of bright blood as my head cracked. And my missing toe, of course, a flap of skin sewn neatly over the new space in my body; I stuff tissues into my shoe to stop my foot sliding around. Still feel the itches and twitches of sand or water between a toe you can't see.

Some trekkers bark at each other as they make their way up the path, eyes fixed on the peaks ahead. Himalaya, the 'abode of the snow'; home of blue sheep and snow leopards, yogis who slow down their heartbeats to ward off the cold, like the bears who sleep through the winter in

164

caves. Maybe Yeti live up there, too. A mythical land where temples are carved out of rocks and bodhisattvas meditate, chewing their rice slowly. But a twelve-hour flight from England, a few days in Kathmandu and the trekkers are here, walking up on to the roof of the world. The porters speak with Kishore, squat down and light beedies. Nyala stokes up the fire for chai, but the trekkers hold back.

'Come and have some tea,' I say, and their surprised eyes tell me they thought I was Nepali. I'm wearing Nyala's cotton trousers and a scarf over my head, no shoes; my skin is the same colour as hers.

'You're English?' says a short, stocky bloke; northern accent, thigh muscles straining out of his skin-tight leggings.

'Yes.'

'Have you done your trek?'

'Er, no . . . I'm living here.'

They stand around awkwardly, packs still on their backs. 'Sit down,' I say; the porters will want to exchange news, collect messages to pass on in the valley beyond. I could set them at their ease, ask about their flights, the route they're planning, the hills they've already climbed in Scotland and the Alps. But I don't want to make it easy for them; they *should* be awed by this strangeness and mystery. They should tread lightly and understand that they're small.

'How's England?' I say.

'Huh?'

'England. That rock in the Atlantic.' A tune comes into my head – dum di-dum di-dum di-dum – *The Archers*, Mum used to listen to it. I can see them fiddling with their shortwave radios getting all nostalgic, up there in a blizzard going dum di-dum di-dum di-dum. 'Bloody Radio 4,' I say. 'Those people think moving *house* is stressful. As if you've got any problems if you've got a house.' Words, thoughts which have been twisting round my head, spill

165

out of me, nonsense, gibberish, but liberating. No wonder Dom always seemed calmed after one of his volleys.

'You know. Man United – I shouldn't say that really, being a Brummie, but the whole world's heard of Man U. Cornflakes. Shreddies. *My old man said be a City fan, but I said bollocks you're a . . .* Swearing, that reminds me of home. HP sauce, Marmite, seaside B&Bs. Dogs. Pubs. Balti houses. Kebab shops. *Blind Date*. Where you've just come from – how is it?'

'Er . . . fine.' They're backing off.

'The *Big Issue*. Soup kitchens. Soup dragons. Frilly fucking duvets. The M1. Weston-super-Mare; me and Sonny were going to run away there once, live under the pier or something, if there is a fucking pier in Weston. Every Englishman's nightmare, he was. Couldn't be trusted to remember his own name but the biggest dick you've ever seen in your life . . .'

One of the trekkers blanches on the word *dick*, the others turn and scarper, leaving their porters behind, laughing with Nyala and me.

*

Sonny. We were both on the run the day we met, me from the kids' home and him from the Army. Ten seconds that change your life. I'd been down to Enoch's Miscellaneous. *We Buy Anything* it says on the door, anything except the soggy books I'd found in a skip. I did try to dry them out first. I was just back in Digbeth when a police car spotted me. Down between the warehouses as quick as, skirting metal slag-heaps in the yards, feet slipping, under fizzing electric cables strung between buildings. Into a derelict shop scattered with burnt-out cider cans and quickly up the stairs to the glassless window, a good view of all the nearby streets and a way out the back if necessary. Panting, breathing quickly like a boxer, my head out of the window for a scan before I even noticed Sonny, bare-chested, scrambling out of his khakis into a pair of Kappas.

'You'll have to do something about those boots,' I said. Polished toecaps poked out from under his tracksuit. The poppers on the trackie bottoms were knackered; glimpses of his legs tattooed with vines and daggers.

'Where've you been all my life?' he said.

A line out of a film or off the telly. I was only fourteen, that's my excuse. At fourteen you dream of someone saying words like that; your prince will come and then it's happy ever after. And he was my sort of prince: fugitive and renegade. He was nineteen, had joined up at sixteen before he battered his dad back.

'I knew I'd fucked up,' he said, as we sat under his army blanket smoking dog-ends. 'But once you've signed up the only way out is with cash. I put up with those bastards screaming in my face for two years.'

'Will they be after you?' I said.

'I'll have to lie low for a bit.'

I didn't tell him the police were after me, too; that I should have been in the kids' home. We went to a flat in Weoley Castle where some mates of his lived, and dossed there for a few weeks – luxury: a dry floor to sleep on, a bath, a telly. We both begged for a while but it wasn't long before he was running errands for the local dealers. On call day and night, answering their mobiles – great big bricks in those days – and driving this mad van in and out of pub car parks; blacked-out windows and chrome bumpers and a tropical sunset painted on the back. We lived off take-aways and dressed in knock-off designer gear; Sonny was wired, couldn't keep still, pacing up and down the concrete floors in his shoplifted Nike Airs. I was the only one who could calm him; he'd get shoved back through the door with a tight, 'He's out of order, sort him out, will you?'

I could. Even right at the end. That's what kept me with him – that's what I tell myself anyway.

Then one day he shot through the door without a kick up his arse. 'We're out of here,' he said. 'Come on. Quick.'

'Where we going?'

'Come on. *Move.*'

'All right, keep your hair on. I'll just get my stuff.'

'No time for that. Out the window, *now.*'

I was down the drainpipe in a flash. Years of escaping from locked bedrooms and dormitories had made me fast, up onto the garage roofs pulling Sonny behind me and then lying flat, breathless, while the boyz roamed around below us, bellowing threats. 'Too stupid to look above eye level,' I hissed to Sonny as we slid down into the alley with baseball caps over our eyes, past the Moby Dick Fish Bar and straight on to the bus into town.

'Where we going then?' I said, giggling with relief into my cuppa in Rosa's Café.

'Dunno.'

'I'll have to go back for my clothes,' I said.

'No way, Romany.'

'No one'll see me, promise.'

'*You're not going near the place.*'

I should have left him then. Tight-lipped, scowling at me like it was my fault we were on the streets again. But my memories of holding him steady, his amazement that I was still around in the morning, the pure cheek – and stupidity – of ripping off those guys, all bound me to him. I knew he'd soon crash without me; it was fatal.

'You've got to find us somewhere to go,' he said.

'Me? Since when did I have the key to the door?'

'I've got to hide. Someone'll see me if we sleep rough.'

So we went to the squat where Karen lived. A mate of mine said there was space; everyone else had left because Karen was just too disastrous to be around. Sonny stayed in and I begged, but he couldn't stand it for long and went out, more wild-eyed every time he came back. Tommy showed up, took Karen away and told me to get my arse round to Mount Street. But I wouldn't. 'You're not giving up on *her*,' I said. 'What's the difference?'

Nyala's coming up the path. She's carrying a baby in a white bonnet and a string of multicoloured prayer flags flutters behind her like the tail of a kite. She left me alone last night for the first time and my head fills up with this: desperate times with Sonny. I wonder what Ty's thinking, alone up in the mountains, if we need to be alone to really face who we are, what we've done. I wrote him a letter last night, in my head, hugging myself in my sleeping bag and wishing my arms were his:

Ty, I know I should've asked about you, that you might think I don't love you because I didn't care enough to ask. I was too wrapped up in me, in the miracle of escape. But then you were wrapped up in me too, weren't you, Ty? You wanted to think about me and not you . . .

I wrote to Kate as well. Rambled on about how much I love her and miss her but can't come back just yet; couldn't find a way to finish it because I know what she's waiting to hear. I lick and seal the envelope and give it to Nyala. She sits down with the baby, makes him smile with claps and peek-a-boo. We both do. He's adorable, chubby and smiling, dressed in a pink embroidered waistcoat.

'Kishore's?' I say, pointing at the baby and Nyala nods, sweeps the child up in her arms and dances round with him. She claps her hand to her chest – *me* – then rocks him, strokes his brow. *I'm looking after him.*

'Great,' I say, giving a thumbs-up sign.

'Grrrrr,' says Nyala, with both thumbs.

She strings the prayer flags between two stunted trees either side of the hut, then sets about cooking for all of us.

The baby crawls on the spongy grass, plays with sticks and pebbles – I find some nice shiny ones, bright colours, and wonder if he might like something from the bag of scraps I've carried all around India with me; a domino, one piece of a jigsaw, a teddy pretty much loved-away. We giggle at the baby's games, squeeze his flawless feet, seduced by this child, this perfect baby, and I think of Mum, the secret attic room. I say a prayer for her, watch the flags fluttering and snapping in the breeze, hope that the wind will carry the prayer halfway round the world, to a house that's slipping into the sea. I shiver, feel ice moving up my spine, and a cloud slides across the morning sun.

'Don't go out today,' I said to Sonny. He was getting tooled up: blade in his shoe, cosh in his jacket. Karen was down-stairs; she'd just come back from wherever Tommy had taken her and was gouched on the sofa. The three of us on the run: me from the police, Sonny from the Army and the boyz, and Karen from rehab. Anyone in the street could be after one of us; no wonder he was paranoid.

'I'll go where I like,' he said. That was how it had got. No point in arguing – he was too edgy to cross. No punches yet but I could see them coming. The wrong words from me and *bam!* In my face. Sometimes he screamed at me like the sergeants had, nose to nose. *You useless piece of shit, think you can make it out of the gutter, do you?* We lived from day to day, I narrowed my mind to deal with that.

'You'll have to get some money, then,' he said, shrugging off his jacket.

'OK,' I said quickly. 'I'll be back as soon as I can.'

Out the door and up the street, running begging sites through in my head. I would've gone shoplifting but I was too shabby to get away with it; all the security in the city knew me anyway. I just wanted money, fast, so I could get back to Sonny – *please be there, please be there* – and that's another day done. Thinking hard about cash, scanning the gutter for dropped coins. I banged right into him, this wall of bloke, T-shirt stretched over his chest. He grabbed the hood of my sweatshirt, dug his nails into my arm. 'You're coming with me,' he said.

Straight into a van, three blokes, blacked-out windows. 'Where is he?' they said.

'I don't know what you're on about,' I said. 'Let me go.'

Bam!

'We're not messing.'

'So I see,' I spluttered, spitting blood out of my mouth.

Bam! 'That's for your cheek.'

'Anyone ever told you you shouldn't hit girls?'

Tape across my mouth and eyes, they drove me off. Stuck me in this room with boards over the windows, bolted doors. God knows where it was – city streets sound the same: traffic, sirens, kids thumping footballs, 'Greensleeves' from the ice-cream van, the thud of bass. I tried to tear the boards off the window, cursing that I'd rushed out without tools myself; I *always* had a screwdriver on me. I yelled, rained fists on the wall, praying for someone to hear me – *Help, I'm locked in. Someone help me* – thinking of all the times I'd heard shouts from the other side of a wall and ignored them. *Never again, God*, I said, *I swear*. Creeping panic, crawling over my skin; about Sonny, about the thugs, about being locked up and no one knowing where I was. There's no way Sonny will still be at the house, I thought; he'll have gone out to score, be deeper in the shit than we already are by the time I get back to him.

Then it came to me. What am I worrying about him for? I'm the one who's fucking locked up.

19

And now Ty's left me in the shit too, drained by fever, travelling, the intensity of me and India, me and him. Washed up on this meadow under the sacred mountain where there are no clocks and we chop wood, draw water like the monks who live on the high, frozen ledges. A simple, good life, without the past; it pulls on me like a dangerous current. Nyala's here most of the time with the baby; we're working out a language – circling our stomachs for *are you hungry?* Fist on chest – *me*; stirring action, *I'll cook*. Signs for *sleep* and *eat* and *wash* and *tired*; they're universal. *Walk* and *happy* and *sad*. Nyala's got one – drawing her hands together and bowing her head as all Nepalis do to greet you – *Namaste* – but then she throws her arms open and stares at the sky. It reminds me of Ty in Varanasi, flinging his bad energies into the Ganges. She wants me to understand this sign and I do, kind of; it's about wonder; being truly out there.

The baby starts to grizzle. Nyala picks him up and wipes his snotty nose with her scarf. She nods at him and circles his stomach. *He's hungry.*

I'll cook, I say, with my hands.

Sometimes I just lie and listen: the brook tumbling down from the mountain, the whistle and swoosh of the wind, goats' hooves on the rocks, the heavy breaths of the buffalo. Ty's out there now, pitting himself against nothing less than the biggest mountains in the world; Kate's in Northumberland trying to untangle the past; and I lie here listening to wind, water and rock. I know that this simplicity is what Ty's after, imagine him coming back over the pass and putting his arms around me, saying, 'It was here all the time.' Then his troubles will fall out of his mouth, as easy as the stream burbling over the rocks and we'll be able to see them, cast them off into the vastness along with the bad energies and prayers. That's what I did when we got to Bombay; told him my troubles, and it only made him love me more. So what is it about him that he thinks might make me love him less?

But I can't stay still for long, shift about, fiff, faff. Can't hear the brook or the buffalo any more, only whats and whys and why nots in my head. Nyala scowls at me; it's a few seconds before I realize she's copying my face. She drags me outside to watch the light catch on the angled rock and ice of Machhapuchare, blood orange and glinting, grainy gold. As if a volcano has suddenly erupted and slicked sheets of golden lava down the mountainside. A cloud swims over the sun and we're blinded by whiteness until the fire chases the cloud away and the holy mountain glows again.

I didn't see daylight for four days.

They made me write a note to Sonny, then the biggest thug took his pencil from behind his ear, licked the tip and wrote 12 Leasow Crescent – the address of the squat – on the envelope and gave it to a boy to take round.

'You knew where he was all the time,' I said.

'He can't get the money if we lock him up, can he?'

'Bastards.'

Someone came, left food and emptied the bucket. This young kid, a runner for them, holding his nose and making exaggerated noises of disgust, as if it was my fault I had to shit in a bucket. Once the boss-thug came. 'Seems like your boyfriend's having trouble raising the cash. A few more days and we'll have to put you out to work.'

'Fuck off.'

'Not very reliable, is he?'

'You think I'd ever work for you?'

He moved closer. 'Tell you what, I won't mash your face up this time, just in case you have to.'

'I'd mash it up myself if you were my pimp.'

But boss-thug was right. Sonny could've got the money. He could have robbed it, robbed a house, found Tom even. I lay curled up in the dark, trying to block out those thoughts. But when I woke with a start from a jumbled, paranoid dream they'd be there. *He's out getting wrecked. Just left me here.* I'd get up and exercise like a maniac: sit-ups, running on the spot, stretches and jumps and hand-stands against the wall. Accompanying myself with shouts; one, two, hup! Three, four, down! until my sweat was smeared over the floor and walls, my chest beating too fast to count along with *onetwothreefour, onetwothreefour.* Only then could I reason it out: anything could've happened. He might not even know I'm locked up. Please, Sonny, please get me out of here.

By the third day not even twenty minutes' flat-out sprinting could keep the dark thoughts away. On day four I was ready to kill him. *Bastard.* Tearing at the boarded-up window, bloody handprints on the walls along with the sweat. *Bastard.* Closing my eyes and trying to conjure light, sunshine, air, freedom to move.

'This place fucking stinks,' said the runner boy, inching a packet of cold chips towards me.

'That's what happens when you cage people up,' I spat. 'You'll have nightmares about this for the rest of your life.' He flinched. '*You're* responsible for this just as much as them,' I said.

'There's nothing I can do,' he whined, suddenly small and cowering.

'Tell Tom,' I said. 'Skinhead, pocked face, one eye. Everyone begging in town knows him. Tell him Romany's in trouble.'

That night I woke up hot and dizzy. By the morning I was coughing and by afternoon I could hardly breathe. There was nothing to ease myself with; no one to ease me. The room was freezing but I was burning up, hyper-aware. My dark thoughts weren't of Sonny any more, but me: look at the state of you, living with Karen, that's what it is, anyone looks healthy next to her. You've no strength. Your skin's falling off in lumps, your cuts don't heal. You start coughing and can't stop. Even the bones in your fingers ache.

The boy came and backed out of the door, shaking his head, recoiling at the smell of my sickness.

'You've got to help me,' I croaked, stretching out a bloody hand. 'Don't lock it. Let me get out of here.' But I couldn't move fast enough and the click of the lock was followed by the slide of bolts and footsteps down the stairs and fast away.

An hour later I fainted through the front door of 34 Mount Street. Tommy – the real prince – in through the window and out through the door; a screwdriver and a sharp kick.

'I'm not getting you out of here unless you go to them,' he said. 'I'll leave you right here on this floor unless you promise.'

'I promise,' I said. 'Tommy, please. Just get me somewhere safe.'

The sun's high in the sky and the magic mountain pristine again. If I stare hard at it I can block out the thoughts – *Is he coming? Is he coming back at all?* – because life on the mountainside's simple and sweet. I think about my life back then – would never have believed it could happen. Going to India and Nepal, with my own money that I'd earned? What fucking planet does that happen on then? Getting off the streets and into a proper home where I was loved, where everything was possible. I could be a doctor or a scientist; make films or books or journeys. And I could leave as well, drift about, hang around and think. Dad encouraged me: 'Do it now, while you can, before you get caught up in something else.' When I finally announced I was going he said, 'Great. So what do you want to get out of it?'

I raised my eyebrows at Kate. *Stupid question.*

'No, come on, Romany,' said Mum. 'Your dad's right to ask.'

'Everything. Freedom. Different cultures. Experience.'

'We've got all that on the Soho Road,' said Dad.

'OK, I'll spell it out . . .' I said. 'I'm going because you gave me an atlas and a globe. Because Kate gave me an A–Z and made me read books. Because Ty says he'll come too. I'm going because it's possible. Me, an urchin, a beggar and a thief, can get a passport and a ticket and step on a plane to the other side of the world. I don't want to *get* anything. I'm going because I can.'

20

Thrunton Wood
Near Alnwick
Northumberland

Dear Romany,

Well, I made it. Pretty good going, considering I could hardly get out of the house in Brum. Tom's death cured me – I couldn't be a coward after that. I'm staying in Jack's cottage. He's given me his room, with a real fire and a view out over the woods; even put a rocking chair by the window for me to read and write letters, to you and Vaz. It's good to talk to Vaz; he knew Tom, knows the loss. Otherwise my only company is Jack's cat Spartacus; foxes, owls, badgers, red squirrels, starlings, buzzards, rabbits and hares. The first day I was here an enormous hare, as big as a dog, just appeared on the path in front of me. The woman in the village shop says it's a good omen; that hares are protectors, faithful consorts to mythological queens. The Hindu gods have consorts, don't they? Or is it vehicles – Ganesh with his rat and Vishnu with Garuda, the half-eagle, half-human? I can't remember now, don't have all my books here with me.

I think of you on your mountain, with your fire and your view. I'm still into mountaineering; reading how a climb is managed – step by step, with fortitude, endurance and moments of crazy heroism – has given me new language, new ways to think about what's happened. And you're up there in the middle of them; waiting for Ty. Sometimes I can almost see him, strolling back over the dip in the distance. A tall, loping figure with fair hair and a slight twitch, covering the ground quickly, eagerly. I'm willing you both home, Romany. I'm pulling on the string. We need you here now.

I've seen Ty's mum. At the post office counter, in the shop, always brisk and purposeful. Everyone's very polite to her. Mrs Waterson this and Mrs Waterson that. Yes, Mrs Waterson; how are you keeping, Mrs Waterson? I haven't had the nerve to talk to her yet. There's hardly anyone in the village Ty's age: older folk, yes, and families with young children, but hardly any contemporaries of Ty's. They leave for the coast or the cities, apparently. Jack says we can go for a day out by the sea soon. But it's odd that everyone his age is gone from here, a hole in the community which no one wants to talk about.

Mum and Dad need us, Romany. It's our turn now. He doesn't know how to reach her and you know how things have been between me and Mum over the years – she'd never lean on me. So it looks like it's down to you, sweet. I'm tugging on Ty, too.

Love you,
Kate xx

Kate in Northumberland, out there on her own. What did she say? – she could hardly get out of the house in Brum? But she was sound in her letters – how come she's been in on her own all these months? Mum made hints, I suppose – 'I've told you how Kate was before', the usual faff – but Kate promised me she'd be OK if I left, it wouldn't change things. I remember us spinning the globe to see which country our fingers rested on when it stopped.

'Ecuador!' I said to Kate, who was brushing her hair in front of the mirror, levitating strands with static. 'What's in Ecuador then?'

'The Andes,' said Kate. 'Jungle.'

'Malaysia . . . no, hang on, it's still going round . . . Hawaii . . . Chile . . . Christmas Island, Senegal, Nigeria, the Congo . . . God, there must be about fifty countries in Africa.'

'I learned the capital cities of all of them in junior school. Ouagadougou, Kampala, Cairo. That's about all I do know though, except from stories.'

'More than me.'

'I'll do you a reading list.' She'd started to weave her hair into thin plaits. I helped her, taking the licks of hair and flicking them across each other. The next day her hair would be rippled all over, black as water in an underground pool. I squatted down, my face joining hers in triplicate.

'Kate, I don't want to *read* about it. I want to *go*. I'm just one of the herd here, into kids' homes, off the street, into schools. A McJob here, a council flat if I got pregnant. Keep me docile with TV and cheap booze.'

'Romany, that's all in the past. You can do anything you like now.'

'What I want to do is *leave* . . .'

I guess I should have known it'd hurt her – but Kate was always cool, with me, anyway. 'I've always dreamed of it,' I said, that night as we lay in bed, the globe spinning on the low table between us. 'To be somewhere else. Another place where life was better. I told myself that my mum and my dad were trapped in Borneo or Afghanistan, salt-mined in Siberia; couldn't come and fetch me for some proper reason – they'd lost their memories, got wrongly locked

179

up. Any story except that they dumped me. I imagined myself out there rescuing them. The social worker gave me a load of fanny about how my mum must be ill, but then I heard her talking in the office: "The house is boarded up, the neighbours say she's done one . . ."

'I sneaked out of school the next day and went there – must've only been about seven. Walking up the road remembering houses, lampposts, even neighbours: someone here might know me, might've known me as a baby. Little kids on tricycles, kicking a football across the street. The gate off its hinges, blown rubbish in the hedge. Snatching a glance at the shuttered-up house – my dreams gone with it – then running off, running and running, till I could do nothing but gasp for breath, and as soon as I'd got some I ran and ran again.'

'You never told me that,' said Kate, stopping the globe with her fingertips, holding it still.

'I never told anyone but you.'

So she understood. She knew. She wasn't convinced, mind, that there was a better life 'over the rainbow' as she put it. 'You'll come back,' she said, although at the time coming back was the last thing on my mind. 'Anyway, you're not going anywhere unless you get some cash together.'

'You haven't got any spare, have you?'

Actually, I liked earning the money to go away with; anything would do. Joining the strong-armed women with their overalls and headscarves, buffing office floors and emptying bins.

'You go for it, bab,' they said, giving me addresses in Jamaica and Pakistan. 'Come and see us when you get back.'

It was around then that Kate came back from college with Ty. Mum was fed up with me never being home, we'd had a row and I'd snapped back at her, 'Well, I'll be gone

180

for good soon!' Then bang, walking into Kate and this lanky bloke who said it, straight away: 'God, you look so alike!'

He came right into the house like he was always meant to be there, like me. I rambled on about my plans that first night, but he seemed more interested in Kate's books and Dad's workshop, I don't think he quite believed me – they were all like that. 'Oh yeah, Romany's off to see the world,' they'd say, gathering up my maps and books from the kitchen table for the fifth time that day. They were right: it's not real until you're gone. Kate knew that. She was cool. 'Go, go, out of my hair,' she said. 'You're driving me mad anyway – haven't sat still since you got hold of this travelling idea.'

'I'm not going if I'll lose you,' I said.

'Romany, you're stuck with us whether you like it or not. Family, remember?'

We hugged. Ty was with us. He stood up and walked to the window. Over Kate's shoulder I saw him staring into the garden; his shoulder and chin jerked backwards quickly, a shiver down his spine, a twitch upwards from the balls of his feet.

'Where are you going, then?' he said, after a while. Kate was in the bathroom. I was searching for a tape I wanted to play her.

'India, I think,' I said.

'Whereabouts?'

'All over. The south, the north. The mountains.'

'My dad was a mountaineer,' said Ty. 'The Lakes, the Alps a few times. But he always talked of climbing "proper" mountains, said all we have here are little bumps really, drew me scale pictures of Ben Nevis and Everest.' Ty's arms made shapes – a hillock, a huge rock as high as his arm could stretch. Kate slid back into the room as he was on tiptoes.

181

'Here it is,' I said, passing the tape to Kate. 'This is the one.' She closed her hand around it, but she was looking at Ty. Ty making mountain shapes. Ty before he decided to come.

I go back to her letters: always about me, about Ty.

She was fine about my plans when I was going alone.

21

You, says Nyala, by stretching her hand out to me. She points at the col and then up at the sky where an aeroplane cuts a path through the blue. *You go there*. She shakes her head and stamps the ground. *Not here*.

'I know,' I say. I've started talking to her as if she understands. 'I should go, but without him I'll be no use to anyone, all lovelorn and moping.' A black thought slips in, deadly. What if he's not coming back?

Nyala's neck stretches an inch; she's looking up towards the col. She's totally still, like an animal who catches a scent on the air. Then she shakes her head, relaxes, turns her uncomprehending attention to me.

'. . . not that there's anywhere to go back to. No house, no Ty, no Tom.' No fishtail mountain breaking the choppy surface of the foothills like a fin, glaciers foaming around its base. No lazy afternoons with the water buffalo's grunts, no nights watching the stars reeling around the heavens. No Nyala stroking rocks and whispering secrets into the goats' ears.

'I know, I know,' I say to her. 'Kate and Mum and Dad need me. You're right. I should go.'

But I can't even make it to the village at the moment; stalled by the wide sky, the burbling stream, the whirling hand-held prayer wheel that Nyala brought up from Kishore's hut. We're all fascinated by it: me, Nyala, the baby. It looks like an oversized rattle, carved nuggets which click against each other as they spin, the whole mechanism turning on its handle, wheels within wheels. I slip into this world easily, naturally, like Kate on her window seat with her books.

Like Kate when she wouldn't go out.

The sun's shifted in the sky, more time sliced away. Ty took our only watch with him. I made a sundial, a piece of shale notched into a flat rock. Nyala thinks I'm mad. She spins her finger around her temple – *you're crazy*. Time for her is written on the sky, the tiny flowers closing up for the night, the colder mornings – she's alert to all the changes around her, no need to keep checking. *Someone is coming*, she says to me, with her eyes. Thumping her chest and tapping her temples. I know.

Please let it be Ty, please let it be Ty, I think, pacing around. *Please, please, please*, to any of the gods or spirits out there. Then we can go home. We can sort the house out, try and make it up to everyone for being away when Tom was killed. We could have a wake for him – get all his old mates together with Mum, get angry and political instead of this deadly sadness. It couldn't be as bad as sitting here on my own asking endless pointless questions: *Why, why, why?*

That's what Mum's doing. Without a reason it's all alien to her.

Come, says Nyala, beckoning me, miming a scrubbing action. *Come and help me wash*.

'I'm going to write now,' I say, my fingers scratching across the grass in front of me.

I watch her walk off up the slope, red skirts billowing, the baby strapped on top of her basket. She's started taking in washing from some of the other Westerners who are staying around here, although I always do my own. The only chore I've had for these last six months, to keep my clothes clean, joining the locals at the stream or well or street-corner tap. The lure of living day to day: no cleaning, no bills; if in doubt stick your thumb out, get on a train. Blessed and cursed by chronic restlessness – I think of Dom and Ty with their twitches and tics. But back in Brum, Ty wasn't one to blatt off at a moment's notice; didn't spin globes and spread out maps on the floor, the future in every contour.

Blatt off – that was one of Tom's expressions – to leave on a whim. Just go, go, go; such power in those words. *C'mon, let's go.* Pressing Ty with it. *C'mon.* Him blinking and twitching and then steady, decision made – *OK, I will.* I said to Kate, 'I hope he doesn't get cold feet when we're out there.' But Ty loved it straight away, like it was fresh air to him, being so far from home; put the wind in his sails, he said.

Maybe he realized it was possible, that he could escape. Again I think, that's him, gone now. Never emerging from the mountain kingdom, trekking further out to places with no tourists, no lodges or fly-in hotels. Walking in valleys where monks and potato farmers live. Growing his hair until it knots into red-gold shanks, or maybe shaving it completely, like the girl in Varanasi, then back to the valley as a madman, a maverick, one who's spent too long on the ice. Here there are always wild men and mad village girls to remind us there are other ways to be.

Here you can rattle a few cages without being battered to death.

A breeze slithers down from the col. I look up and two figures have appeared, one leaning heavily on the other. 'Ty!' I yell, up on my feet and running towards them before my brain will accept that they're stocky, dark, not lean like Ty, and Nyala has stayed at the pool. *Shit. Shit, shit, shit.* Trekkers – one of them sick by the looks of it. I stoke up the fire, stir the chai.

They're close. 'Hi? Any chance of some tea?'

'Here. I started warming it when I saw you.'

'Oh . . . right. Thanks. This guy – he needs some help. I found him high up on the trail. Altitude, I reckon.'

The sick man is the northerner with the thigh muscles, straight out from England, invincible. 'He came through here a while ago, with a group of Brits.'

'He was alone when I found him.'

I wrap the man up in my sleeping bag. 'Kishore will take him to a lodge, get a doctor,' I say, knowing he'll appear soon, won't have missed this happening in his valley. 'Were you on your way down anyway?'

'Yeah. You reckon his mates just left him?'

'I bet he told them to go on. He was that type – you know, "I'll be fine, catch up with you later."'

'He was far from fine. Altitude, I've seen it loads of times. There's no way of knowing how you'll cope till you get up there.'

'A leap into the unknown, then.'

'Yep.'

He yawns and stretches out in the sun, shattered. I indent the spongy grass, feeling the water collect in my fingertip pools. The earth is getting wetter. Ants and beetles scuttle towards tussocks, drier ground. It'll start raining here soon; the high valleys will fill up with snow. Clouds muster behind the mountains and winds whip across the lake, streaking it with wake from invisible craft. My wide sky will soon be shrouded by mist and sleet; time will move on.

'Rrr Rrr Rrr . . .'

Nyala is shaking my arm, grunting urgently. It's pitch black. I sit up, rubbing my face, blindly patting the earth floor for matches. Nyala's face is frantic in the sudden fire-flare; *me*, she thumps, and points towards the col.

Me go, and then at me. *You too. Now*.

'Why? What's happened?' I say.

She shakes her head. *I don't know*. But it's bad; I can't read her eyes but her limbs are jerking, wanting to get up there fast. I grab my jeans and she pulls me out of the hut and up the slope, sleep-grit in my eyes. In the far distance there's a streak of grey, the start of the sunrise, but here it's still dark. I can't see the path; without Nyala I'd be hopelessly lost already.

'Is it Ty?' I say but she ignores me, stopping instead, hardly breathing.

She taps her ear. *Listen*. A distant whistle or cry; high, sustained. Did I hear it in my sleep, before the *Rrr Rrr Rrr*?

We scramble on over shale and rocks slippery with dew, a crunch of frost in pockets. The grey line is widening, streaks of pink appear and the landscape around us jumps into relief. I can see the col now, and the fishtail tip floating on top of the mist. Nyala moves so fast I can hardly keep up, images of twisted bodies on hillsides in my head. It's Ty, injured; badly. Will he recognize me, be able to speak? What if I'd already left here and he died without seeing a face he knows? Like Tom. My legs gain a burst of strength; I must get up there. I race past Nyala, lungs burning.

'Rrr Rrr Rrr.' She stops, swivels her head. Rocks, choppy waves on the river far below, the col just ahead.

'Come on,' I say, pulling away, but she grabs my arm and drags me towards some huge boulders, bigger than a house, carved mani stones all broken up on the ground. And a cave – the cries are coming from inside. Nyala rushes in but I stop dead. Is it him? Broken; maimed? Black, frostbitten legs?

Nyala's calling me from inside the cave but my body won't move. 'Rrr Rrr Rrr.' She runs out and points at Kishore's hut across the valley – flooded with pink light now, and a green haze as the mist lifts off the grass. *You go*

187

down. Get Kishore. She wraps her scarf around her thigh. *And bandages.*

'Is it Ty?' I say.

Nyala shakes her head, pushes me forward. *Go, quick.* I pelt downward. When I get to the hut Kishore is already on his way.

'Boil water, make tea, broth, bring it up,' he says. Two rescues in one day; the trekker's safe in Pokhara by now, saved by chance, luck.

'It's her cousin,' says Kishore, as we stand at the cave entrance, oil lamps flickering over Nyala who is feeding broth to the exhausted man; there's a rapid, winced exchange in Nepali. 'Her uncle has died,' says Kishore, 'and now there's no one else to care for her grandmother. She must leave us.'

'Just like that?'

'Of course,' said Kishore.

I go back to the hut and watch the mountain, build up the fire and make more chai, handing cups to Nyala and her shivering cousin when they come down. *Why?* I say, with my hands. *Why are you going?* Pointing at the col. *Here is good. The baby* – rocking my arms; *your washing* – scrubbing mime; *Kishore* – hands on my heart. I know she loves him.

'Mmm mmm mmm,' she says earnestly, holding both my hands.

Light floods around the mountain, like the fin is rising; the great fish or whale might break through any moment and we'll see it all, the wholeness, in a trick of light and rising mist. *I* says Nyala, thumping her chest. 'I mmm mmm . . .'

'You mmm mmm?' I say. She nods, smiles quickly.

'Mmm mmm ssst ssst.'

'Sisters, yes, we're sisters, of course.'

She rips a piece of her skirt, wraps up her skull and

presses it into my palm. *You go*, she says, hands reaching up to the wide sky. *You go home.*

My hands are still shaking and I'm not sure they'll stop. As I pelted down to Kishore all I could think of was Mum, with the same dry, scared voice asking a man on a mountainside, 'Is it Kate?'

That time the answer was yes.

Part 3
Kate

'The secret of an opal's colour lies not in its substance but in its absences.'

Australian Geographic

22

'Is it Kate?' Her voice as high as the screaming wind.

We'd had a row. 'Kate, just stop sulking and help us unpack the car.'

'No.'

'Pardon me?'

'Unpack it yourself.'

'Just who do you think you're talking to, young lady?'

I marched off, up the hillside, away from them. Into a storm, a hooly: rapid, vicious, from nowhere. Storming off into the nascent storm. Crags and ridges cut away by squalling clouds – bitten off, snatched – and with them, me. Tents were flattened by sudden downdrafts, boats ripped from their moorings. The sea churning, heaving, thickening, as if a beast might break through its surface and charge roaring across the land, scattering houses, grabbing fistfuls of children and waving them in their parents' useless faces. That would have been easier, perhaps. Then it wouldn't have just been me.

'Ambulance, quick,' said the man, the climber, to Dad. 'Poles, bandages, make a stretcher, quick.' Dad galvanized into action: *do this, then this, then this, then this*. Mum paralysed, desperate, in the way.

'Is it Kate?' she said, grabbing the climber's arm. He tried to shake her off, but her hand was like a vice, tighter and tighter. '*Tell me what's happened. Is it Kate?*'

Prising her fingers away, handprint bruises. Pain and fear igniting rapid fury. 'I expect so, missus,' he said; hard words, tacks shot from his lips. 'Unless you know of any other kids who went up the mountain on their own today.'

That's how Dad told it to me. Mum doesn't know that he has.

I didn't like talking about it. Could never find the right words, the right place to put myself in the story – my story – because Mum's guilt and Dad's helplessness were understood; my territory unknown. Then Romany came. 'Give us a break,' she said, 'how can I just *ignore* it?' – and I told her because I knew by then that to survive it I had to at least try.

'I almost feel like me again,' she said, fingering the scabs on her ankles, at last beginning to heal. 'Halle-fucking-lujah. How long did it take for you?'

'I'm still trying,' I said.

We were sitting in the bandstand in Handsworth park, watching the kids running round and round us in circles, endless energy; like wind-up toys their feet wouldn't stop. Collapsing on the grass – playing dead – trying not to laugh, or sneeze, or choke on dandelion fluff. The air still, quiet, except for the sawing of branches somewhere near by, *nee nee nee*.

'Come on,' said Romany. 'Spill.'

The park, gloriously normal all around me – a girl pushing a pram full of shopping, dogs pulling on a ball, geese feeding off scatterings of stale Bombay mix. Storms and snapping bones and terror in my head.

'*Kate* . . .'

'*OK*. We went on holiday to Scotland. I was twelve, in a strop about having to go. Mum found that hard – I'd always been so eager to please when I was a kid. But I wanted to be with my friends in the city, and they dragged me off to Skye, mid-summer, midges everywhere driving us mental. Dad said he'd make a fire to get rid of them, but all the wood was wet and he got into a right strop. Mum was going, "Mike, just leave it," in this you're-an-idiot voice, then, "Kate, come and help unpack," and I just thought *sod this* and stormed off up the hillside to get some height between me and the bloody midges. Mum called, "Kate, come back here right now," and I turned round and yelled back, "Make me." You should've seen her face – she was so used to me behaving. That was the last I saw of her before intensive care.'

The summer evening haze in the park thickened. People pushed at the air, staggered shadows behind them. There was no wind; the playing-dead kids had crashed, stretched out motionless in the grass.

'Go on,' said Romany.

'I powered up there, straight upwards towards the spiky ridge which jutted out like a line of teeth against the sky. I felt the grasses springing up as I lifted my feet, driving me on. It only gets dark for a few hours a night in summer up there and I thought, just keep going, follow the sun, stay with it, hold the moment. I was up there free and strong and *myself*. Sounds mad, now.'

'Sounds ace,' said Romany.

'It was. But all Mum could say was, "Why did you have to go off like that? What did you think you were doing?" I didn't mean to make her feel worse – *well, if you hadn't dragged me off to Scotland* . . . But what did they expect me to say? *OK, my fault, arly-barly?*

'I climbed up really high and it was amazing – all these mountains and islands and water rippling out in every direction. Thunderstorms cracking the sky in the distance, but where I was it was still. It was like I could touch everything on the planet; it was all there, laid out for me. Then suddenly I was cold, frozen; the sweat from my climb turned to ice on my T-shirt. No coat, no protection anywhere. A storm cloud racing towards me, sharp flecks of rain on my arms. Thunder hit the rocks, stones tumbled down the scree, crashing, growling. Icy clouds all around me, a hailstone the size of my fist hit my head. I can still feel the thwack now, still hear my roars and howls. There was a strip of light below the clouds, on the slopes which led to the campsite. Then it happened.'

'What? What exactly?' said Romany.

No one had ever asked me that; it was always 'the accident', 'Kate's accident'. Never the detail, the sequence, the facts.

OK, here goes. Only for you though.

'There's this rumbling above me – like a giant clearing his throat – and the scree's moving. There's nowhere to go. Hail pelting down, blistering my skin, lightning ripping up the sky. I scramble for an outcrop thinking, *shelter, quickly*, but it all hit too hard, too fast. My right leg slams down a crevice – nothing but treacherous emptiness under-neath – and I lurch to a halt, the air full of rocks, as if a massive invisible hand is hurling them straight at me, at my trapped, exposed left leg; sinews, skin, ripping and tearing. Then it's gone, buried. I scream as my thighbone splinters and snaps; feel the life being crushed out of it and the pain racing through my body. I know my leg's gone, not consciously, but physically, deep, deep body-knowledge, as true and permanent as *I am a girl, I am a human*. I'm pinned to the mountainside with boulders hurling around my head and hailstones exploding into ice-shards and my right leg hanging through a tear in the earth, and I know instantly that everything else is gone too. Everything that's mine, that's me. My life, grabbed by a hand from the sky and ripped into pieces.'

Romany and I looked straight ahead, squinting. The park was still, freeze-framed. Footballs hung in the air, aeroplanes stalled above us.

'It's true what they say, you know. Your life does rush past you – but it's not just the past, no one tells you that. If something's really shocking it tears holes in time. There I was choking on panic and snot, staring at my twisted, lost foot poking out of the rocks at an impossible angle and in barged the future, hitting harder than the pain. *You'll be ill, sicker than you can imagine. You'll be desperate. It's all changed; for ever. You'll never get over it, not really.* I saw Mum torturing herself, Dad with no place for his rage. Everything I ever did, from that moment on – if I lived – would be skewed by this. *And that'll hurt*, said the future; *that'll hurt much more than this.*

'In hospital they knocked me out cold and cut what was left off. Some people actually hear it happening. I met a bloke at the limb centre who couldn't have an anaesthetic because his heart was weak, so they gave him an epidural and he had to lie there listening to the sawing. *Nee nee nee.* Every time he hears that sound he's right back there, he says, unable to move or feel or shut down his ears for the life of him.'

Romany grabbed my hand. After a while she pulled me upright, eddies and swirls in the air around us. We moved off. Footballs continued their arcs in the sky and the playing-dead kids stirred and blinked, every blade of grass, every stick and stone in the park just how it was when they'd drifted off.

*

*Jack's House
Near Alnwick
Northumberland*

I wake to the chattering of birds. They start as soon as grey creeps into the night sky; some mornings it seems that their song pulls the sun upwards and shores it there all day with

197

well-timed hoots and caws. When I first came here I found it too quiet. No traffic, no sirens, not even house noises: creaking boilers, clicking thermostats. But now my ear is tuned in and I can hear the snap of bird wings as they land in high branches, the hiss of the wind through the undergrowth, pebbles tapped together by the tumbling brook.

Vaz and I exchange letters almost daily now – we have since Tom died – and I write about this place, how it sounds and smells; tiny changes each day, a leaf unfurls, the stream swells. Vaz says he can feel what this wood is like, that some mornings he wakes and thinks he's here, listening to my wood pigeons cooing and the feral cats yowling outside the window, calling to Spartacus to come outside and be wild.

Some days I think I could, like Romany. Being here makes it more possible. I don't tell Mum this, though. How would she feel, with both of us gone? Whatever I do affects her and Romany: my move up here, Mum's to Frieda's, Romany's travels now stalled up on her high, green shelf. All tangled together, invisible skeins attached to our wrists and ankles, and to each other, no matter where we go. Like puppets – a twitch on one string and across the world another one jerks. Frieda says we've got to sort it out.

Frieda thinks it's time.

Jack calls, 'I'm off to the village if you want a lift.' I've been watching his shadow move through the gap under my door, listening to the fire fizz and crackle.

'Here you are,' he says, nudging my door open and handing me a mug of coffee.

'I'll do it tomorrow, promise.'

'We've been waiting years for you to let us spoil you,' he says.

Today, I think, as I'm getting dressed; I'll go and see her today. A clear thought, suddenly formed and whole, like a soap bubble blown from a plastic dipper. I'll introduce myself. *Hello, Mrs Waterson, I'm Kate, Romany's sister. I wonder if . . .* She must have heard of Romany, even if she doesn't know about me. All the other options have drawn a blank – down at the coast the other day, nothing, no one who knew Ty. Jack said we should have gone in the evening, that all the young folk commute down to Newcastle to work, said he'd take me back if I want, but today I'm ready to talk to her. I tell Jack; he pinches my arm and I punch him softly in the chest.

'I have to do it in my time,' I say.

'No rush,' says Jack.

There might be though. Another clear, round thought. Romany will come back. A few months ago I'd have taken this as a sign – she's coming down from the hillside right this second. But now I'm less trustful of our telepathy, wonder if it was wishful thinking by both of us. Perhaps there's a whole part of her life that I don't know about, that's invisible to me, that would shock me to the core but which I'd know was true: the jolt of veracity, the click of things falling into place . . .

Something as big as this. In my head I've been with him.

With him. Every day as I studied, read, wrote letters, made phone calls; but the second the phone was down, the door closed behind me I made myself with him. Just a hint, the possibility that he liked me, and I made up a whole world. Saved up stories to make him laugh; he'd call me babe, honey, unable to help it, affectionate names falling out of his mouth like sweets from a jar. Blissed-out scenes complete in my head, no complications. Fantasies. Then Dad would call me. 'Kate? Griz and Carla are here, come down and be sociable.' Or I'd have to placate Mum with a trip to the shops; she always wanted to buy me clothes, dress me up nice, but I hated it: the changing rooms, sleek bodies and easy, cocksure gaits. And I'd have to push him

199

out, think about the family, the suckers pulling on my wrists.

Dad had an inkling. When Romany first left he asked me about Ty. We were in the garden clearing brambles and I tried to pluck the notion out of his mind, press soil around the gap with my protests – *I'm missing Romany, why wouldn't I?* But now even Dad seems to have forgotten that Ty was my friend first, that we used to be close. Romany and Ty. Ty and Romany. It trips off everyone's tongues like there was never any question.

The post arrives, a letter from Vaz, but I don't have time to read it because Jack's in a rush. We bump down the lane, Jack looking out for broken fences or torn bark, talking me through his day. 'What are you going to do then?' he says, as an afterthought, eyes pulled by a flicker of movement deep in the woods. 'Knock on her door?'

'I don't know,' I say. 'But I will talk to her.'

'Good,' says Jack. 'It's about time we found out something more about that Ty.'

I want to know but I don't. Do I need more reasons to give up a life I never really had?

Adrian told me some stuff in his letters. Thin slivers of information, transparent almost, no more significant than *boy, rural*. When Ty was eight he broke his arm falling out of a tree; they used to make dens in the woods and hide things there – knives, matches, forbidden magazines. He shot up six inches in a year when he hit thirteen, trouser hems flapping round his ankles. He missed his dad and felt guilty about his mum – obvious really, but coming from Adrian, who knew him back then, they were precious facts. His mum was exceptionally stern, but Ty knew how to work her. She'd drop him off at the youth club perfectly turned out; pressed trousers, buffed shoes. Ty would wait until her tail-lights faded and then dash to the toilets, mussing his hair along the way, jeans and faded T-shirt layered underneath his one-size-too-big shirt and trousers. 'Room for growth,' he said to his mum, apparently. 'Six inches in a year, remember?'

I wanted to ask – why did he latch on to me? But then Adrian wouldn't know why he wouldn't. I think about the timing, the library, the attention; every bloke in the damn city trailing after Romany and no one – not even her – so much as thinking that I might want someone, need someone, be lonely for a lover. They couldn't even approach it: that I might be too damaged for love. Then along came Ty, charming, good-looking, happy in my company. Is it any wonder that in my head I got carried away?

A contact with the outside world, that's what Ty asked me to be for Adrian, and that's what I've been. Sent letters telling the tale of Ty telling the tale of a ride across India on a train, of head shaving by the Ganges, of barbed mountain air. Images, sensations refracted through their eyes and pens, my reading and imagination. The flood from the attic: describing how the water froze at the junction into the tank, the whole lot crashing down with the thaw. Trying to bring the world to life for him while he's stuck inside the hub of the wheel, unmoving, as the spokes whirr around outside. We both knew it was a poor substitute; imagining the thump of heat on a summer's day in Delhi can never be like feeling it, metal hot, on your forehead.

Don't you want to go? he wrote. *You could be there now.* The implication – *I can't, poor me.* I wrote back tersely, *There's a reason why you're stuck inside. Think yourself lucky.*

Lucky? he wrote back. *Now you're really taking the piss.*

Sorry, Adrian, I think, sitting in a café in the village. Caught me on a bad day. What I wanted from you was never going to happen, anyway; your loyalties were to Ty.

He didn't forget you when he was halfway round the world. One pull that he couldn't ignore. Me, the family, Tom, even Romany he could resist, stepping into the mountains without her, lured by that space and silence. But you, no.

I score the pitted skin of my orange and peel back sections one by one. The girl behind the counter chalks up the menu laconically – teacakes, toasted cheese – but she eyes me, slides over to fill my teacup. 'You're staying with Jack up at the lodge, aren't you?' she says.

'Yes,' I say.

'Keeps himself to himself that one.'

'Do you know him?'

'Not really.' *But I'd like to.* I can hear her thoughts, see them in the jut of her hip, the way her hand smoothes her apron down. 'Might brighten up this place if I did,' she says, sitting herself down opposite me.

'You're from round here?' I say. She's about the same age as me, as Ty.

'Yeah, worst luck.'

'Do you know Ty Waterson?'

'Ty? Haven't seen him for years. We used to knock about together when we were kids though.' There's a customer tapping a squelchy foot up at the counter. She pushes herself up, pops an orange segment into her mouth.

'He's in Nepal with my sister,' I say. 'I'm after some info on him, actually.'

'Tell you what,' she says. 'You invite me up to the lodge to meet your dreamboat ranger and I'll see what I can remember.'

Deal done. I head up the road, rehearsing what I'll say to Ty's mum.

'So . . .' says Jack. 'What happened? Did you meet her?'

It's evening and the sky's purple. The hills rise behind the

202

dark woods, smooth and curved, glimmers of silver from lakes and streams caught by sun that's left us now. It's all I want to do, sometimes: watch the landscape move and swell under the changing light, longing – waiting – for its movement to pull me out of my world of books and fantasies into that physical, tactile space, where contemplation is a luxury, not a torment.

'Wait . . .' I say. 'Look.'

The shadow of a cloud drifts over the camber of the hill and vanishes into the darkness behind. The last of the light slips away and with it the hill subsides, like a giant's shoulder nestling back under his blanket of earth and roots. A bird cries, far off, harsh and piercing.

'What was that?' I say.

'Never you mind,' says Jack. 'Out with it.'

'She didn't want to know,' I say. 'I told her who I was, spun out some line about families getting to know each other. She just stood there. So I start wittering on about how I just happened to be in the area and does she know you and it would seem rude not to drop by. I thought she might be softening for a moment.'

'And . . .'

'I said, "Mum and Dad thought the world of your boy, he was always welcome in our house." Wrong words – I knew straight away, like I was accusing her. She said, "I don't know who you think you are. But you'll learn about him," and she shut the door in my face. God knows what Ty's done to her but she's not forgiving him in a hurry.'

Jack looks crestfallen. Not for himself, I know, but for me. They've all been hanging their hopes on my mission to find out about Ty. More whispered conversations my sonar doesn't miss. *She's doing fine, Mum. Much brighter. Tell Jenny to stop worrying and think about herself.*

'Not much else you can do then, I guess,' says Jack.

I'm staring at the sky – feeling the planet move, slowly

203

spinning, light captured by faraway stars passed back to us in patterns: warriors, scales, twins. Gathering strength from the hills and the light and Jack's sure friendship; storing it away like the squirrels in the wood, so there's always a reserve, a hidden stash to draw on. You have to.

'Don't worry,' I say. 'I've got a plan. And it might even mean a love life for you.'

23

Jack has an ancient free-standing bath with claw feet; the water comes straight from a well on the hillside, brown and brackish but sweet as strawberries, leaving skin and hair soft, flyaway. The light comes in through the high, square windows, casting geometric patterns on to the tiles; I slip under the water. My breasts and knee break through the surface of the water like the hills outside rising up from the woodland and I tip them backwards and forwards, up and down, changing my landscape, getting to know it. Maybe even to love it.

'Kate! There's someone here to see you.'

Must be the girl from the café – couldn't wait to be invited before turning up. I won't hurry; it's Jack she's come to see.

I flick my toes, sending ripples up and down the water, sprinkle droplets over the surface. There are voices next door but I screen them out, listen instead to the rumbling purr of Spartacus who's nudging my dangling fingers. I reach for the slippery, rose-scented soap and lather myself slowly, watching the steam billow and disappear as it nudges into walls along with all thoughts of her and him. Here there's only me, and me is fine.

'Kate!' The urgency in Jack's voice reaches my underwater ears. 'Kate,' he hisses, creaking the door open. I lurch upwards, spilling waves. 'Didn't you hear me?'

'I'm in the bloody bath,' I say, grabbing a towel, the water churning and slapping.

'I know you're in the bloody bath but I told you. There's someone here to see you. He says his name is Vaz.'

Vaz?

Vaz *here*?

No, no, that can't be. I've thought about us meeting up – of course I have – but couldn't work out how to tell him without changing things. The thought of writing it down and posting the letter and waiting was too much, back there on my own in Brum.

'Kate? Did you hear me? I've got to go out now so I'll tell him you'll be through, OK?'

Icy lumps are pushing up through my skin, set off by a jolt straight through me when Jack said *Vaz*. Like the Himalayas, I suddenly think, irrationally, and then I'm irritated beyond belief, by this intrusion, these feelings, this stuff I have to deal with. 'All right,' I snap. 'For God's sake, I'm allowed to get dressed first.'

'Rather you than me,' I hear Jack say to Vaz. The front door bangs. It's just me and Vaz. I hear him moving about, sweeping ash from around the stove, opening the heavy iron door and poking the embers.

'Kate?' he calls, tentatively. 'Are you OK? I did write to say I was coming.'

I'm grabbing clothes out of drawers. Nothing is right. Sweatshirts, jeans, a long skirt maybe? Where's my dress? I brought a dress with me, I'm sure. One that goes right down to my ankle.

'Kate?'

'I'm coming,' I say. Unnerving glimpses of emptiness in the mirror. More movement out there. Fiddling with window catches. A pause, cigarette smoke, a creak of sofa springs and then he's up again, pacing about. Brief, useless fantasies of climbing out of the window and up the lane on my own, finding Jack, persuading him to come back and make up some excuse to Vaz. But Jack won't do that, I know. Don't be silly, Kate, he'd say, you're you. It's enough.

I'm me. Riddled with fear and minus a leg – but me.

Take it or leave it. At least he's got an option.

Out on to a precipice. Vertigo on flat earth.

I nudge open the door and go through. 'Hello, Vaz.'

He turns round too quickly, stumbling slightly. He looks exactly how I imagined: two or three pairs of holey socks, muddy combats, cropped hair except for one thin dread down his back, a fisherman's hat which he quickly grabs off his head and clutches, twisting it with both hands.

'Hi . . . Kate . . . Listen . . . I . . .' He looks me up and down. Twice. Eyes snagged by the space, wincing at the absence. Look at my face, I think. My arms, my breasts. See what's *here*.

'I . . . err, look, err, sorry to just turn up like this, but . . .'

He's trying. I should be kind to him, but I can't manage kind when I'm teetering on ice, trying not to slip, be jolted, jilted. 'But what?' I say. *Go on, say it.*

He looks at his hat but finds no salvation there. 'Kate . . . What the hell's happened? I mean . . . Did you . . .? Have you . . .?' He swallows hard. 'You've only got one leg.' He mutters it into his chest, embarrassed by the blindingly obvious now I'm here, physically here, not just someone he imagined, built up out of letters and shared impressions and loneliness.

'Ten out of ten,' I say.

'But . . . *Shit*. When did it happen? I mean . . . Have you always –?'

'It was an accident. When I was twelve.'

'God. *Shit*. Kate – why didn't you tell me?'

'Would that have made any difference?'

'It's a bit of a shocker. I never even dreamt that . . .'

I turn on my crutch. Hop over to the stove, move kettle

and cups around, something to do, pottery and metal and plastic handles blurring in front of my eyes. I hold a cup in one hand and the kettle in the other and for a moment can't work out what the hell to do next – stalled by the fact that there's no sense in any of this. Vaz leans forward then stops himself, twists his hat again.

'I tell you what,' I say, turning. 'I never dreamt it either.'

Romany saw what it means instantly. That I'm a living image of loss; a bogey out in daylight, a monster with a pretty face – her pretty face. All of us cripples are: warnings, red flashing lights, *This could be you*. People veer off because they can't stand the thought of it. They don't have to. But Romany knew in a flash, on that bridge over the canal as I crutched it and stumbled; she saw the drop-jawed stares and the double takes and the kids going, 'Mummy, she's only got one leg.' Fingers pointing, wavering in the air, itching to lift my skirt to see for themselves, to comfort themselves with the lie that it might be temporary; a sprain, a fracture, something fixable.

But Romany saw that part of me had been stolen by chance, by fate. And I knew, too, when I looked at her, a black-eyed teenage girl no older than me, begging on the city streets. I knew that she must have lost pieces too. She could hide her losses, pull her face into a smile, straighten her shoulders and her stride and no one would see the gaps inside. 'Lack of imagination,' I always said, and Romany would smile properly, from the inside. 'How can they think you haven't lost out?'

'I'm young, tough, won't take any bollocks,' Romany said. 'People think that makes up for everything.'

'Can't see past their own noses, then.'

We were good for each other like that. No one had ever stood up for me like Romany. The first day she came to school – I was using a wheelchair at the time – I found that my history class had been switched to an upstairs classroom, no lift. *Sorry, Kate, but you can see how we're fixed* . . . Teachers, administrators, willing me to agree, to collude, thinking it was all right to ask this of me. I was different now, after all, a logistical headache, not a student.

'See how you're fixed?' said Romany sharply. 'You're supposed to be learning us, why should Kate give a flying fuck how you're fixed?'

The whole room stalled. Queues of kids, teachers behind desks with lists. 'If there's not a law against this there fucking should be,' said Romany, her voice cutting through the heedlessness. 'Do something decent for once in your lives, will you?'

The class was moved to a Portakabin with a temporary ramp and Romany chose the same options as me. 'Never let them treat you like shit,' said Romany. 'Because they will. Don't kid yourself otherwise.'

'I wish you'd told me, Kate,' says Vaz. 'Why didn't you *say?*'

We're out in the woods. I've got my artificial leg on and he's easier with me now. I don't walk well – slow progress on bumpy ground – but I look OK, the absence covered, masked by plastic and foam, by awkward steps and silent winces.

'It'd have been easier for you,' I say.

'Is that why you didn't?' he says. 'To make it difficult?'

'Vaz, I didn't know you were coming.'

'True.' He looks sheepish and I laugh. The sound surprises me.

'I wanted you to think of me as whole, to feel what I *am*. Trust me, I know what I'm on about. People do treat me – think of me – differently, given half a chance. You might say "I wouldn't" but that's just too easy. I'm so sick of being defined by what's gone.'

'Like Captain Ahab.'

'One leg to the eye but two to the soul.'

'What I said in my letters is as real as this,' I say, thumping my chest.

'Your letters got me through the winter. And brought me here.'

'I'm trying to explain, honest.'

A breeze flicks at the tree leaves, setting off a vibration, a thrumming which spreads through the wood. Ripples move through the carpet of bluebells, just appearing, only on a second glance does the haze separate into distinct flowers with stalks and petals of their own. No one else is here or anywhere near us, except for Jack, distant thuds betray his whereabouts.

'Your mate's working hard,' says Vaz.

'What have you come here for, Vaz?'

'To see you. I'd like to stay a while, if that's OK.'

'What, still?'

'Give us a chance, Kate.'

We walk on. I know he'll like the wood, and that makes it easier, takes the attention from me. We point out birds' nesting places and finger the tiny pea-green ferns shaped like sea horses, unfurling out of last year's crisp brown remains. I'm wrong-footed by him seeing me without my leg on; only people I know well and trust absolutely see me like this. Mum, Dad, Romany, Frieda. Ty and Jack and Chrissy. That's about it. Tom, but he's dead. Strangers are too shocked. They can't match my face, my youth, with this gap; they never know what to say. Say nothing, *idiot*, I think. Just ignore me, like you're ignoring every other human being on the street. You're making me a freak.

It happened too often when my leg was first gone, before Romany came. Mum insisted I had to go out, that it would be good for me. 'I'm not ready,' I told her. 'I don't want to be pushed around.'

But she couldn't think what else to do and had to do something. 'Come on, Kate,' she said, grabbing the handles of my wheelchair and jerking it down the ramp outside the front of the house. 'Do you good to get some fresh air. Let's drive down to Tesco's and buy something nice to eat.'

Food, I thought. Yuk. Never again. Food makes me puke. She wheeled me down aisle after aisle but I just shook my head, don't fancy anything. The looks shocked her as well; her hands gripping my chair then my shoulders as if she, too, was in danger of falling into an unknown, darker place. *Ahh*s and *oh dear*s and *poor thing*s. Faces rapidly recomposed; quick, terrified smiles; children passing their hands through the space to be sure the leg was really gone.

Vaz did quite well, considering. Seven out of ten. I did think about putting my prosthesis on before going out to him, but what was the point? I couldn't hide it for long – can't wear this thing all day, too much scarring on my stump for that. 'What's wrong with your leg?' people say, when they see me limping and gimping around. 'Nothing,' I say, poking in a pin or grinding out a cigarette on the foam; another hole, a whiff of burnt plastic. 'I just haven't got one.'

Take it or leave it. This could be the first time I've actually lived that phrase.

The bluebell carpet shimmers and rolls under dappled sunlight. 'As lovely as I imagined,' says Vaz.

Back at the cottage the red light on the answer machine is flashing:

'Kate? It's Dad. Got an email today from Romany. She's on her way home, waiting on standby in Kathmandu. She's written to you but might beat her letter back. You'd better ring me, love, because I'm not sure which home she thinks she's coming back to.'

'Romany's coming home,' I say, turning to Vaz. 'I'm going to have to leave.' With Ty? I think. Or on her own?

'When?' says Vaz.

'I don't know. Soon. I have to talk to Dad. And Mum.' My artificial foot slides on the wooden floor; every surface seems slippery and difficult. I want to get my leg off, and on the phone. I can't deal with this and Vaz all together. 'I need to get myself sorted,' I say lamely.

'I'll go and see if Jack needs a hand,' he says.

'OK.'

'OK if I come back later?' His manner is light, easy.

'Course.'

I watch him stride away. For a second I'm crippled by jealousy, doubling me up like a knife in the stomach. To walk, just go. *Things are tricky, I'm in the way, I'll get out of here now. Blink and I'll be gone.* Years of hidden envy leaking out. I don't try and catch it, bottle it back up. Love and resentment's a deadly mix, I know that now, but I couldn't rid myself of either.

Let's just go, Ty. Romany at his elbow, her breath in his ear. *Let's go.*

I said I wouldn't be jealous. I promised her, watched her face as I lied. 'No, honestly, you go, I'll be fine.' My voice sounded good, steady.

'Are you sure? I know how I'd feel.'

'You can't stay because of me. Anyway . . .' I moved my face sideways so I could watch my mouth in the mirror, saying it.

'Anyway what?' said Romany.

'We'll have to cope without each other some time.'

Her mouth flickered on the word 'cope'. She'd had enough of that – the slow, sticky grind, hour to hour, day to day. We'd both done too much coping and she was ready – able – to fly. *Who the hell are you to stop her?* I said to my face as it looked back at me from her.

'You don't have to go back because of Romany,' says Jack. He's warming his hands in front of the fire, Vaz is in the kitchen chopping veg. 'It suits you here. You've said so yourself.'

'What, just not be there when she gets home?'

'She can always come up here.'

'There's too much to sort out. It's going to be hard for her – Tom, Mum, the house.'

'Harder for her than the rest of us?'

'What is it you've got against Romany all of a sudden?'

'You can't cushion her. It doesn't work – wouldn't work for Romany, either.'

Jack stops rubbing his hands, the coal dust in the air still disturbed by the friction. 'Listen, Kate,' says Jack quietly, crouching down close to me. 'I'm not saying you shouldn't go – of course you want to see her – but think about it, that's all. You're doing well, now. Romany wouldn't want that to change.'

You're doing well, now.

Romany rescued me from all that – from kid gloves, from anxious, useless whispering in hospital corridors, on telephones and behind doors. *How's she doing? Any better?* 'Oh, leave her be,' said Romany, blithely sure that I'd come through fine, stronger; cutting through the layers of guilt and fear and caution which had been choking our family since that day on the Scottish mountain. 'Why does everything come back to her leg, for God's sake? Stop fucking tiptoeing around. She's got PMT, the blues. Wrong side of the bed; bad day on planet earth. Happens to bipeds even.'

I laughed. 'So you won't curse Barnardo's next time you're feeling down?' I said to Romany.

'Only if it's really their fault.'

'And who decides that?' said Dad.

'Me,' said Romany, beaming through her contradictions. 'Come on, Kate. Let's get down that hospital.'

My mood lifted when it was just me and Romany. Mum watched my every move; any dip in my mood and she'd start to fuss. Romany would jump between us saying, 'Fuss me, I'm the one with no mother.'

'I can't stand it,' I said to Romany as we went into the limb-fitting centre; crutches and half-made legs and stump moulds piled up in corners; boxes of single shoes donated by M&S. 'She wants me to be heroic. Smiling through the pain; good old English stoicism. Sod that. The only person who that's good for is her.'

'Too right.'

'I'm not like I was before. I can't be that person. It kills me enough as it is, without knowing it's broken her heart.'

A sudden twinge in my phantom – electric shocks digging into flesh long-gone. I grabbed Romany's shoulder and we staggered as we realized we weren't the only ones expected to smile through the pain.

A tap on the cottage door. 'Hello?'

The girl from the café. 'Mmm, smells good,' she says. Onions browning in cumin – Vaz has pockets full of spices; never travel without them, he says.

She brushes past Jack and comes to sit with me as if we're old mates, which makes her irresistible. 'Hope you don't mind,' she says. 'I was just passing, thought you might like to look at these.'

The cottage is the only building at the end of a long track; no one just passes. 'Want to stay for dinner?' says Jack.

'Ooh, yes please.'

'This is . . .'

'Fran,' she says, standing up and kissing Jack swiftly on the cheek. 'Photos,' she adds. 'Of when we were kids. Me and Ty. Loads of people. My nan had them all stuffed in a drawer.'

Photos.

I take the packet and leaf through, then move over to the table and spread them out under a lamp. Fran is in and out of the kitchen, dipping her finger in sauces, chattering to Jack – his job, his cottage, his CDs. I stare at the photographs. Teenage parties, bodies sprawled on the floor, furtive smoking. Fran squeezed on to a sofa with three blokes, Ty behind her shoulder. He looks about ten – eager, boyish face on a lanky body. Another of a crowd of kids celebrating, hands punching the air.

'That was our last day at school,' says Fran. 'Last time I saw Ty, too. I went down to Newcastle, didn't come back for years and when I did I found that everyone else had left as well. Not surprising, really.'

'But it's lovely here,' says Vaz.

'Oh, it is. Lovely. This cottage is straight out of a fairy story. But you can understand why all the young folk went.'

That explains it all then, for her. No mystery, no complications, just boredom with rural life, an itch for something different, a city buzz, meeting people you didn't go to school with. She doesn't know anything about Adrian, though – only that him and Ty got closer after Ty's dad died.

And now Ty's further off than any of his friends in the photo, lost at high altitude. Dad told me on the phone – Romany's coming home on her own. I haven't heard Dad so weary since, well, since my accident. Clipped, resigned. Chilling, for me – Dad's always been putty in my hands. It was the one thing that didn't change when I lost my leg; Dad would be there, whatever, reassuring as a bedtime story. His voice always softened on hearing mine. 'Mike Jackson,' he'd say briskly on the phone, but after my 'Hi

Dad, it's me,' his throat relaxed and his words flowed gently. Not today, though.

'You'll have to talk to your mother, see if she's coming back to the house,' he said. 'It's habitable now. Just about. No thanks to the rest of you.'

'Dad, what's the matter? Are you OK?'

'Just tired, Kate.' Staccato.

'Are you moving back in soon?'

'I suppose I'll have to. Although if I had a choice I'd rather you three sorted yourselves out well away from me.'

So I have to face it. We've eaten our dhal and rice, Jack and Fran are playing Scrabble at the table. She needs no excuse to lean towards him, to slap his hand playfully, to wriggle on her seat as she mulls over her next move. It looks so easy, this flirting, but I've never been any good at it. Romany used to say, 'Kate, it's a piece of piss, flutter your eyelashes, hold his eyes just half a second too long, he'll get the message.' But I never could, was just getting my head round it when I lost my leg and then afterwards, after all the sickness, it was hard to feel alluring while dragging this big dead weight around; this empty, twitching, itching space. Vaz is sitting in the corner with a book, unobtrusive, and I like this containment, his physical neatness. He would never sprawl, except in bed perhaps, a lazy stretch, toes catching the edge of the mattress . . .

Stop distracting yourself, Kate. Think about it. You, Mum, Dad, Romany.

Perhaps I can do it as a story. 'Once upon a time –'

No. Straightforward this time. A family. Mum, Dad, daughter. Happy, on balance, give or take. They would have liked more children – baby after baby, Mum said – but knew they were lucky; most of their friends had harder, poorer lives. I was loved, and grew up strong. They were proud of every new inch, each flex of my arms and legs as I beat Dad at tennis, Mum in the swimming pool. I became brave under this love, stabbed horses' flanks sharply – craving the wild gallop, the rush of speed; sailed boats close to the wind and scrambled ropeless up bare rock although Dad warned me not to. We went on holiday to Scotland, Ireland, Wales, Cornwall; they wanted me to know the countryside, not be scared to sleep in deep quiet like some of my classmates. I wasn't frightened of anything; there was nothing to be frightened of because my mum and dad loved me and my body was strong.

Then, in a second, it all changed. One second. That's what really rattled Mum – that it could all have been so different – the jungle trap missed by a millimetre, the disaster averted by one tick-tock. 'Why my Katie?' said Mum. 'Why us?' Dad knew that the answer was 'Why not?' But he wasn't sure his wife could stand that – her perfect only child broken for no reason in the world. He couldn't stand it, but knew he had to; he had to because I had to. My leg was gone and there was nothing anyone could do to bring it back.

The creak of Jack's bedroom door brings me to. The photos are still on the table, Fran's sandals on the floor; I catch sight of a flick of her skirt before Jack's bedroom door is quietly closed. Vaz is curled up in his sleeping bag – something tells me he's still awake but he doesn't move as I leave. I thank him silently and slip into my bed knowing that he, too, is awake, listening to the wind bang against the walls, soft explosions and shudders eddying through everyone in the house.

*

Katie, Katie, how I miss you babe.
I'm in Kathmandu waiting on a plane. From my room on Freak Street I can see the roof of the Monkey

Temple – the painted eyes follow me through the mesh of TV aerials and dust. Not that I'm doing much, except thinking of you, and Ty, and Tom. We have to find out what happened to Tom, Kate – I know you've all tried but there must be more. I feel so badly for him – I had chances, once I came to you, but Tom never had anything close to that. I'll be looking at something – a boy on a bicycle moseying along, the temple roofs, a warm, grassy slope with a view of the pristine mountains – and then I think of him and it's like a hole has been punched in the scene. *Bam*. It all seems lovely but there are cracks through to dark, terrible places. So what if some days I only want the surface, the pretty, glittery, slick coating? Is that what Ty's gone searching for? A place where the ice is so bright that the holes can't get you?

Now I don't think that I ever knew him.

I've left a note with Nyala and Kishore – must've taken me half a day to write. 'Dear Ty, I've gone back to England.' 'I had to go, my family need me.' 'Thanks for leaving me (bastard).' But I couldn't stop him; still think the instinct's a good one. For kids who've come from nowhere to have the chance to leave, travel the world, it's the most amazing thing; blinding, dazzling. It dazzled me – that's the only excuse I have. I just hope I haven't lost you. Coming home to nothing – my worst fear in the world.

See you SOON.

All my love,

Romany xxx

Her contrition makes me not want it any more. I did want you to go. We're OK. I'm doing good, apparently; everyone says so. It would never have worked anyway; hanging on to Romany's life in the hope that I could be happy in some kind of reflected glory. I need to find my own way – always hated that when I first lost my leg, the way everyone thought they knew best how I should cope.

Energized, I get on the phone to Mum at Frieda's and tell her we're going home, book my train tickets, think of twenty things I can do in the city that I can't do here: shops, hairdresser, library, swimming pool, cinema, even clubs and pubs I haven't been to since Romany left. Dad's amazed when I tell him we'll all be back within a week. 'How did you get your mother to agree?' he said.

'I just told her.'

'And she said yes?'

'Yes.' A pause. 'Dad, you do want us all back there, don't you? And the house is OK? I mean we can live there?'

'The flood damage is fixed, yes.'

I cook for Jack and Vaz. They both know it's my last night in the cottage. Vaz tidies up his bits; all he'll have to do in the morning is roll up his sleeping bag and be away. He's off to Scotland next; some mates who're building yurts up on old crofting land. They chat about organic farming, LETS schemes, wood husbandry, which reminds me of Dad, his rain gauges and compost heaps and slug pubs, digging his politics into the urban garden – and I think how much he'd like to see the places Vaz knows, where people live out the ideas, test them, risk failure. Then Vaz takes me outside to see the comet, Hale-Bopp.

'I've been watching it for a couple of weeks,' he says. 'It'll loop right round the world.'

The smudge in the sky that I can cover with my thumb is made up of thousands and thousands of stars, a million of our suns. The light from it shines on our faces; a dog somewhere nearby howls, although the moon isn't out tonight.

'He's a sound bloke,' says Jack, when Vaz is clearing up in the kitchen. 'You should think about it, Kate.'

'Think about what?'

'You . . . him . . . you know.'

I look at Jack. He's lounging on the floor teasing Spartacus with his bootlaces. His body's at ease – like the cat's – joints and tendons soothed and slackened. Something's changed in him since last night; muscle has settled on to bone, there's no tension in his skin. My phantom spasms invisibly and Jack sees me flinch. 'Sorry,' he says. 'Didn't mean to pry.'

I go to bed with a picture of Jack and Fran falling together in an easy tumble, knowing they'll wake in the morning with someone to hold.

24

Romany

Five a.m., circling above Heathrow. Runway lights in strips and loops spread out beneath me for miles; planes hang in the air waiting for clearance. The sky is crowded and turbulent. Last time I was up here I was with Ty. We were off on our great adventure and the world was ours, a gem-sparkled carpet just waiting for us to step out on to it. Now it feels as if I'm inside a tired, lumbering beast: Royal Nepal Airlines out of Kathmandu straight to London. Everyone's weary of being up here; we want to get down to earth where the air and food are fresh. England. Dad's down there now, waiting to take me home to Kate and Mum, to Mount Street.

It's cold up here but the real chill comes from inside: will I ever stop longing for that moment again? The day we left, when love was beginning and anything was possible. It's bad enough that the past spills into every day, but the future, too? I'll have my future unknown, please, bubbling with potential.

Like it was then.

The captain tells us we're in a queue. A queue of planes in the sky, linked to the planet by radio signals, sound waves, electric impulses; invisible things. I'm so jittery I daren't even blink, can't nod off in case the invisible breaks down – fear of the future, leaking in again; it makes me think of Kate. How her whole life since the accident has been about plugging that gap, not giving in to the knowledge that things could get worse. Every time she gets stared at, pitied, patronized; every time a kid runs away from her, an adult is repulsed, the patch over the fear thins, starts leaking. So we have to change the future, it's the only answer; believe in change and don't get scared.

That's what Mum used to say, anyway. They were going to change the world, live differently. Their world would be just, humane; they would vindicate the struggles of their parents. It was going OK, too: Michael hanging on at the factory that his dad had slaved in, keeping it alive; Jenny taking her energy to the streets; Kate a bright beam of hope. Then the unjust, the inhumane landed slap on their plates, a big, scary mess that they hadn't a clue how to clear up. Especially her. Give us poverty, give us capitalist oppression – we understand that, know how to rail against it, but don't give us this, don't make me flinch at my own daughter . . .

I'm up in the sky which can fall on your head. A memory of the story, of standing in the corner shop with money Dad had left for food. But Mum didn't eat so I bought comics and sweets instead, spent ages choosing – good tension, for once – cola-chews or gobstoppers? That day it was refresher lollies and a comic-strip version of *Chicken Licken*; I liked the sharp-nosed fox, his red coat and wiliness. *The sky's going to fall on your head.* When I got home Mum was rocking at the top of the stairs – red alert danger sign – and Dad came in just after me. As soon as she saw him all her sodden energy flared up. Dad shoved me into my room and I tried to shut my ears with sweets and *Chicken Licken*. It wasn't long before the social workers came and took me away. Mum hardly got out of bed – manic depression, people would whisper – and Dad was out most of the time. I'd watch him leave from the upstairs window, never even a glance back at us.

The sky's falling on your head. Panic!

Can't you see it? Don't you know? The sky's going to fall on our heads!

Sugary bile in my throat as I heard the front door slam. Dad's footsteps fading quickly into the grind and scrape of the city. It's all right for you, I thought. You can go. I never forgave him, or her. That was my family pretty much finished. Into the kids' home with a load of other anchorless, holey children, making up stories about princes and dustbins and death-in-childbirth while sneaking off down the narrow streets of Aston, seeing my old home become tattier, dingier; trying to wish my mum sane.

It's because of Nyala that I'm on this plane, that I'm thinking of the past. 'Mmm mmm ssst ssst,' she said. We never spoke a word of the same language except for *namaste* – she goes 'nn-te nn-te' – yet I gave her the Buddha I'd bought in Varanasi, dipped in the Ganges and everything, and she gave me her tiny alien-head skull, wrapped in cloth ripped from her skirt. It's in my pocket now. An orphan, rescued, taken in by an ordinary family; slowly making a place for herself, then the past came piling over the col and into the cave, her sixth sense drawing us up there in the middle of the night.

'Mmm mmm ssst ssst.'

It was only after she'd left that I worked it out. 'You must.'

Back to England and all that's in my head is the house in Aston – how could I ever have thought I could leave it all behind? It was always cold; Mum's eyes glaring at me, clear as day that I was the one who'd sent her mad. I took Kate there once. The bus routes had changed and we had to walk a way; Kate hitching her prosthesis over cracked paving slabs and piles of rubbish. The house had been repainted. 'It was boarded up last time I came,' I said. 'I hated that, as if those boards finally killed my family off.'

A man opened the door, toddlers gripping both of his hands.

'Look at that,' I said. 'All happy families.'

Kate squeezed my arm. 'You've got us now.'

'I know,' I said, scuffing my boots against the kerb. They seemed too new, somehow. 'Not the same as a real one, though.'

'Tell me about it,' said Kate. A group of kids dashed past us, pumping skateboards, sliding across kerbs and skidding into alleyways; not an inkling that one day, without warning, the sky might fall on their heads. 'They shouldn't have to think about it,' said Kate, her eyes glittering, protective. 'They should run and run.'

As I sit here suspended above England, I wonder if she'll ever forgive me for leaving. And if Ty will ever be bothered that I have.

*

'Romany? Wake up, chick, we're nearly home.'

I open my eyes to roads and fields. The car zips along the motorway and the motorway cuts through the country-side; there are no family picnics or donkeys or cows spilling out on to the tarmac. I fell asleep almost as soon as we set off from Heathrow – soft seats and good suspension luxuries, like Dad's arms, his wrinkly skin smelling of tobacco and Imperial Leather. 'The wanderer returns,' he said, smiling. 'Your mother's going to say you're too thin.'

'She can fatten me up then,' I said, thinking of custard, and baked beans, soft white bread and Marmite, sausages and chips.

Dad's jumper is underneath my cheek – he must have tucked it there when I fell asleep. Tears spring to my eyes. 'Not crying at the sight of Brum, are you?' says Dad, as we move off the motorway, past the Hawthorns, crawl down towards Handsworth past shops with familiar names – Khoobsoorat Saree, Ambala Sweets. The old pub sign with a painting of Jesus, a Union Jack and a Rasta flag all hoisted on the same pole, then the chevron-shaped street-lights of the Soho Road. Fruit spills off the shop fronts into the street; the mosque is strung with coloured lights, looking like a ship floating in the haze.

'Did you want to adopt me, Dad?' *Or was I just thrown at you, at your liberal conscience?*

The car jolts – a patch of oil on the road; a cat, belly-down as it scuttles between rows of parked cars. 'Of course,' he says.

'It wasn't more Mum?'

'No. We all wanted it. What's brought this on, love?'

'Bet you wish you hadn't now. All the stuff with Tom. Mum being so bad. If she'd never known us then this wouldn't have happened – all that pointless tragedy right in her face . . .'

'It's been on its way for years.'

We've stopped at some traffic lights; Dad's hands are clenched tight on the steering wheel. 'I've seen it coming since Kate's accident. Tom was the straw that broke your mum's back.'

Out of the sky, I think, like a meteorite. It was always going to hit and there was nothing he could do to stop it.

We go to a café, Vietnamese, I think – white-washed walls and plastic tables, cups of tea that taste like medicine, old men in slippers playing Mah Jong. Kate and me wouldn't have given it a second glance as teenagers – *boring* – but now it fascinates me. I imagine us coming here to read and gossip and watch the street outside.

Dad's never actually spoken to me about Kate's accident, but it looks like I'm about to get it – the truth. Mum did once – only once – staring firmly out of the window, eyes following the traffic as she told me of the climber running

225

down the hillside, chased by storm clouds, meeting her and Dad on their way up; her anguished cry.

In the café Dad looks me straight in the eyes and tells me how it was. 'A freak storm, from nowhere. It was mayhem: ships driven into fields, power lines down, nothing but flattened grass where our tent had been. No one saw it coming. Kate was helicoptered to hospital pretty quickly, considering, but when I saw the faces of those paramedics I knew it was serious. One of them even said it, feeling her leg for bones that weren't smashed. "Dead meat, that, it'll have to come off." Your mum couldn't take it in. "You've got to save it," she said. "For God's sake, we can fly to the moon and you're telling me you can't fix my daughter's leg?" "It's crushed," the surgeon said, as gently as he could. "The bones are shattered, an artery is severed; there's no blood supply to her foot. We need to take it off now – she's very weak, the infection has already spread . . ."'

Dad's voice is a low monotone; charged. The café is quiet: sucks and hisses from the coffee machines, clicks of ivory, a quickly hushed whimper from upstairs. I can't think of one thing to say that'll make this any easier.

'I signed the consent for the amputation,' says Dad. 'Your mum couldn't, and someone had to. I'll never forget her face when she saw Kate come out of theatre: this empty space where her leg should've been, the stump huge and swollen, wrapped up like a mummy. She shrank away – just an instinct, but she's never forgiven herself – and started crying, "My perfect baby, my perfect baby." I had to drag her out of recovery in case Kate came to and heard her. It was the worst hour of my life.'

Dad's skin has gone grey, his eyes lost under harrowed brows. I rub his hand and he smiles, automatically; even now he's reassuring.

'When Kate came round she said she knew her leg was gone, had known on the mountainside. "My body knew,"

226

she said. Your mum went into practical mode – healing, rehab; books, information packs, support groups, relentless positivity. "There has to be a way to fix this," she said. "There has to." She stayed that way until Tom got killed; his death seemed to snuff out the light at the end of her tunnel. There was only one other time when I saw any change in her and that was the day we adopted you.'

I remember it well. Kate and me late back from school, our dinner money spent on fags, but they made Kate sick so we stayed in the park until she stopped heaving. Her wheelchair got a flat and I couldn't push the sodding thing without bumping and bruising her so it took us ages to get back.

'She's not on the step,' said Kate, as we turned the corner into our road.

I pushed the wheelchair up the ramp, calling cheerily, 'We're home,' and spitting chewing gum into the bin. Mum was at the kitchen table, smoothing her hands over a letter. There were tear streaks down her face and Kate lurched towards her, saying, 'Mum, soz, it's OK, it's my fault, we went to the library to fetch that book I've been waiting for.'

But when Mum looked up it wasn't at Kate. She looked straight at me and her face flashed with animal joy. 'They've said yes,' she said. 'We've adopted you. You're all mine now. You're Romany Jackson.'

25

I meet Mum off the train at New Street and she seems smaller, less lean.

'Kate,' she says, 'you look taller.'

'How are you feeling?' I say, reaching for her bag; she lets me take it. She's holding Hutu in his basket, I bend down to say hello and he pushes his nose into my cheek.

'OK,' she says. 'Better. Really.'

'And Frieda?'

'She's great. Batty as ever. She's got herself a new bloke, a fisherman.'

'A *fisherman*? Frieda hasn't eaten fish in donkey's years.'

'I know. They have fantastic rows about it all the time, but are completely mad about each other. Then he goes off to sea for weeks on end and she stares out of her windows all wistful, fretting every time there's a storm.'

We must have seemed like storm victims when we arrived at Frieda's after Tom and the flood. I had to get her away. She couldn't walk the streets any more; just the sight of a child beggar or snappy parent filled her up. We had to retreat somewhere quiet, underpopulated; find some different rhythms.

I listened to them talking round the kitchen table night after night, Mum's voice rising until it cracked, then Frieda's murmurs, as soft as the tide slipping over the shingle outside. They went for long walks with Star, strode for miles and miles up the empty beaches while I tried to write my dissertation. Mum seemed to find the blanched pebbles and sluggish seas soothing; though when the wind rose, nudging into the tunnels under the house, hooting and mewling through the fissures she shrank again. So we prayed for good weather and long, calm days.

'What's happened, Frieda?' I said. 'Why has Tom's death set this off?'

Frieda clasped her hands around the back of her neck. 'She's been running on empty for years,' she said 'People do; all their lives sometimes. She can't find a point to it – she was brought up to believe that everything's part of God's plan, remember. I think her crisis of faith hit the ground when Tom was killed.'

'Have you talked to Dad?'

'He doesn't have any answers. And that's what your mum wants.'

'Poor Dad.'

When Dad came to visit, Frieda sent them off on walks and then left the three of us alone in the house with homemade lasagne or chilli in the oven. We did as we were told but they were hungerless meals. I longed for Romany, thought she might be able to cut through the family impasse with a joke, a gibe, even a tantrum. I thought about throwing a fit myself – 'Just because Tom's dead it doesn't mean we all have to fade away' – but I couldn't do it; Mum was way beyond being snapped out of it. If only Romany would write, I thought. A letter from India to take us away from this, into the unknown, the thrilling. Dad tried – *We've got responsibilities, Jenny* – but Mum's eyes stayed disengaged, and Frieda said we just had to have faith. Only time and faith would heal this.

Sometimes, in the early mornings when I was crutching it to the toilet, or up on the window seat reading – always a legless activity – she'd look at me and see it, the space that can't be healed, and we'd exchange a fearful glance.

'Where's your dad?' says Mum, looking round the station platform for him.

'At the house. Getting it ready.'

'It's not ready?'

'Just a few bits and pieces.'

When I arrived back from Northumberland a couple of days ago Dad was frantic. 'He's been a bit slack,' Carla said. 'The basic work's done but he can't bring the place back to life all on his own, can he?'

We bought flowers, painted skirting board; a quick prune round the garden, Dad's experiments buried in brambles. I dusted each room, turned on radios, cooked some food hoping that the smell would lift the atmosphere. Our old sofa had been re-covered and re-sprung – no more fighting for the corner which didn't throw you to the floor – but I found my fingers feeling for the old shiny patches on the arms. 'It'll be better when Hutu's back,' I said, before I went to bed, into our room on my own.

I couldn't sleep for hours, twisting the sheets; too hot, too stuffy. Eventually I opened the windows and scented jasmine and night stocks drifted up from the garden. I put an extra blanket on the bed and let the cool air fall into the room, into the musty corners of wardrobes, behind book-shelves, under beds and into plastic bags full of old clothes – I'd found Mum's running kit, unwashed; she hadn't even taken it with her to Frieda's. By morning the room smelled of nudged-out dampness and I knew what to do.

'Open every window,' I said to Dad. 'Get some air in the place.' A breeze had risen during the night and was twisting rubbish and dirt on the road into little devils. Dad opened all the back windows and propped every door open and the wind found its way in, under lips of carpet, rattling the *Welcome Home* cards on the mantelpiece; up and down the stairs with a scouring whoosh.

In the taxi Hutu drops a paw out of the basket-mesh on to Mum's thigh. She holds it, like you would a child's hand. As we dip and swerve through the city Mum stares out, sunlight catching on the sharp-angled buildings; bus-shaped shadows falling on pedestrians and then sliding away leaving them sunblind. I watch Mum's thumb stroke Hutu's paw.

'I'm OK,' she says, before I ask again. 'Better than before, anyway.' Her eyes are on the Hockley flyover, the runway which skims over warehouses and faded shops and roundabouts and will soon land us back home in Handsworth. 'I've started taking the pills,' she says. 'Frieda said I should at least try.'

'They help then?' I say.

'I don't feel so useless – can do normal things like talk on the phone, go to the shops.'

'People always doing for you,' I say. 'I hated that. It wasn't until Romany came that I felt anything but a burden.'

'You wouldn't take any pills though.'

'The pills were for other people's sakes.'

'Maybe,' she says and withdraws. I can almost see the screen drop down between us. But I don't push it – it's the most honest conversation we've ever had about that time. Now we're both damaged, I think, almost laughing at how terrible this is. Mum stays quiet and it suddenly occurs to me that maybe she knew Romany would save me; that as soon as Mum saw her face around the back of the burger van Romany was burdened with being the way out for both of us.

The taxi turns into Mount Street and Hutu starts pacing around his basket, sniffing the air. As soon as we get out of the car – Dad is on the steps – Hutu flings himself around, scratching to get out. Dad takes the basket and swoops a quick kiss towards Mum, sits her down in the kitchen, then

231

takes the basket into the garden and opens it up. Hutu darts into his bushes down at the back.

'Well, at least he's glad to be home,' says Dad.

'Dad, don't be like that. I'm glad to be back, honest. It's just difficult.'

'How's your mother?'

'On Prozac.'

'Happy pills.'

'She's trying.'

Dad's chest sinks inwards. 'I know. We all are, aren't we? It's just that most of the time it seems to get us sodding no-where.'

He plods back into the house. I stare at his footprints, sunk into the damp earth. That Dad is defeated too seems awful – me and Mum have clashed since the accident, although I've told her millions of times that I was going my own way anyway; the accident just heightened her sense of having lost me. She had her ideas of how things should be, how I should be and how she should cope; Dad was more flexible, more accepting of life's quirks and oddities, the strange patterns we make for ourselves. But we've gone too far this time, all of us – me, Mum, Romany. Abandoned him, and now that shows – of course it does. I wish he'd let it all out. Rant and rave and stamp his anger on to us, on to the house we fled from. Like I imagine screaming at Romany sometimes: fantasies of cathartic anger, regretted seconds later but somehow magnificent in their righteousness.

Careful, Kate, I think, slipping into the bushes after Hutu. Mum was always the righteous one. Remember what it was that made you most angry, that's at the root of your estrangements. Her ragged voice squeezing through floorboards and door cracks. 'She really should have moved on by now, she's no better, it's been six months . . .'

She *should* be better, she *should* get out more, she *should* have come to terms with it by now. I said to Romany that if anyone ever managed to explain what 'coming to terms' actually means, in a real life, then I'd saw off my other leg and hand it to them on a platter, garnished with rosemary. What it really means is stop moaning, put on a cheery face and don't bother anyone with your loss. Certainly don't try and explain what that means, how you saw the life you'd glimpsed for yourself receding in an instant, to blink like a rarely seen star on the edges of your consciousness, removed from all possibility. Seeing all that on a hillside as the sky fell on your head.

But Mum lost the daughter she'd glimpsed too; had to deal with me, sick, scared. I knew how hard it was for her, that her bustle and briskness – turning me out of bed to change the sheets, not satisfied until they were snapping in the wind below my window – signalled desperation, really. She couldn't fix my leg but she could fix my clothes, my room, my activities, my future if there ever was a God on this earth. Mothers behave like *this* when their children are felled. Then along came Romany. Romany; with her face like mine and the body that should have been mine, too.

'Hutu . . . Hoo – too,' I call to him softly. I'm completely hidden from the house now, in cat world; worm-bulges in the soil, creeping chickweed, stones shunted up to the surface from the restless rocks below. He'll come to me, but I'll have to sit very still – any movement and he'll be off, arching his back and skittering back to blend in with the dark undergrowth.

Zulu's still at Frieda's – she disappeared a few days ago, vanished utterly and only emerged from the old crab pots under the house when Mum had left. Frieda says she's gone feral now, snacking off fish-heads and pushing her territory further and further; the shiver of her tail on the blackened thorn-trees, on rocks that are swamped at low tide.

Hutu's nose appears, his whiskers flick out from a bush.

'Hello, Hutu,' I say, stroking his back and tail right up to the tip. He circles around me, in contact all the time, then sniffs me carefully – my trainers, my leg, my hair. Hutu judges by smell, not appearance, and I seem to pass. I stroke his back, stare into the bushes and long for a man like that, who'd start it all off by taking a great big lungful of me.

26

They're here. She's back.

Car yanked to a halt outside; doors slammed, footsteps, key rattling. Mum has baked bread – pounding the dough in the early hours – and is just pulling it out of the oven as Romany bursts into the kitchen.

'You're so thin,' says Mum and we all laugh at the predictability of this remark, even Mum. 'Well,' she says, 'you know I can't stand these girls who starve themselves out of existence.'

'And you know that Romany eats for England,' says Dad.

'Or for India,' I say.

'Give us some of that bread then,' says Romany.

Within minutes we're all sat round, passing butter and cheese, a bowl of tomatoes on the table, Dad mixing salad dressing in a jam jar. The map of India is back on the wall, slightly wrinkled from the damp. Hutu butts through the cat flap – Romany feeds him, gossiping into his ear. She's full of chatter about her wait in Kathmandu, the flight and the journey home; keeps saying how weird England looks, how weird. Dad has secreted a bottle of champagne in the fridge and we drink it in seconds, the bubbles swallowed easily into all of us. Seeing Romany's face across the table makes me feel unsteady, as if the house really is floating; dipping and rocking underneath us, a ship with bad ballast.

'We've only just come back here ourselves,' I say, in case it seems to Romany that nothing has changed except for fresh paint on the walls.

'I didn't quite lose it out there, you know,' she says, meaning *I know*. 'Where's Zulu?'

'Gone walkabout at Frieda's,' I say. 'You'll see her when you visit.'

'Tell us about Ty, then,' says Dad. The question I've been wanting to ask, unable to say his name – *Ty* – casually, curiously; so unable to say it at all.

'Chasing his tail in the mountains,' she says. 'I think they call it "finding yourself".'

So that's how she's going to treat his disappearance – a quirk on Ty's part, something to be indulged. She must be hurt though, inside, that it was more important for Ty to 'find himself' than be with her. The way she blanches slightly as her eyes meet mine tells me that, but she's facing it out and I admire that; can never help but admire Romany.

When I wake up the next morning, Romany's asleep in the chair next to my bed, a blanket pulled up over her head. We stayed up late last night, whispering about Mum and Dad, gingerly peeling back the layers of our family's life.

'I guess we'll have to get used to worrying about our parents now,' I said, amazed that we'd never anticipated this – so obvious now, their fragility tangible.

'The whole thing just makes me want to eat sweets,' said Romany, so we piled on old jumpers over our pyjamas and sneaked down to the all-night garage to buy Dime bars and Skittles and chocolate milk.

Romany's face emerges, chocolate-stained, and she grins on seeing me. 'You don't half know how much I've missed you,' she says.

'Me too,' I say.

'Shall we go and look for Tom today?' she says.

My stomach plummets like a lift cut from its wires. 'Romany, Tom's dead.'

'I know, babe. But that's about all we know. It might help Mum if we get some answers. Me too.'

'Asking why only makes it worse. It just happened. Like me. Like you.'

'I know what you're saying. Your accident came out of nowhere. My mum and dad just couldn't get a bloody grip . . . but Tom was *killed*. Someone did that and I want to know who. Boatman Freddie, your leg, my family – I guess they got taken by fate, and OK, it might have been some psycho turned out to care in the community, in which case Tom was in the same boat as us . . . but there might be a reason. Someone responsible. Someone who could get banged up for life.'

Her mention of prison makes me think of Adrian. I filled her in last night – as much as I know, anyway – and told her about Ty's mum, Fran and the photographs. The skin around her eyes creased and she nodded, digesting the information, then dropping a shutter down over the subject.

'We've got places to start,' she says, her turn to be detective. 'The street kids, of course; your mate Vaz; even the police might be able to tell us something.'

The mention of his name causes a small, cold scoop inside me; involuntary, like a hiccup, or a suppressed urge to speak.

'I'll write to him now,' I say, reaching for the pad next to my bed. I had a letter from Scotland a few days ago. *There're lots of things I'm not, Kate. Rich, clever, handsome . . .*

'Oh no you don't,' says Romany. 'You're coming into town with me.'

We cross the park, arms linked, and hit the Soho Road. It's busy, as ever, clogged with traffic streaming between

Brum and the M5. Romany buys some mangoes, squeezing them expertly and waggling her head sideways before agreeing on a price: 'Acha.' Old men in trilbies and fifties suits stroll out of the patty shop with their rice and peas; girls with cardboard caps slide trays of iced buns and chocolate concrete into the bakery window. Romany's eyes are everywhere, like they must have been in India, but I notice the crossovers, the merging of styles and cultures. Indian men in kurta pyjamas wearing argyle socks and brogues; white blokes with long, snaky dreads; Asian girls in six-inch platforms; white women who've taken the hijab.

We're buoyed up by the energy of the city, by being together again. The fissures under our skin silt up and for a precious moment we're whole. When we get to New Street there's a familiar voice belting out 'Waterloo Sunset', his voice bouncing off the plate-glass windows of the gleaming shops. It's Crow – he does a double take when Romany says, 'You remember Kate, don't you?'

'Yeah, yeah, course, man. The twins. How was India, babe?'

'Mind blowing,' says Romany. 'But we need to find out about Tom.'

All noise dies. A moment of complete silence before the street jerks back into motion, the pigeons start babbling, the smell of coffee curls past again.

'Bad, bad, bad,' says Crow, his head swinging on his neck.

'Does anyone know what happened?' says Romany.

'Fancy a sherbert?' says Crow. 'You buy and I'll tell.'

We go into the Temple Bar, a lone refuge from continental cafés with metal counters and chain pubs with 'no workboots' signs. Loud rock music is playing; the landlady sings along as she pulls pints.

'The word is that it's something to do with Karen,' says

238

Crow. 'He kept coming back here to sort her out, again and again. But that Karen . . . She was like water draining down a plughole, man. There was nothing you could do to get her back.'

'Where is she now?' says Romany.

Crow shrugs. 'Ask me one on football.'

'She wasn't at the funeral, was she?' I say.

'Had some shame, then,' says Romany.

Tom did get Karen away from the city for a while, Crow tells us. Took her on the road, let her cold turkey all over him, tried to heal her abscesses with tea tree and fresh air. But there was smack on the sites, too – dealers fanning out from the cities to towns and villages; even a caravan in a lay-by or a bus in an old gravel pit wasn't safe.

'I got into it myself for a bit,' says Crow, holding his hands up. 'Tom deffed me, wouldn't believe I was clean. He got a bit mental about it, really. Not that I blame him – Tom was golden. His heart fucking broke every time he looked at that girl.'

'I bet she did come back,' says Romany. 'Where else would she go?'

'She got in a bad way with a dirty hit and Tom freaked. Manhandled these guys off the site, trashed all their gear into the river. Karen screaming at him, "What am I going to do now, you fucker?", like she really expected him to go off and score for her. Tom was nothing compared to Lady Morphine – couldn't pretend any longer – and I tell you, you've never seen a bloke so low. Disappeared for weeks on his own, roaming around. Poor bastard. I only saw him a few times after that, once or twice here and there. I don't know . . . I'd say he was asking for trouble, if it didn't piss me off so much when people say that.

'He sat with me once when I was busking. This woman got her bag snatched and Tom shot off after the mugger – this raggedy tramp bloke gone loop. Got the bag back,

239

though – that woman gave me a quid every time she came past after that.'

'What happened to Karen then?' I say.

'I don't know,' says Crow. 'Let's face it, no one but Tom ever gave a shit.'

My beer tastes flat and sour. I leave it on the table and we trudge up Corporation Street, cold trickling through me. The city's lost all its glitter and I'm missing a tenner from my purse. 'Crow,' says Romany. 'Must be back on the gear.' It's harder for me to walk than ever. I just don't have the energy to drag this lump of metal and foam around any more; long for the days when my body carried *me*. Romany's feeling much worse than me though, and I know why. Tom saved her from Sonny's avengers, and where was she when he needed saving?

'Don't blame yourself,' I say. 'You can't put your life on hold in case something happens to one of your mates. I saw him while you were away – he was fine. He asked about Karen, but no one knew where she was and he left it at that. I mean, he was still carrying it around with him – he loved her, didn't he? – but it didn't stop him getting on with his life.'

'You really think so?'

'Yes.'

'So who killed him?'

'Romany, I just don't know.'

'We have to find out.'

'Mum's been down that road already. It nearly finished her off, Romany. You can't tear up this family all over again.'

'I can't just leave it.'

'Is that for your sake or for Tom's?'

We're standing at the bus stop, glaring at each other. I'm hot with fury, with an urge to shove and shake her. Coming back here, stirring things up before she's even eaten breakfast twice. She's breathing hard, her eyes are thin. I daren't speak in case something horrible slips out. *You weren't here. You didn't see it, didn't see Mum.* And lower down, deeper. *You bitch, you left me,* like Tom said I should. *You left me and you took him without a thought.* I was shocked that Tom spoke of Romany like that, he'd always guarded her like a dog; recklessly loyal. But Karen had left him by then, rejecting his protection, his care and his love. Bitch.

'Do you think we've been slack?' I say. 'That we don't care about what happened?' She knows we do – I realize that as soon as I say it. She cares so much that it rips her up inside, nothing she can do except thrash and flail.

'I can't believe he's gone,' she says forlornly. Her breathing is slowing down. I'm cooling.

'Well, he is, Romany,' I say. 'You'd better get used to it.'

*

Dear Vaz,

Again, I'm writing to someone on the move, not knowing if the letter will reach you before you're gone. I hope so. I hope you're having a good time in Scotland. Romany's back now. Blunted in some ways – who wouldn't be, losing Tom and Ty? – but completely herself in others. It's weird: as if a mirror either side of her would show different pictures. But then we all show what we want to show, if there's any choice; and we hide what we can, if we can.

I'm sorry I didn't tell you about my leg. I just wanted you to think of me as whole – to have a picture of me in your head which wasn't missing a piece. I liked the way we'd become friends through our letters, didn't want it to change because I said, 'By the way . . .' It's virgin territory, being disabled: there's no way of telling how you'll handle it till you're there. Like the mountains – except no one ever gave you a choice and there's no way back. I wonder if you've got two pictures of me now – the one you built up and the one you actually met. Is there any way of sliding the two together, so that they match perfectly; no edges overlapped or patches blurred?

How are the hills, Vaz? I want to come out there. I always did, ever since I was a child. I always imagined I'd be adventurous. I remember the day of my accident, when I set off up that hillside on Skye, thinking, this is what I want to do. Stride out further and higher and wilder because out there you can touch something, sense something; when your blood is high on oxygen and your muscles pull and throb. I understand why Ty has gone, the sparkling, impossible mountains luring him like a siren; ready for it – honed by months of travel and meditation. I understand because it's what I want, whereas Romany wants what I have: flesh and blood parents, unshakeably, immovably mine no matter what else happens. We used to know this about each other – we still do, I think – but we're dealing with so much more now, strands of muddy water leaking into our once clear pool of understanding. I thought that clarity would last for ever; that nothing would stain it.

I didn't intend to write all this. I meant to ask you about Tom. Romany wants to find out what happened, answers to why? Her mother's daughter. She wants to track his movements, his last few weeks. Get close to his life to cope with his death? Maybe. I said I'd ask if you could help.

Write to me.

Love,

Kate xx

27

It's quiet in the house for the next couple of weeks. Dad's out in the garden when he's not at work, digging, mulching, planting and feeding, rescuing his experiments. I watch him from my reclaimed window seat. He doesn't disturb the areas the animals have made their own; talks of attracting birds to the newly dug pond, of ducklings and great crested newts and water boatmen. There's no wind, and every morning spiders' webs lace across the window in front of me, droplets of water trapped and then dried to nothing by the sun. Mum reads a lot and has taken to scribbling furtively in notebooks, as if this is something she's not allowed to do. Romany is out, on her missions. Sometimes I go, sometimes I don't – pretty much like when we were teenagers except she doesn't bug me now if I say no. We're all careful with each other, polite; no tantrums or accusations, but no denials either. The truths have quietened us all.

I hand in my dissertation and am finally signed off from college – all those years of part-time study over with, and now I have a degree in English Literature and a library gathering dust in my head. I've done it though, learned to cross at least one of the roads again. Mum thinks I should go into research, but I want to do something different for a while; go somewhere, move out of the house, maybe. No rush, they say. It'll take some thinking about. They've never pushed me, asked what I'm doing with my life. I sometimes wish they would, like Vaz's parents. 'You're eighteen now, you can look after yourself,' they said – he's ten years younger than his brothers, grew up with his dad's model railway running round his room, half converted when his mum fell pregnant. They weren't impressed when he chose a bus as his new home, but had blown their argument by then. Romany's brows furrow when I mention leaving. 'Mum and Dad are staying here, though?' she says.

'For a while, I suppose,' I say. 'Not for ever.'

'If it was up to me it would be,' says Romany.

'We have to make our own homes one day,' I say.

When I do go out with her it's to the grimiest, grottiest, most forgotten corners of the city; places I haven't been since she first came and made me go out. 'Anyone stares at you we zap them,' she used to say, as I hopped up and down kerbs on my crutches; I was out of the chair but scarring still stopped me wearing a prosthesis. 'Zap, zap, zap,' she said, nodding her head towards the gap-mouthed, the look-away-quickly, the stumble-and-stare; and I zapped too, hundreds sometimes, imagined them all lined up on judgement day.

She's tracked down the hooker who found Tom's body and discovered that some of these girls, too, were watched over by Tom, his networks much wider than even Romany knew. We go and visit.

'Either a pimp or a punter, I reckon,' says Lou, the one who found him, a beautiful black girl whose long, thin fingers twist through her long, thin braids. 'Girls were getting battered and robbed out there and Tom took to hanging around the streets with us, just in case, like. Yeah, it was safer with him about, but we had to send him packing – business was drying up. The punters sent him mental. I remember he jumped up on a car bonnet one time, nearly gave the old giffer a heart attack – Tom's mad scarred face banging on his windscreen. We wouldn't hear anything for weeks and then he'd send us stuff – condoms, safe addresses, even money sometimes, although he was the skintest person I've ever met. I told him loads of times: "Tom, it's not up to you, mate," but he'd just scowl and say, "Well, who is it up to then?"'

All the time she speaks Lou moves around the room, polishing her plants, positioning photographs, straightening books, back to the plants. 'He was a hard-knock, Tom, but you still felt he could just crumble, like there was nothing holding him together. And he got people's backs up; certain sorts always started on him – coppers, security, ordinary blokes too, like he had it written on his face, *Come on then, come and have a go* . . . And they did. He was forever swatting people away.'

'How did you get into this?' I blurt out, before I can stop myself. 'I mean, you could do *anything*.'

'We all could, darling,' she says. 'Given the chance.'

It's noisy and grubby out on the street again in contrast to the clean tranquillity of Lou's room. Romany's spitting. 'I should've been here,' she says. 'If I'd been here I'd have known, got him away.'

'You mightn't have known,' I say.

'Tom didn't have secrets from me.'

'Looks like he did. Anyway, things change, Romany.'

'Jesus – what's happened around here? No one trusts me any more. It took me a week to talk Lou into letting me into her flat. Mind you, she doesn't half protect her space; said she always made Tom strip off when he came round. He had to leave his clothes out on the landing; sit there bollock naked with his hands over his dick.'

'Mum did that to him once, remember?'

'People were always trying to clean him up.'

245

I remember the day. I'd been upstairs reading; didn't even know Tom was in the house. Romany was out and he came round and chatted to Mum for ages. I was on my way to make a brew and he was sitting in the living room naked apart from a pair Tasmanian Devil boxer shorts, an old Christmas present of Dad's. He was covered in scars, even worse than me, and tattoos – *Mum* scrolled under a heart with an arrow through it; *Karen & Tommy for keeps*. Like a map of his life, a history, the latest chapter a slice above his eye which Mum had taped together with steri-strips. Pockmarks everywhere, glassy patches of burnt skin, one ear caved in by a punch, an amateur tattoo around his neck, dotted line and scissors and a wobbly *cut here*.

'Hi, Kate,' he said. 'Your mum's reclothing me.'

'She does that,' I said, leaning into the doorframe. I was still on my crutches, wary of visitors, distressed by people's stares, the way they fixed on the space where my leg should have been, suddenly mesmerized by the patch of lino or crack in the pavement which they shouldn't be able to see.

'How're things with you, anyway?'

'OK.' I slipped into a chair, kicked the crutches out of sight, tucked my leg up and pulled a cushion on to my lap.

'Why do you try to hide yourself, Kate?'

'Why do you think?'

'Maybe it'd be better if we all went naked,' said Tom. 'Everyone's flaws out on display.'

'Ugh.'

'Ugh to you too.' He made a face; an ugly, monstrous face, like a storybook troll. I imagined him living under a bridge snatching gold from the greedy, casting spells on the arrogant, stretching out wires to trip up the mercenary. I wanted him to live for ever.

'We're all ugly but we're all fucking gorgeous too,' he said.

'Fucking gorgeous,' I said.

In the street outside Lou's flat damp rises and hits the sun at knee level; small rainbows flash in puddles and on the flanks of cars, off Romany's silver bracelet and the mirror shades of the boys swaggering past. Oily smears on the road become iridescent in the unexpected light, music breaks out of a window high up above us; calypso, sunshine music, and a woman in African robes sways past us, dancing for a few steps. Romany's eyes are bleary and pained but she smiles at the dancer, raises her arm to someone she knows across the street, who flits through the silvered stream of traffic and plants a big smacker on both of our cheeks. Romany crooks her arm for me and we move on, through light and shadow, talking of Tom, of all the people left exposed now; and how fucking fantastic he really was.

The next day I fall over hard while I'm on my crutches and bash my stump. Mum and Dad start arguing over whose fault it is: the wet patch that didn't get mopped up or the fact that there's stuff – boots, overalls, magazines, files, tools – all over the tables and work surfaces and floors. I can't negotiate mess, I'm just not nimble enough.

'Oi, oi,' says Romany, just back from the chemist with my script of co-prox, 'stop bickering, will you. We just need to sort the space in this house out, that's all.'

'I need a bigger workshop,' says Dad.

'And I need a study,' says Mum.

'I was hoping I could store some props and stuff here,' says Romany. 'I've got an idea for a show to take round the festivals.'

'What about the attic?' I say, running my mind through each room in the house. 'It's huge, isn't it? And didn't Dad replace some of the floorboards after the flood?'

A fly buzzes at the strip light. Mum's work file falls open

in her hands and the clip breaks; paper dwindles down-wards like falling sycamore leaves. A sudden stillness has landed. Dad stares hard at Mum and then starts to pull his overalls on.

'It's time,' he says, throwing a heavy glance at her and then backing out into the garden. 'I said we should have cleared it after the flood.'

'Time for what?' I say. 'Cleared what?'

'Not now, Kate,' says Mum. 'You need to rest. Romany, help Kate upstairs and I'll bring you up something to eat.'

'No way,' says Romany. 'You've got to tell her.'

'You know?' says Mum to Romany, whitening, gripping the edge of the table.

'Know what?' I say.

'You really think I've never been up there?' says Romany.

'Up where?' I say. 'The attic? What are you on about?' Pain throbs through my stump – it's badly bruised – down into the severed nerve endings, to my phantom leg, trapped for ever in a Z-shape – foot, calf, knee – by the rocks which fell from the sky. The untrainable part of my brain still thinks if I wriggle and shake enough I can fling off immutability by force of will although I know – I really do know – that this awkward, invisible Z is with me for ever, distorting my space. I spasm severely, even black out for a second or two. Dad's face appears behind the glass of the door and he comes back in.

'She won't be able to get up there on her own with her stump all bruised,' he says. 'Come on, Kate, I'll carry you.'

'But . . .' stutters Mum. Whiter than the cloud-blanked sky outside.

'But nothing, Jen,' says Dad. 'You know how I feel.'

So it's in Dad's arms that I'm taken up to the attic, back to my childhood, to the time before my accident. The lacy frill around my duvet is yellowed and my swimming cups are tarnished but I'm there, two-legged; poised, expectant.

Dad puts me down on the bed and I remember exactly the dips and creaks of its old springs, the dusty smell of the mattress; how I curled under the covers with my torch reading Bruce Chatwin, dreaming of the strange and foreign. Mum and Romany have followed us up and are standing, necks bent under the sloping roof, shifting from foot to foot. Romany picks up photographs of me from the bedside table: as a baby, a toddler, a sunburnt girl climbing cliffs with Dad. I'm using a pink rope and seabirds tack in and out from the rocks; I remember the smell, the beat of their wings.

'You knew,' I say. 'You knew and you didn't tell me.'

'Shit, Kate,' says Romany. 'I couldn't handle *this*.' She stops, pauses. 'Sorry.'

I try to remember what happened to my things when I finally came home from hospital. Redecoration, a new bed, change the furniture round – it all made sense at the time. 'Make it as nice as possible for you, love,' Mum said. But all that time my old room was up here, in a space at the back of their minds; reminding them what I could have been, what I wasn't. It makes sudden, sickening sense, like a film reeled backwards, a detonated tower block pulled back upright from the scattered debris. Blocks of concrete fly up through the air, pieces of masonry are sucked back into their slot in the finished jigsaw of walls and ceilings and the tower is preserved in pictures, if not in time. I reel at the thought of it; me preserved in space only, haunting the house and her mind, taunting her with lost potential.

'Who did this?'

'Kate . . . I'm sorry. I always meant to tell you . . . thought that one day we'd come up here and remember together – have a cry together – but we were never like that after . . .'

'And you put it all back together? After the flood?'

'I said we shouldn't,' says Dad.

'But this is like I've died, like a bloody shrine.'

'I didn't know what to do with your things,' says Mum. 'Couldn't bear to throw them out, Kate – please, try and understand how awful it was for us. My little girl . . .'

'I *know* how awful it was.'

I came home a smoking pile of rubble and she tried to piece the building back together. 'What am I? Humpty fucking Dumpty?' I say to Romany, who's sat down next to me, her hand hovering around my shoulder. I flinch it away. Don't want anyone touching me. I pick up the photograph of me climbing and we both stare at my black hair and sturdy, salt-flecked legs, realizing instantaneously that it could be a picture of either of us, an arc of connection like the day on the bridge. This could have been Romany's childhood; I could have roamed around the world.

'God, soz, Kate,' says Romany. 'This is awful, like you're your own ghost or something, like you haunt yourself. I guess I blanked it out . . . too familiar, all that family shit –'

'Lucky for you lot you can blank it out.'

I turn to her. No sounds except breathing. 'So what was your plan, Mum?' Rage boiling inside me; energizing, powerful, cruel. 'Embalm me up here? Did it help you? Did it?' Wind rattles the tiles above us and the room shudders. I wish it would all crash down on us; that we were in the middle of the storm hanging on for dear life instead of being here, damaged, with the aftermath strewn all around us.

'Katie, you were my baby . . . I didn't know what to do. I mean I just didn't have a clue.'

'And where did Romany come into this, huh? When you realized I wasn't going to do the heroic bit and para-lympically overcome everything? You'd have loved that, wouldn't you? Cheering me round the track, right beside me when I picked up the prize. And there was me, reading books and getting an education – what a fucking dis-appointment. Still, you could come up here for solace, couldn't you? And you had Romany – shame she's not the sporty type really.'

Mum is crying.

I've made her cry. Good.

'You bullied me,' I say. 'Wheelchair racing, swimming classes, gym, yoga. God, I hated them – only went to shut you up. And all that time I was failing to live up to your little cache up here.'

'You didn't fail at anything, Kate,' says Dad.

'God, it drives me mad. How am I supposed to live up to *this*?' I've been squeezing my stuffed dog Banjo, picked up from the tatty collection of toys on the bed and now I throw it – him – violently against the wall.

Mum gasps and grabs Banjo, clutches him. 'I only kept a few things . . .' she says.

'A few things? Part of me has been up here all this time and I didn't even know. You've made me into a bloody phantom.' Bitch, I think. Breathing hard, concentrating on not saying it. Bitch bitch bitch.

'OK. Kate, that's enough. I think we know how you feel about it,' says Dad stiffly.

She's leaning on him now. He tries to kiss my forehead before taking her down but I turn and he misses. My hands feel too big as I watch my parents leave. I want to say something to her but am scared of what might come out if I start again.

'What do you want to do about this lot then?' says Romany, once we hear the door to their bedroom shut. 'Get rid?'

28

Romany

Dear Romany,

I've just got word from Kishore via some porters that you've left the hut, gone back to Birmingham. I wonder what you'll think when you find this letter on the mat at Mount Street. I try to convince myself that you'll be OK. You're strong (true), but I know it's not enough and I'm sorry. I shouldn't have left you like that. There're lots of things I shouldn't have done and that's kind of why I'm here. I knew you'd be OK though, which isn't fair I guess. People shouldn't have to take things just because they can.

How's Kate? Your mum and dad? Is it good to be back?

I'm sitting at the top of a pass under the prayer flags, bright against snow and rock. The sky is deep blue and ice crystals glitter in the air. Half a day's walk away there's a village where I'll give this letter to some porters heading back towards Pokhara. I'm tempted to just fling it upwards, let the wind bring it to you along with the prayers on their way to the gods. The right words that you'll instinctively understand. That's what I wish I could send, but what you'll get is these scratchings, my pen blotched by cold, my fingers numb.

It took me three days to get up to this pass and now I can see what's next – a long, slow descent. The paradox of climbing – the glory is at the top but the hardest part is coming down: hard on your knees, your back, your mind as you leave the pureness of rock and ice. Only noble creatures live up this high – snow leopards, eagles, bodhisattvas – rare and perfect creatures who remind us what gods might look like, what perfection is. And I'd never have come without you, Romany; never have given myself the freedom to leave. Either side of me are two huge basins sculpted by glaciers – rocks straining under the ice, breaking free to scoop out this gigantic valley, leaving thin veins of rivers behind. It's like watching the earth being made, broken and remade, in front of your eyes; thousands of years swept along on the wind, by the clouds which speed past me, blotting out the sun, turning everything dark and cold.

You'll be angry by now – your eyelids will slide over your eyes. But Romany, up here I can cut it, think hard, maybe even reach something. Down there, even with you, I'm a fraud, hiding parts of myself from everyone but me. Up here I don't have to pretend and that's so much better.

Kate will have said about my friend Adrian who's in prison. He should be out soon and he may come to you, I don't know. He doesn't really have anyone else except me and I'll be staying here. I need these big spaces, this ice-tinged air to tackle my demons, otherwise they might have landed on you and that would be worse.

It would, honestly.

Love,

Ty xx

*

'Tosser,' I say, crumpling up the letter and kicking it into the corner. 'What the fuck is he on about . . . *demons*?'

'Maybe it's best,' says Kate. She tucks her hands underneath her legs, eyes on the letter.

'How can you say that? He left me alone on a fucking mountainside and now it looks like we'll never see him again.'

'It might be for the best, you know,' she says, turning her face away, walking to the window, tripping up on nothing as she goes. 'God, Romany, I don't half feel woozy, must be the painkillers. I'm going to have to lie down for a bit.'

She hitches her prosthesis up carefully over the rug, trying to walk well but it must be hurting too much for that. Her shutters have gone up since the row in the attic, as if the rest of us somehow conspired, although she knows we didn't.

Mum's fantasy Kate was never going to happen anyway; we'd both moved on from what she wanted, but I guess I did kind of cut Mum out once we were together – we were soul mates, see, twins in the womb. God knows what she was doing, really, keeping that stuff up there. Keep a little bit of the past perfect, maybe. Anything but let her loss hit her. Then in came Tom from the blindside.

The two of us sat on Kate's old bed in the attic and tried to work all this out, Kate smouldering, me catching sparks of her anger and flaring: I was just a substitute; they never really wanted me at all. And did I betray Kate by not mentioning the attic? 'I'd only just got here,' my excuse. 'Was still expecting to find myself out on my ear . . .'

'You weren't to know what it meant,' she said. 'And we can't share everything, despite what we thought back then.'

After a while Mum came back up and Kate spoke to her steadily, as if she'd been practising the words in her head. 'There's no way you could have prepared for this. We're dealing with stuff most people never go near. I know you felt cheated and I know you want the best for me.'

'I couldn't stand what had happened – for ages I couldn't. How were you going to cope?'

'But that's up to *me*, Mum. I couldn't stand you thinking you knew best. Especially after Romany left.'

'But you stayed in so much. I thought you'd get depressed.'

'You're the one on Prozac, Mum.'

Mum managed a thin smile, reached out to touch Kate but stopped.

'We're going clear this lot out,' said Kate, looking around the attic. 'I might keep a few photos, nothing else. Then you three can fight over who gets the space.' She shifted on the duvet; damp was seeping through. If we didn't make a move it would soak into our clothes, our skin.

Mum was fingering Banjo's furless ear. She wanted to ask Kate if she could keep some bits, I could tell; was checking herself every few seconds, mouth opening and closing. Let her, I thought, be big about this; be as big as you are, sis.

'I . . .' said Mum.

'Do you want to look round first?' said Kate.

'Just a few things, love.'

'We'll come back up later then. Romany, give us a hand to get downstairs, will you?'

'It's your decision too,' said Mum. 'What we do with the attic.'

'I'll pass on climbing ladders, thanks,' said Kate.

I hit the streets. Have to get out of the house; Kate needs space, so she says, and Mum's trying not to try too hard. There's a bloke from the community centre I met while I was scavenging wood from one of his skips, he's been asking about my shows.

'Why go touring? We have festivals here,' he says,

opening the door to a store room stuffed full of sequinned costumes, headdresses, ostrich feathers, giant animal masks, wire-skirt contraptions decked with streamers. 'And this is just for Carnival,' he says. 'Theatre can be any-where – why not here?' The masks and costumes remind me of India: papier-mâché heads and glitter; drumbeats and chants cranking the rock-hard life of the streets up a level with whistles and horns and wild dancing.

I've been finding it hard to love this city again – stabs of loss as I move around Tom's territory; they're still sharp as I corner into Brewery Lane where he lived for a while, down by the canal in a old hut at the tunnel entrance, taunted by air rich with yeast and molasses. But today his absence makes what's left here special. A thousand places to hide in a city like this, he used to say. You can tuck your-self away in the creases and wrinkles; the secret streams, the overgrown cuttings, the back end of a breaker's yard, behind metal and rust too thick for anyone else to tackle.

I roam around all my old haunts, checking out the distant past of my life, over barriers I never thought I'd cross. The backyard where I tottered in the grass – we had a dog for a while, I remember as I spy through a fence hole, a mad puppy, fur and tongue and quick-beating heart. The crumbling, red-brick infant school where I refused to show how miserable I was, making myself the loudest, the brightest while wishing I could lose myself instead, reading books in the dim library next door, with its church-arched windows and sleepy assistants.

Nyala will be back over the col now, in the landscape of her past. She whispers to me in my dreams: *Rrr Rrr Rrr*. Something Dad said in the café is stuck in my mind. 'The shapes of the past will always be there,' he said, talking about Mum, recoiling at the state of Kate after the accident, and trying to make me feel better about Ty. 'You can't rub them out or ignore them; somehow you have to make space for them in the here and now. Me and your mum, we didn't intend to have a kid so quickly but when Kate came along we just took our luck for granted: this lovely chuckly baby, the house on the cheap, work for me when none of our friends had a hope in hell. That's part of our lives, too, in there with the loss and struggle and the big fat mistakes. Your travelling's in you now, a store you can always draw on. When Kate lost her leg your mum longed for our bright days back; she had to make them physical.'

He was talking about the attic, of course, but I didn't click – seems like I never do until it's too late. 'She saw the holes,' I said. 'Couldn't pretend any more that they're not there.'

I brush up against wet hedges, swing around lampposts, down the streets in long loopy patterns. As I trace the shapes I feel part of it again, made by the concrete and cars and tree-lined roads which dip and rise. Tower blocks sprout out of greenery, light flashes between high windows like secret signals arcing across the city. I end up on Barr Beacon, a Black Country oasis of gorse and pine, and when I reach the top I stand and watch the lights come on, the ripples and twists of the land. Needle-thin spires and bronze mosques, factories and forts and football grounds and backstreet warrens threaded through by the motor-way's giant arms.

'Maybe I'll stay,' I say, to Tom. 'How can I run away from something that'll always be here?' My past, my land-scape. Them, even.

I'm not going to talk to bloody Ty, though.

'What's he hiding?' I say again to Kate, in desperation, a day or two later. 'What are these sodding demons?' She's taken to her bed to rest up – can't wear her leg on top of the bruising – and is garrisoned in there with half a damn

257

library. Every time I try to talk about Ty, about the thousand little heart-stalls every day when his name passes through my head, she seems to withdraw – but not blatantly, you'd feel like a tit if you said anything. 'What is it, Kate?' I say.

'Something must have happened before he came here, to do with Adrian. That's as far as I've ever got,' she says.

'No, what is it with *you*?'

'There're some photos in that drawer that Fran gave me in Northumberland. Have a look, see if you can find a clue in there.'

I go to the drawer and pull out the packet. Pictures of teenagers squashed up on sofas. Out of focus, fingers over the lens, for the bin really if you didn't know any of the people, but I can't resist them – Ty before I knew him. He looks so young – a close-up of his face, wisps of hair on his chin and his floppy fair hair. I think of him being shaved in Calcutta; the zip of the cut-throat razor and the aniseed shaving tonic, burying my face in his neck, his smell. I clutch my stomach, maybe gasp, because the next thing I know Kate's arm is round my shoulders and I can smell the blue soap on her.

'He's been on the run since Calcutta,' I say. 'Got to the mountains and leapt clean away from everything.'

'We wondered why you left there so quickly,' says Kate.

'We saw an accident,' I say. 'This boy got knocked over by a car right next to us – I wrote you a letter about it. Bang, dead. Ty freaked.'

'I'm not surprised,' says Kate.

'No, I suppose not.'

'I'm sorry he's hurt you, Romany.'

'So am I, babe.'

'Why didn't you go with him? To the mountains?'

'He didn't want me there. He never said it but I know when I'm not wanted. I couldn't stand being . . .' I know what the word means to Kate, how hard it presses on her, but saying it is better than leaving it hanging '. . . a burden. Imagine me trailing miles behind him, killing myself to keep up. And . . . I was pulled back here eventually – Nyala leaving without a second thought – I couldn't carry on blocking you all out.'

'We've got degrees in blocking things out in this family.'

'It's mad, though, out there. We both got lost in it – Ty just took it that one step further. There're thousands and thousands of kids moving around like some great big twitching sea; no roots, no shackles, they just unhitch themselves and disappear.'

'He wrote to me about Adrian,' says Kate, 'but never got in touch for any answers. It was like I didn't exist after that.'

'He passed his last tie on to you then.' Kate as the problem solver; unlike me, idling around on the green shelf, shirking, till the past almost literally hit me in the face.

We can hear Dad shifting around above us: drilling, hammering, and a new sound – whistling. Making a study for Mum, they told us firmly; the house is for us now you girls are grown up. We looked at each other, thinking, 'grown up?' But Kate *is* different, more self-contained, less needy, a stirring in her. And I've changed, too; can't shake off my disappointment over Ty – it leans on me, casts a shadow over everything. Once or twice I catch it under my feet and stamp on it, grind my heel on disillusion, but it always leaks out again, dark stains on the pavements and kerbs where I've been. More shit to live with, to take into my life.

Kate's back in bed dozing, eyes flickering under her closed lids. I wonder what she's dreaming of. I leaf through the photos, peering closely; the spaces between people, where a hand slips into darkness, a foot disappears. This is all I have of Ty's life before he came down here. I took him and Kate on tours of mine: the streets where I'd slept, the emptied markets where the homeless wait for soup vans. All my landmarks. I felt again the cut of window ledges, the jolts of jumps for freedom, the scrages as I fell; physical memories. Bile in my throat as I dragged them past the house, unable to even glance at it then. No wonder I was so desperate to leave, to travel; the lure of a place with no memories, where alleys and subways and street corners don't trigger aches and fury. I don't think Ty quite got it until we were out there, but it dawned on him fast: *I can be different here.* Was that the day I lost him?

Kate groans, pulls the sheet over her head so I wander downstairs. Mum's working on the computer, absorbed. I stand in the doorway, idly thinking about scanning in my photos from India when I'm caught by what's on the screen. Montages of me and Kate, our faces overlapping, our arms and legs mixed up. Eerie images of us when we were younger, my face overlaid with Kate's, matching almost exactly, my mouth slightly wider. But now our faces are starting to separate – Kate's is sharper, more canny than mine. Lines are appearing in different places on our faces – a small fan-burst at the corner of each of Kate's eyes; my forehead rippled.

'Mum, what the hell are you doing?' I say. 'That is weird.'

'I'm looking at the past,' she says. 'Been away from it too long.'

'God, we were identical. You must have been spooked when you first saw me.'

Mum stares at our flickering faces on the screen but then she turns to me, flesh and racing blood. 'When I first saw you, Romany, it seemed that you were a gift, for me and for Kate. Your face was the sign, the gift-tag. *The Lord giveth and the Lord taketh away.* That's what my dad used to tell me, when I was a child. It was hard for me not to

think of you as a kind of compensation. But I was wrong –
you were always more than that. It was wrong for you but
especially for Kate, to ever think she's a case for redress.'

'Kate will be fine,' I say. 'Look at her face.'

'I pray so,' says Mum. She needs something from me:
reassurance, comfort, perhaps just plain love.

'Have faith, Mum.'

She nods hesitantly, then steadily, as if swallowing
medicine, making sure it's gone down, then turns her face
back to the screen and starts moving the faces around,
jumbling and layering them – I can't work out who is who.
'Is that me?' I say, placing my finger on the screen. 'The
eyebrows are a bit thick for Kate . . .'

'That's not Kate; or you,' says Mum. 'That's me.'

29

It's another week before I can put my leg on and I'm
screaming to get out by the time the bruising has faded.
Good, I think, I still want it, this freedom. Romany's out
all the time, comes home smeared with grit and grease-
paint, evidence of her two preoccupations – out on the
streets asking after Tom, and rehearsing for the show she's
planning to take on the road this summer. I'm jealous – of
her show and her plans, but not the obsession with Tom's
death. I've let that go now; I had to.

Mum gives me a lift down to the Soho Road and
manages not to ask me, 'Will you be OK? Where are you
going? Shouldn't you take your stick with you just in case?'
I should, probably, but I don't. I'm sick of carrying things,
want my hands at least to be free. My love/hate relationship with who I've become embodied in this false limb of
plastic and foam. Embodied; even I smile at that. Captain
Ahab, eat your heart out.

'Morning, love,' says a passer-by I vaguely recognize. A
breeze flickers down the street, snatching hair from underneath veils, ballooning under skirts; the newspaper seller
picks up a brick and pins down the *Evening Mail*. Lads
swagger past in bright yellow shirts, two-finger rings
catching the light. A girl is strolling, elaborate coils of
pinned hair and kiss-curls shaped down her forehead, so
precise they could have been drawn with eye-pencil. A boy

on a bike weaves slowly along next to her, twisting his handlebars this way and that to stay at her pace.

I buy bargain-basement toiletries with exotic names and sit on a bench letting the traffic blur in front of me; smells of curry patties, perfume, drying concrete leak through the fumes, an occasional gift of freshness from an invisible place. I walk back through the park. It takes me ages but there are plenty of benches and verges to rest on and my slow pace means I really get to look – at an oak tree spreading into the sky, names tattooed into the bark, a disused nest high up splintered by gusts.

I've been expecting Vaz for a few days – hints in his letters, I notice them now – and when I turn the corner into our road he's there, sitting on the steps talking to Romany. They're laughing, I can see that, but their voices are snatched by the wind and it's as if I've gone deaf for a moment. I hurry as much as possible, jerking and stumbling along the road, my hands on hedges and walls and lampposts. I want to walk well, smoothly, as much as I want to be calm and composed, but can manage neither, already running lines through my head: 'Glad you could make it, good to see you,' or even, 'This is my sister, Romany,' as if he hasn't worked that out for himself.

The wind changes direction suddenly and I can hear them now, something about Womad, and a sharp, burning pain bores down to my toes that aren't there. My face is crumpled by the spasm and just at that moment Vaz looks up. 'Hey, Kate . . . you OK?' he says.

'Fine.'

'I'm sure you shouldn't be walking on that yet,' says Romany.

'I'm sure you shouldn't be telling me what to do.'

Romany bridles. 'Excuse *me* . . .' she says.

'We were just talking about the festivals,' says Vaz.

'I'm not deaf.'

'Kate, don't get shitty,' says Romany. 'You know you can come with me if you want. We always need musicians.'

'Very benevolent of you I'm sure.'

We stand in the street being bashed about by the wind which rushes past us grabbing up rubbish and sticks and silvery dust, dumping them randomly. 'What's your problem at the moment?' says Romany. 'Spit it out, Kate.'

'Nothing,' I say. 'It just hurts, that's all.'

'Let's go for a drive,' says Vaz. 'You've got to see my new van.'

Romany moves as if to come with us, but then takes herself up the steps into the house. I concentrate on the new dwelling: a bottle-green Bedford van with a chimney pipe poking out of the roof. 'What's the engine like?' I say, stupidly – I wouldn't know a decent engine if it landed on my head, but it's better than the only other comment I can think of, *nice colour*.

'Great,' says Vaz. 'Came down from Scotland no problem. I could go anywhere in this – France, Spain, over to Morocco . . .'

'I thought you were off to the festivals.'

He stares at a tyre, pokes at a bit of rust. 'Depends, doesn't it?'

We drive out to Clent, the motorway rumbling underneath us, and then cut away into the hills which eddy off towards Wales. Vaz is on the lookout for stopping places, lay-bys and unmarked roads where he can blend into the trees at dusk.

'Great colour, this van,' he says. 'Easy to camouflage.' I smile and Vaz does too. He reaches over and squeezes my shoulder. 'You OK now?' he says. 'What is it with you and your sister?'

I couldn't even begin, I think, shuffling down in my seat and watching the sunlight bounce across the windscreen. But I wish I could keep her away from you. Instead I tell him about Mum, and the attic room, which is of course about Romany too.

'Nothing much has changed between me and Mum, though,' I say. 'On the surface, anyway. I always knew she was torn up about my leg; thought if she'd finally admit to it, talk about it, there'd be this great catharsis and then we'd slot nicely together again like pieces in a jigsaw. But it's never like that really. We rub along together much like we did before but without this unmentionable cloud between us – a bit more room to breathe, I suppose . . .'

'Sounds like quite a big difference to me.'

'Maybe.'

'You'd have changed as you grew up anyway.'

'No, I wouldn't. I'd have stayed perfect.'

Vaz laughs. A tape is playing on the stereo, something Irish with repeated phrases which mimic our rolling movement, whistle then mandolin then fiddle or flute as we dip into another valley. 'I like this music,' I say.

'D'you play?' says Vaz.

'Flute, when I was younger. Haven't touched it for ages though.' Since Romany left for India.

'Take it up again then. Go with her if you want.'

'She's mentioned it. But I wouldn't want to slow her down. And . . . I need to do something for myself. Don't ask me what. I keep telling Mum and Dad I'm going to leave home – they just look at me thinking, and live on what? The only things I'm good at are reading and studying and no one pays you for that.'

'You could teach,' says Vaz.

'Maybe, one day.'

'There's always a way to get by. I'll do anything – mending walls, clearing out rubbish, fruit picking, fixing engines – for food, fuel or cash, anything will do. Hasn't let me down yet.' There seems to be more weight behind these words than just passing the time of day.

'What are your plans now?' I say. 'Back to Wales?'

He hesitates. 'Maybe . . . I could stay around here a bit. Romany says there's plenty of work building the set for her show – painting and all that. And there're loads of places for me to park up. You could come out in the evenings, bring your flute . . .'

The tune changes to something more jumpy, syncopated. I've an urge to press the button, rewind to the gentle rippling of the previous one, but my thoughts are already in time with this new tune: *I want you to stay for me, I want you to stay for me.*

'What do you think?' says Vaz. 'Should I stick around for a bit?'

'Whatever,' I say, staring straight ahead. We turn a corner and the brooding shapes of the Black Mountains fill the windscreen. The light is fading and my own face is reflected on top of the black; dim and fuzzy and scared to say yes.

When we get back Mum, Dad and Romany are sat around the kitchen table. Something else has happened, I know immediately, and feel a flash of resentment, that there's never a clear run; no time to sort one thing out before something else intrudes. I'd been thinking on the way back that I really should talk to Romany, about Ty, me, Vaz. But that's not going to happen; the tinge of nerves – alarm – in the air tells me that. 'What?' I say. 'What's happened now?'

'Ty's Adrian's out of prison,' says Romany. 'He says he's coming here.'

'Did you invite him, Kate?' says Mum. She doesn't want him here, her clipped voice tells me. Scared to let more strays through the door, more needy kids she can't protect.

'No,' I say. 'But Ty's letter . . .'

'Ty thought he might come here,' says Romany.

'Who's Adrian?' says Vaz.

266

'This is Vaz,' I say. 'He knew Tom. I've been writing to him.'

'And who else have you been writing to, Kate?' says Dad. 'Do keep us informed.'

At the mention of Tom, Mum's torso sags just slightly; she rubs her eyes hard. We all exchange glances. I try not to, because I know how this feels – to have the whole room passing meaningful looks over your head, knowing exactly what they're thinking but unable to think of anything to say except *don't*.

'Bloody hell, Kate,' says Dad, switching glances between us and Mum. I can read his thoughts too. *Just when we were beginning to settle. Your Mum taking an interest again.* Romany and I squirm. There's no point in protesting, trying to explain the reasons I may have had for attaching Adrian to our family. *I felt for him, locked away from the world, and anyway, Ty asked me . . .* Because right now Mum's more important than any of that. My foot is twisting on the lino; both of Romany's are.

'Can I have a look at the letter?' I say.

Dear Kate
(and Romany who I've heard so much about)
   I'm OUT!!
   You'll be pleased to know. I hope you'll be pleased to know.
   And I'm on my way to see you and catch up with Ty. I would've phoned but you didn't give me your number.
   Why didn't you give me your number??????
   Anyway my old friend Ty said you were people I could trust so that's good enough for me.
   Hope this finds you well
   Adrian

The letter's dated yesterday. He could be here any minute.

'Why don't you go to Frieda's, Mum?' I say. 'Me and Romany'll deal with this.'

'Will we?' says Romany.

'Dad, you can take a few days off, can't you?'

His eyes say *not easily* but his mouth says, 'Yes. Yes, of course.'

'Oh, let him come,' says Mum. 'What do I care?'

'You don't need this, Mum,' I say.

'I'm *all right*,' she says.

'Jenny – we're going,' says Dad. 'These girls can clear up their own mess for once.'

She's easily ordered. Mum being told what's good for her, shielded from problems, whispered about behind closed doors – I'd never wish that on anyone, least of all Mum. I move to the kettle – something to do, a cup of tea – aware that Adrian could be walking down the road, up the step, a knock on the door at any time, and this shunts away my other thoughts, worries, jealousies, longings. Got to deal with this first.

'What's up with your mum?' says Vaz after they've gone upstairs: phone calls, packing, quieted protestations. 'I got the impression she'd cope with anything.'

'She can. Could,' I say. 'I guess Tom's death set it off – sent her into a spin about all the other pointless crap that happens. Happened. She's on pills now and they help, but she doesn't find it easy. She should just tell us that Adrian can't come here and not give it a second thought, but Mum beats herself up when she's not the perfect hostess to every lost soul in town.'

'Nasty business, depression,' says Vaz. 'She'll come through though.'

'Do you really think so?'

'Sure.'

I make toast and soup for everyone – carrying food up

the stairs to Mum – and then phone Frieda. 'I feel terrible,' I say. 'We really thought . . . you know . . .'

'Well, nothing goes away totally, does it? But I'm optimistic. Your mum's not blanking her problems out any more; she doesn't deny them or lash out at your dad or you two instead. She'll come through.'

'That's what Vaz said.'

'Jack liked your Vaz. You'll have to bring him over here.'

'He's not my Vaz.'

Frieda goes quiet and I picture her standing in her clean, spacious room overlooking the wide sea.

'I've been talking to the council,' says Frieda, 'about that idea we had – kids from the city coming out here. We could set something up, dedicate it to Tom. Your mum might like that.'

'She might.' The idea curls around my brain, hope from some stubborn, unassailable place. 'Thanks, Frieda,' I say. 'One of these days we'll stop running to you.'

'Don't you dare,' she says.

'Is your fisherman there?'

'He's on his way. Probably arrive in the middle of the night stinking of fish and I'll have to hose him down on the doorstep.'

'I bet you get fed up waiting.'

'I've waited long enough, I can cope with a few more hours.'

'You miss him when he's away, though.' It's a statement; she doesn't answer. Underneath the silence I fancy I hear the soft hoot of the wind beneath her house between crackles of static and my own steadying breaths.

30

'Bloody Ty,' says Romany, after Mum and Dad have gone. 'More head-fucks he's just swanned away from. What the hell did I ever see in him, Kate?' She grabs one of Dad's beers out of the fridge and starts to swig, fast.

I don't know. I don't know if it was the same things I saw or if he was a totally different person for you. I don't even know what I saw any more except the charm, the gloss, the easy manner.

'Oh, bollocks. *Bollocks*,' says Romany. 'Couldn't we just do without this crap?'

Vaz agrees; he nods as Romany curses. He seems taken aback that I've been writing to Adrian as well as to him but I can't start explaining that now – *I did it for Ty, cos he asked me to, cos I wanted a bit of him for myself . . .*

'It's not you he's coming here for, or even me,' I say.

'Who then?'

'Ty, of course.'

Romany pours beer down her throat a can at a time, like a seabird swallowing fish. '*Fucking* Ty.' She crunches her can and stomps around, picking up curry house menus and cheap furniture promos and flyers claiming to 'heal your whole life' – screwing them up and lobbing them in the bin ferociously. She shoves a can in Vaz's hand and he sips politely but that's not good enough for Romany. 'Drink,' she says, 'come on.'

'We've got to get up early,' says Vaz, 'to look for a good comet-spotting place.'

'Fuck comets,' says Romany. 'You're both drinking with me.'

'Do you see the same stars here as in India?' I say, reaching for the newspaper and looking at pictures of the night sky opened up into segments.

'Fuck India, fuck stars. Fuck *everything*,' says Romany.

'Especially Ty,' says Vaz. Romany sputters into her beer, spraying it around the kitchen.

'Fuck Ty,' she says, 'fuck him.' She leans on Vaz's shoulders to steady herself, laughter hiccuping in her throat. Vaz looks at me.

Then there are just hiccups coming from Romany's throat, but she doesn't stop drinking. Fetches vodka from the sideboard and swigs from the bottle, pacing and ranting and muttering like some mad woman in the street, except it's more scary somehow, inside. Vaz makes sugary tea for us and the clock ticks round and Romany still drinks. The phone rings – we ignore it – and Hutu comes in, jumps up on the table and winds himself around Romany's head – crashed on the table now – cat fur clinging to her hair. My heart creaks and burns for her, but all I can do is stroke her head saying, 'You'll be fine, everything will be fine,' thinking, he's hurt her bad, like she never thought he would.

'How come he's not bothered?' she says. 'I mean how can that happen? He's just switched me off. Well, two can play at that game. It's not like I haven't done it before, when I lived out there. Enough cider and glue and you never feel your boots pinching your toes, the crusty seams in your armpits – fucking bliss.'

'You don't want to do that, Romany,' says Vaz.

'No, you don't,' I say, furious, in her face. I can hear her creaking, close to a snap, the final break. 'You don't need

271

him, Romany.' *We don't need him.* 'Fuck him. Fuck Ty Waterson,' I say, surprised at the vehemence, the truth of how I feel.

We're all in bed before dark but still can't rouse Romany when the alarm goes off at two a.m.; she's under the duvet, only a curled palm and a hank of hair showing. We head off to Malvern without her, a note left by her pillow. It's a good night for star watching – cloudless black sky – the roads are empty and before I'm even awake properly the ancient hills loom before us like dinosaur fins.

'Where shall we go?' says Vaz.

'British Camp,' I say, pointing out the sign. The highest place we'll be able to park. From there it's only a scramble to the top, a hard scramble for me, but I make it and lie back in the soft grass and stare upwards.

'We won't see Hale-Bopp now,' says Vaz. 'It's still visible in the southern hemisphere though.'

'Where was it?' I say, thinking of the giant smudged thumbprint we looked at up in Northumberland, how it seemed a mistake when I first saw it, an accident in the sky.

'North-west I think,' says Vaz. 'There're others out there; we just can't see them.'

It's cold. I shiver and Vaz puts his arm round me; we huddle together. Everything around us is silvery-grey: the feathery grass, the monument, the silhouettes of trees – and silent, as if the earth is holding its breath, waiting for mysteries to become visible in its skies.

'There should be one around there,' says Vaz, pointing north to Brum, and then upwards into the black. I look hard for a smear of light behind the stars and planets I already know, then feel sudden vertigo as the sky jumps from flat screen to 3-D, our earth just another planet spinning and whirling and dancing in space.

'Look!' I say and glance at Vaz as he looks at the sky:

272

snubby nose and chin and a neat ear with two holes for earrings he doesn't wear any more. His arm is heavy on my shoulder, but I wish it was heavier; that he'd pull me close, clasp me with his rope-veined, dirt-smeared hands. He turns to me, pupils wide and black. He blinks.

'It's making me giddy,' he says.

'Me too.' His arm tightens; he breathes me in.

On the way down, the hills seem slippery, insecure. Even Vaz can't walk well. Two people stumbling and staggering and laughing as the earth spins and twitches and birds sing joyously at the new shafts of sparkling sunshine.

It's two more days before Adrian arrives, but when he does I'm glad Mum's not here. A short jab on the doorbell and the three of us look up from our toast and move together to the front door. A pale, slightly bloated face, a failed attempt at a smile – like he's forgotten how to, or maybe never quite got the hang of it in the first place – testiness around his eyes.

'You must be Adrian,' I say. 'I'm Kate.'

I hold out my hand and he jerks his forward from his hip. 'This is my sister Romany and our friend Vaz.'

'Can I come in then?' he says. He's been edging closer to the door and darts inside as soon as we move aside. 'It's taken me ages to get here.'

'How inconvenient for you,' says Romany. She's taken an instant dislike to him, which is understandable, but not very helpful. For the last two days she's been scanning photos into the computer: the three of us before she and Ty left; India photos; the pictures Fran gave me. Zooming Ty's face in and out, unable to cut him out despite saying it: *fuck you, Ty*.

I usher Adrian into the kitchen and make food for him, feeling more like Mum with every movement, every sentence. 'Do you want a bath? I'm sure we can find you

273

some clothes if you want to stick those in the wash.' His clothes are terribly pathetic. Prison-issue trainers with the soles worn through, a patchy shell-suit, no socks. He's not impressed though, when I hand over some stuff from Mum's store.

'What am I going to look like in this?' he says, holding up a perfectly decent sweatshirt and sneering. 'And why are you limping?'

'I've only got one leg,' I say. Adrian looks as if he doesn't believe me and I hold on to my patience. Why would I make it up?

'I'll have that top if you don't want it,' says Vaz, kicking his boots on the step before coming in from the garden, scattering zigzags of mud on the metal-grid mat. A cool green breeze flows into the house with him.

'That's about right,' says Adrian. 'It looks like something a crusty would wear.'

'Oh yeah?' says Vaz. My eyes plead with him not to fight with Adrian. 'So,' he says. 'Tell me about this Ty then. I've heard plenty about him, but only from the girls . . .'

Adrian's face eases a touch and I instinctively fade into the background. 'I've got to find him,' says Adrian. 'He was my best mate. I've never had a mate like that. We had a laugh, you know. Dares, all that stuff. We were the maddest. Where is he anyway? I thought he was in India with that Romany.'

'He pissed off into the mountains and left me,' says Romany. Adrian seems to have sparked off some deep fury in her; she'd ignite if touched. 'You'll have to go to Nepal if you want to find him. But in the meantime you can do us all a favour and get yourself washed. This kitchen stinks like a fucking prison.'

Romany's contempt for Adrian backfires though. Prison disease, Vaz says; he's used to being yelled at. He hangs

274

around her, sliding along the hall to watch her working on the computer, drifting outside to where her and Vaz are building props; a dragon with evergreen scales, a staircase to nowhere. Her activity, her grim determination to get on and do things makes me edgy. I know I should be making plans, too; that I've come far enough to think about moving on.

Dad phones and won't let himself be diverted by my questions about Frieda, Zulu, the boys. 'You leave your mum to me now, Kate, think about your life. Once you've got that boy out of the house, of course.' At one time Mum would have sorted Adrian out a bedsit, a McJob, but now they stay away; Dad's taken leave and a loan from the bank. 'Now matters,' he says. 'We've all been living in some fanciful future for too long.'

And what was that? I think. A future where I'm suddenly, miraculously, whole and perfect. Where what I've lost doesn't matter any more? There's more truth to rage; more power. Adrian is angry too. When I mention that I went to Northumberland and tried to talk to Ty's mum his face tightens and his lips spit bullets.

'That old cow,' he says. 'You'd have to be a fucking saint to satisfy her.'

'What about your parents?' I ask. 'Do they still live there?'

'Moved away when I was sent down. Couldn't walk round the village for the shame, my mum said. She even wrote that to me in a letter. Can you fucking believe it? After everything that I've been through . . .'

I wait for more, but he suddenly snaps out of the room, leaving a vacuum in my thoughts which is filled by images from Ty's letter to Romany. Him inching up a sheer mountainside, biting the thin air, brutal lines of rock against blue-black sky, ice crystal blizzards, frost-bitten fingers; ripping out pages of his book as he goes, words fluttering off into the wilderness. Could anywhere be more separate from here; this tangled, restless city? Heathland smothered by road and factory; railways, canals, warehouses, estates. Hundreds and thousands of two-up-two-downs lolloping over the plateau, dissected by hidden rivers and streams where dogs sniff and swallows dart. Trees catching a breeze high up. Wide pavements crowded with pushchairs, phone boxes, kids in school uniform: green pleated skirts, blue blazers, russet jumpers tied round the waist. Trams and trains and buses and cars and bikes – up there he only has muscle and bone. No roads or navigable rivers, a map with no paths. When he wakes on a ledge with frost creeping over his face, does he realize this is no place for humans? A slurp of wind, a missed foothold, a blocked valve on his stove and he's a goner. Only himself to save himself, but at least that way if he does come down no one will say it was his family, his friends that brought him back from the danger zone where disappearing is the easy option. But he's prepared – lucky Ty – his matches are dry and his rice nourishing and the sun cleaves through the dark distances and spreads like spilt oil, chilli-red over the empty, haunting valleys.

This is what I imagine, anyway. No doubt his last thought of me was months ago. At least Romany can lay claim to her losses – *her boyfriend left her in Nepal*. Not that she does, mind; she's never wanted sympathy. All I lost was a dream, a fantasy – as insubstantial as the dandelion fluff which drifts in through the kitchen window, through my fingers, but so tantalizing – the seed of possibility finally crushed by Romany's broken heart.

'You with us, Kate?' says Vaz.

'Sort of. Feel a bit . . . I don't know . . . disconnected today.'

He nudges my shoulder. I nudge back. Experimental touching, leaning, bumping between us ever since our star watching. I long to reach out and cup his face – just a stroke, nothing more, meaning nothing more – but don't have the nerve, and I think of Fran with Jack, her hand on his thigh only an hour or two after they met, the confidence to do that, to carry it through.

'You coming to the community centre tonight?' says Vaz.

'What's going on?'

'Hasn't Romany said? They've given her rehearsal space, she's going to work with some youth group down there – Stairway Theatre Company she's calling it. We're taking the set down tonight, then having a bit of a drink to get it all started.'

'So she's not going off travelling then?'

'Doesn't look like it.'

Do I want her to stay? Yes – of course; I missed her so badly before, our bond, all those shared years when no one else knew us so well as each other. But nothing is totally mine when Romany's around and I want that, for a while at least. I join Adrian hanging around the door to her room. She scowls at the sight of him. 'Twat,' she mouths to me, 'pillock.' His dog-eager eyes follow us to the window where we look down into the garden and the plywood props: curved arrows and giant question marks, a leaping fox; the shapes of Romany's new life.

'I'm going to stay around for a bit,' she says, in answer to my silent question. 'Too used to dossing about, me. Only gets me into trouble. I need to work, create something, you know.'

We both smile at the improbability of this remark a year or so ago and stand at the window, feeling the thud of time passing beating in our chests. 'Can I tell Dad or will you?' I say.

'No way,' says Romany. 'This is my news.'

'Does it help?' I say. *With Ty*, I mean. *With Tom*.

Romany links her arm through mine. We stare at the

shapes in the garden and I know that they're in there somewhere – a lanky, floppy haired gap and a pocked, dark moon-face – cut into her consciousness, attached to her body invisibly, twitching and jarring and occasionally burning out every other feeling except that they're gone.

'A bit,' she says. The shapes flex and wobble in the wind, sending strange, underwater noises into the sky; messages we can't translate but have to make part of us, somehow.

The community centre is in darkness when I get there and I can't find the entrance. The others went down hours ago – Romany and Vaz with stars and swirls hitched on their shoulders, Adrian scuffing along behind, although Romany scoffed that she didn't see what use he was going to be. I meant to stay away – too easy to get drawn into Romany's projects, her plans – but by nine or ten the house was full of empty spaces and I knew that only I could change that; no one was going to come along and take me out of it.

The windows are boarded up, metal grids nailed on top, and only a faint strip of yellow light bleeds out. I can hear voices – rowdy, disorganized – and some broken-up beats in the background. The pavement slides underneath my feet and I nearly take off for home again, but am loath to walk up the road alone, no one to link arms with, everything so much easier that way. My stump is sore and my prosthesis awkward and heavy – something has come loose, a notch, a link – and now nothing is safe, it could all just collapse without warning.

Where's the bloody door to this place?

I feel my way along the walls, looking for a gleam of light at ground level, wishing I had matches or a torch. I feel naked, unprepared – the only things in my bag are a pair of glasses and a purse with a couple of quid in it. The trees at the back of the community centre are black silhouettes,

278

like shadows, fuzzy orange lights blooming behind them, and all I can hear is the zip of tyres on wet roads, in every direction, like I'm the only idiot who walks in this city. My heart clacks in my chest and I can't believe I'm in such a state. This panic again, so sudden, so soon after I thought I was OK. The slipperiness and wetness and swishing of car and branch reminds me of something – fish out of water; gasping, flapping – but I stay off the ground, resist the temptation of a foetal curl, and carry on inching my way around, banging the walls and windows.

'For God's sake,' I say, aloud. 'Romany! Vaz! Let me in. It's me.'

A yellow segment in the wall, a body. 'Hello, Kate.'

Adrian. His eyes darting back down the corridor. 'Thank God for that,' I say, blinking in the light, shaking rain off my shoulders. 'Didn't you hear me? Where's Romany and Vaz?'

'How should I know?' says Adrian. He seems intent on staying in the corridor, has a bruised look about his face.

I feel my exasperation with him rising. 'You came here with them, didn't you?'

'Nothing to do with me,' he says. I head for the door and the voices.

'I wouldn't if I were you,' says Adrian.

'What?' I say, turning my head and pushing on the door at the same time.

Adrian stares past me and says nothing, contrary as ever. He's got to go, I think. His gaze tugs my head round and then I see. A room full of people and in the middle Vaz, Romany; her on his lap, whispering in his ear. His fingers splay across her thigh and back together again, a small movement; he laughs at something she says. Their heads jolt towards me in tiny, precise movements, like robots, and their faces drop: Romany sheet-white; burning red spots on Vaz. I'm back down the corridor faster than I ever thought possible; stumble out into the black wetness. The rain is needle-sharp, flints in the air, but doesn't penetrate the numbness which spreads down my arms and across my face as I stumble on the gravel and wish hard as hell that I could run.

'Kate! Kate, come back . . .'

Romany. No way will I talk to her. I try not to pant, to become a shadow.

'Kate, listen . . .'

'Piss off,' I say, as she moves towards me. 'For once in your life will you just do what I ask?'

'Ah come on, Kate – it's not what you think, honest. It's that bloody Adrian's fault – coming on to me all the time. He's always in my space, standing in the way so I have to brush past him . . . even grabbed my arse tonight. I told him I'm still in love with Ty, could never fancy a little weevil like him but . . .'

'Save your breath,' I say.

'You've got to listen to me.'

'I don't have to do anything.'

She stumbles on nothing. 'Kate, honest, I sat on Vaz's lap to get *him* off my case, that's all.'

I stare at my sister, don't even try to stop envy spreading across my face, feeling it curl my lip and hatch my brow. Those easy tactics with men; grab hold of one to put another off, slide into a lap, brush off a hand knowing it'll only make them want you more. And the men, colluding greedily, knowing she's a prize, that not wanting her would diminish them somehow. I've never wished I was her before, not even the day they left me behind.

'Can't you let me have anyone for myself?' I say.

'It's not like that.'

'Why flirt with Vaz then? You've been doing it ever since he arrived so don't pull the Adrian excuse. What are you trying to prove, Romany? That no one can resist you?'

'No one except my *parents*.'

'And you're taking that out on me?'

She stops. We glare. 'Kate . . . it doesn't mean anything. I do it because it *works*. Unlike trying to fucking reason with people.'

'But why do it to me? You haven't a clue, have you? How I've crawled and scrabbled to get out of the hole you left me in; how close I came to giving up, cutting my own rope, leaving *you* to struggle on your own. You're just like the rest of them, writing me off when it comes to men. You act like I'm not a player, not even in the game. Well, I am, Romany. Just because I don't play like you doesn't mean I'm out of the running.'

Vaz's voice. 'Kate, it was nothing, honestly.'

'Nothing to you, maybe.' I wish he hadn't heard that, that I hadn't seen it; that this could all stay buried, some-where less painful, less hard.

'So you want me off your case then?' Adrian to Romany; his voice querulous.

'Piss off, muppet,' says Romany. 'You've caused enough trouble as it is.'

'You never said you were still in love with Ty,' he says. His shadow falls over both of us, ringed by the orange city glow.

'Well, I'm telling you now. And don't think I'm fucking happy about it.'

'I was banged up because of him,' says Adrian.

'Just get lost,' says Romany.

'You were banged up because you're an incompetent thief,' I say.

'It was because of *him*. I'd never have got into trouble in the first place if he hadn't . . .'

'Hadn't what?' Me and Romany speak together, exactly the same timing, intonation, urgency.

Adrian flicks glances between us and then spreads his

shoulders back, rests his hands on his hips. Romany and I are caught in the shadow-triangles his arms cast. 'You really don't know?' says Adrian.

'Know what?'

'You don't know any of it, do you?'

'Spit it out then,' says Romany. 'Say what you've got to say.'

'Your precious Ty . . .' He's staring at me and I know from the thump in my gut that he knows my secret hankering for Ty, for everything she had. I send him a message. *Not any more. That's over.*

'Your precious Ty,' says Adrian. 'He's a killer.'

'You want to watch what you're saying, you little creep,' says Romany, advancing towards him. I really think she might punch him.

'Miss "I'm-going-to-find-the-murderer" is still in love with a killer,' says Adrian, unfazed, Romany's blows nothing compared to the cons. 'What would your precious Tom say to that?'

'It wasn't him,' she screams, launching herself at Adrian's chest, kicking the ground and the fence and the door and then back to his chest with her fists.

'Romany –' I grab her and pull her back. 'He's not saying Ty killed Tom – they weren't even on the same continent, remember.'

'What the hell is he saying then?' She slides down the wall and squats, head in her hands. Adrian rubs his arms and staggers backwards, shocked by the force of her feelings. I'm scared to watch her, know she won't break in front of them, in front of anyone but me. But it has to come out someday, somewhere, and now is better than later. *Tom's dead. Ty's gone. Cry baby cry.* All my jealousy drains into the gutter at the sight of her grief, over Ty, over Tom, and I know that I love her and we need all the love we can get, to stop our hearts from breaking all over again.

'Come on, sis,' I say, pulling her upwards. We leave Adrian and Vaz and, as we stutter away through empty, rain-sluiced Handsworth, Romany spews out Tom's story – pieced together from mutterings, rumours on the street.

'Lou went to the police and they told her he died from a blow to the head, a brick maybe. They said, "It must have been a punter, seen anyone dodgy around lately?" Lou said, "They're all dodgy, you tit." She thinks he was got from behind – a brick from the sky, Kate – someone who didn't like him hanging around the girls, who doesn't think brasses need protection. "It's moody out there," Lou said. "You never know who's next. Tom was going to cop it sooner or later – he upset people, ignored the pecking order, the rules. He might as well have had a target on his back." A target. That's what she said.'

Romany stops under a streetlamp, rain buzzing around her head. 'That could have been my life, Kate,' she says, 'if it hadn't been for Tom.'

'I know,' I say. Ghosts of the other possible lives close in on us, licking at our heels. Romany doing tricks with a punter in an alley; me brain-dead from the raining rocks.

'What are the police doing, then?' I say. 'Shouldn't they investigate?'

'No witnesses, no evidence. A homeless half-caste troublemaker who hung around prostitutes, travellers and drug dealers – who gives a toss about him? The police shrug their shoulders and the druggies close ranks and any-one who tries to force a path between them, who realizes we all live on the same planet, gets mashed.'

'Tom's life was worth as much as anyone else's,' I say.

'Too fucking right it was.'

Back at the house Romany goes straight upstairs. Adrian is kicking his heels in the garden, grey half-light draped around him. 'She was nasty to me,' he says, grabbing my arm. 'She didn't have to be like that.'

And I know it's true, that Romany brushed him off as a moron to even think he was in with a chance, and I'm grateful that if nothing else I haven't been a fool. Rejection, blunt, unequivocal – that's hard; he's been stung into making up this nonsense about Ty. 'Come on,' I say, as I drag him reluctantly up the stairs, 'you're not saying Ty murdered someone.'

He stops, refuses to come any further. The study door is open and Romany's clicking through her photomontage. She zooms around the screen, close into fuzzy corners, dim spaces between bodies. 'See this, Kate?' she says. 'Ty's got a fag in his hand.'

'Never,' I say, peering at the blur. Romany taps the mouse a few times and the picture jumps into clarity. Ty, smoking, a thin line rising from the cigarette tip, breaking up the air around his face.

Adrian's at the door. Neither of us turns but we both know. 'He always used to,' says Adrian. 'It was only after the accident that he went all evangelical, turned veggie; turned fucking perfect.'

'What accident?' we say.

'What's the point? You won't believe me anyway.'

'Stop fucking about and say your piece,' says Romany, staring hard at the picture of Ty.

'It's true,' he says. 'Why would I make it up? There're ways of checking if you really think I'm lying.'

'Make what up?' I say, a sick feeling crawling through me.

'Pub, Saturday lunch. A gang of girls there from the coast. Got invited to a barbeque but everyone was pissed. The girls were whining, pestering that they were hungry; we tossed a coin for who would drive.'

Ty, I think.

'Two girls in the front seat, three girls and me in the back. Crashed into a tree on the A697, snapped Angela

284

Latham's neck like this,' he says, grabbing a ruler and cracking it over his knee. It splinters, hangs limp.

'Ty changed after that. The police came and he held his hands up – "It was me, officer. I'm to blame." Did it all right; wrote to her family and everything. He used to visit them; her dad even went down to the airport to see him off to India. Community service. That's what the judge gave him; said Ty'd always be paying for what he did. Fixing fences and digging old people's gardens – they all think he's a bloody saint. *She* didn't forgive him though – blew her top completely. "Drinking? Underage? Driving borrowed cars and hanging out with those rough girls? You weren't even wearing clothes I'd seen before when the police brought you home." He stopped smoking and drinking and eating meat; joined bloody Greenpeace and never mentioned it again. A conversion,' says Adrian, gnawing on his words, 'like the road to bloody Damascus.'

'You telling me he was a fraud?' says Romany. 'A fucking fraud?'

'He was whatever people wanted him to be, after that.'

A chameleon, I think. To all of us: Mum, Dad, Romany, me. The poor girl's parents – everyone except his mum. I can see, feel their accident, the truth of it, the sickening thud and snap. Shake my head to rid myself of the picture but it's there; the dreadful consequences spreading out, scattering the youth of the village, leaving Adrian with just Ty, his boyhood friend who wouldn't play any more.

Adrian's eyes crab together as he tells how he took to drink, pills as well, but only so he could drink more. Run out of the village by his debts, down to the coast, the city; Ty the only one who ever kept track of him, bailing him out. 'They locked me up,' says Adrian, 'he kills someone and stays on the out and then they bang me up.'

'Just take your bullshit somewhere else,' says Romany, still staring at the screen.

'It's the truth,' he says. 'You know it is.'

The picture won't fade – I see Adrian and Ty, up to no good, their youthful swagger undented by any hint of tragedy – he wants that back, never got over the loss of his friend. A gap opened up beneath him and he's never got out of it.

'Well, you're out now,' says Romany. 'And you'd better get yourself in gear, because I don't want to see your face around here no more.'

Romany goes to punch the computer screen but jabs it off instead. Adrian steals a glance at her, follows her movements as she leaves the room, a look in his eyes which is something like love.

31

Driving out of the city in Vaz's van the landscape blurs in front of me, as if I'm looking through the window of a passing train. My mind ticks relentlessly, searching for distraction. *Count the red cars, count the blue cars, you've always loved this gentle landscape – see it, see it now. A lorry from Northumberland – think of Jack, think of the woods, swallows dancing out of the roof eaves, the sea.*

Vaz glances over; one hand leaves the steering wheel and hovers in the air, but doesn't get past the first of the rings of resistance which must be rippling out from me. *Am I like this all the time?* my mind says. *Do I do this all the time?*

Shut up, mind. Shut up and count cars.

Vaz parks up by the River Severn near Arley. The water moves slowly around tendrils of weed, eddying and swelling and coursing smoothly over rocks.

'Kate . . .' says Vaz. 'I didn't ask her to land herself on me, you know.'

'You think I'm bothered about that?' I say, hunkering down and tightening my crossed arms, unable to contain this ridiculousness.

'There's nothing going on between me and Romany,' he says.

'So what if there was?'

'If there was there'd be no chance for me and you, would there?' he says.

287

I stare at the water, its lolloping and plunging echoed in my stomach, my breast. Something is stirring in me and I need to be physical – run, jump, scramble up a tree, spin around and around with my hands joined to Vaz's, like Mum and Dad at the dance – but I can't, ever, and think I might explode with frustration. Some moorhens move past, their orange feet cutting efficiently through the water. One dips its neck and disappears and the movement, the shape and ease of it, slides into my brain and ticks, flickers like a fish about to writhe into deeper water. It's still and silent but Vaz's presence thrums through me.

'Kate?' he says. 'You OK?'

'Let's go for a swim,' I say.

I wriggle out of my leg in seconds and plunge in, swim straight to the middle where the water is dark and cold, a few patches of sun-warmed surface between the tree-shadows. Vaz follows. He's a good swimmer – strong, rhythmic strokes, his pale body glimmering under the water. In the river I'm buoyant, my movements fluid, lightsome, like the water which flickers in and out of light and shade beneath the flourishing, waterside trees. Here I'm graceful, roll over and over, round and round, until it feels like the water's flowing through me, easing into every fold and cranny of my body and mind, licking them clean.

'Race you to the edge,' I shout, and we pelt through the water; he doesn't seem to be letting me win, pants hard when we reach the sandy shallows. My hair floats on the surface like angel-hair weed and Vaz slips around me, knuckles brushing my back, knees clutching my waist, just for a second. It's too cold to stay in for long though and Vaz lifts me out and rushes to the van, sprinkling river, and we dry ourselves on an old rug and shiver together till our goose pimples subside. Vaz boils a kettle and we sit out on the grass sipping, his arm tight around my shoulder.

'Great tea,' I say, tipping his cup with mine.

'At your service,' he says. 'Reminds me of Portugal, this – hundreds of miles of hills and rivers with sunshine thrown in. You'd love it. And the van's perfect for you, everything in reach, park up where we want to stay . . .'

I stiffen, Vaz's arm heavy on my shoulder. 'Sorry,' he says. 'I didn't mean to . . . It's just . . . I think we'd be fine . . . if we went.'

Go; let's just go. This is how it feels. Like the earth is slipping away underneath me, the sky tipped upside down. Clouds float past in front of us, edges fuzzed by the limber water.

'All I'm saying,' says Vaz, 'is don't say no because of your leg.'

'It wouldn't be easy,' I say.

'When is it ever?' says Vaz.

A memory slips into my head, something I'd blocked – not deliberately, self-preservation more like; if this had been my first thought each morning I'd have never got out of bed again. 'The first time I tried to stand on crutches after the accident,' I say, 'it seemed impossible that I had to put weight through this tremulous, wasted thing – my good leg. It just crumpled beneath me – I couldn't make proper contact. The ground's never felt solid since, like it might crumble beneath me at any minute.' Like being in a snow cave way, way up high. Any movement and I might fall through, but there's no way to get on unless I do.

'But you did it,' says Vaz. 'You stood up and walked again.'

'After a fashion.'

'I saw Tom like that once,' says Vaz. 'Karen had done one and he went walkabout, backwards and forwards to the city and then out wild, sleeping under hedges, in barns, turning up by the fire every now and again for a brew. He always knew where to find us. I was out walking and up in this tree was Tom, elbowed into a crook, clinging on to the branches. I tried to get him to come down but he wouldn't, said he couldn't let go or he'd fall off the earth. I don't know if he'd been at the mushies or something – saw him a few days later and he was fine, helped us dig some drainage for the site. But it's always stayed with me, that – him up that tree terrified to move, as if a part of him was fixed like that.'

'He had to try and not remember,' I say. 'Let yourself feel how shaky things are and you're done for. That's the trouble with being around me. I remind people. This reminds people.'

'You do all right,' says Vaz. 'You do great.' Simple, solid, real. Droplets of river water fall from my hair on to the rug, sunlight catching the surfaces; shimmering, perfect tension. 'I'm not just saying that.'

'I know, but . . .'

'When I was a kid I was picked for the school play, *Joseph's Technicolor Dreamcoat*, up on the stage singing in front of everyone. I hated it, was much happier sorting things out backstage. I made out I'd hurt my ankle in the end. I still remember how the lie burned in my mouth. But nothing would work if everyone wanted the spotlight. There's no need for you to even try. You're . . . you're a different kind of star, Kate.'

Redness is creeping up his neck, a rash of vulnerability, of courage. 'I mean that too,' he says.

'I know.'

'Want to go for another swim? See if you can beat me when I'm really trying . . .'

We swim again – *thanks, Mum* – and come out starving. Vaz has bread, cheese and tomatoes in the van and hums as he puts together monster sandwiches. I watch him enjoy the task, each movement displaying his lightness of mood, his temperamental gift from the gods. He hands me my food along with a winning smile. A breeze brushes our backs and then travels over us on to the river, breaking up the surface, sending the clouds back up to the sky where they belong.

We don't get back home for hours, but when we do Romany sees the shift between me and Vaz immediately. I fancy that her brow flickers for a second but then she breaks into a broad smile – unfaked – and hugs us both hard.

'Mum and Dad are on their way back,' she says. 'I phoned and told them about Ty and Mum said, "Right, we're on our way."'

'Just like that?'

'Yeah. Weird.'

'Frieda must've been working her magic.'

'Something's changed, anyway.'

'Where's Adrian?' I say. 'Do you think all that stuff is true?'

'Still around somewhere, worst luck,' says Romany. 'Says he's going to the Himalayas to join Ty. I tried explaining the fucking size of those mountains but he's not having any of it, and it'd suit me just fine if they did meet up. Think you can walk out on your past, Ty Waterson? Here comes your worst nightmare.'

'So you believe it?'

'It explains everything, Kate. Think about the timing – the way he went all weird after the accident in Calcutta, how he left just before your letter came, with the news about the house and Tom. As if he knew that things were catching up with us. And the way his mum was – Adrian phoned her, you know, to ask about Ty. And Tom never really trusted him – that should have told me. Everything slots right into place.'

'Except for Adrian. He didn't have to keep in contact.'

'Adrian's his Achilles heel.'

'He could have told us – told you at least. It was an accident. One he paid for.'

'It might not be shocking now, but I reckon it would have been then.'

I see him again, striding off into oblivion, the stark facts of his life trailing behind him; following him everywhere, however far he wanders. At least Adrian reacted, I think. Instead of burying his grief like Ty – like Mum – to erupt years later as a madness no one else understands. Is that why Ty attached himself to me? Because of my accident, through pity? My phantom twitches and jabs, small, burning dots like a hot skewer boring through flesh that isn't there any more but still feels this fire.

'I'd like to see Ty's face when Adrian bursts his nirvana,' says Romany.

'Don't gloat, Romany, that poor boy killed someone.'

It's Mum and Dad, back already. I can't remember the last time she was so direct with either of us, although her tone is as familiar as the scratches on the kitchen table. *Don't touch that, Kate, it's hot. Don't be rude to your grandfather.*

'Quick journey,' I say. 'Want a brew?'

'Love one,' says Dad. 'I've been gasping all the way down, but your mum didn't want to stop.'

'Forget the tea and sit down,' says Mum.

Romany and I sit down obediently. Something in her tone of voice makes us want to do as she says. Even if she tells us off it'll make us feel better, because it means she does care – what we do, how we behave, what we'll become.

'Don't be cruel about Ty, Romany,' she says. 'I know he's hurt you but he never intended to kill. But he did. Nothing can change that.'

'Same with Tom's killer,' says Dad, 'whether or not they're ever found. And you're not the only one who's been hurt, girl. What about his poor mother?'

They've been talking – I always know when, have always known, even before the accident. Their bodies are settled and calm. *Kate, now please listen.* No anxious glances between them now, no hasty qualifications.

'Frieda said it when we told her about Ty,' says Mum. '"Death's the only end; anything else can be salvaged. If you've still got life you can pick it up and remake it."'

I think of Frieda's beachcombing project, the scrap-wallahs in India building business out of other people's discards. Mum's eyes have crystals glistening in the corners and I feel like I've just found something I'd forgotten I lost.

'And as for Adrian,' says Mum, 'you should be ashamed of yourselves, the pair of you. I'm going to talk to him right now, see if I can't get him on some programme. There must be something. The lad needs help and you've just written him off – would your Tom have done that, would he?'

'Look where that got him,' says Romany. Her chin is thrust out and her eyes resent being told.

'I didn't bring you up to talk like that, Romany Jackson. Tom died with a clear conscience – who else can you say that of? He *tried*. He put himself out there for people and he paid the price. There's always a price – you pay it, you get on with it if you've half a chance.' She pauses, letting her words sink into all of us. 'Now, I've no doubt all that junk in the hall is going to evolve into a fabulous creation at some point, but right now it's an obstacle course we could all do without. Can you cook?'

She's looking at Vaz, who glances around him as if someone else might have unexpectedly come into the room. 'Er . . . yes,' he says.

'Good. You can do tea tonight then. I'm afraid we've spoilt these girls rotten on the domestic front and neither of them can so much as stir a pot of soup. If anyone rings, I'm busy.'

293

As she leaves the kitchen she straightens a pile of newspapers, picks up two empty cartons off the table and bins them, rubs the mirror with her sleeve and picks out the dead flowers from a vase full that Romany brought back from the market a few days ago. The room looks brighter, as if it's just been polished.

'Dad, what's happened?' I say, the floor swimming slightly beneath me. I can make it stop though; I know I can.

'You didn't die, Kate, that's what's happened. Romany's back safe, and the rest of it is all small print.'

I go upstairs to put my leg back on – I left it off since the swimming; Vaz carries it for me, hooked over his shoulder. I wash, brush my hair and teeth, fetch clean clothes and smooth my jeans over the false leg first, then pull myself into it; buttoning, zipping, smoothing Velcro, shifting and shuffling till it feels secure. Trying a few steps, adjusting again, testing my weight on my leg and my appearance in the mirror. Good – both – a rare conjunction. If I stay still no one would know except me. So I stand still and perfect – just for a second – captured and frozen in time like a photograph. Even the prickles and jerks of my phantom seem to stall, although I can still feel its ghostly presence. My untrainable brain playing magic tricks again, letting me know that eyes and ears never tell the whole story. With these instruments in place – my brain, my leg, my sticks and my family – I feel prepared, equipped for the vast unknown terrain of the future. As soon as I move what has gone nags me again and I know that I'll always be carrying it, but it can't stop me now.

By my bed is Romany's globe and I spin it, faster and faster until the edges of land and sea blur. The room lurches around like a ship at sea but I steady myself in time and stay standing, poised for the next wave.

*

'What's going on then?' says Romany. 'With Vaz? Are you going away with him?'

We're walking down the street towards the park, leaving Adrian to Mum and Vaz to Dad. Vaz wants to convert his van to LPG – cheap, green transport – and they're trying to fathom out whether it would work for a motorbike, too. The terrace steps gently upwards, ending in another perpendicular block; identical houses individualized by white paint, blue doors, uPVC windows inset with mock-stained-glass roses, sickle moons, Jamaican flags. The city cross-hatched by these flat-fronted dwellings, red brick glowing under the evening sunshine, grit and rubbish in the street, trees rising behind the terraces – clouds of green floating on the breeze.

'I'm not sure yet,' I say. 'What about you? Will you write to Ty?'

'I don't know,' says Romany.

We stop at the entrance to the park, paused by this mutual admission – so common in me but rare in Romany.

'You still love him, don't you?'

She opens her mouth to speak – to ask me about me and Ty? – but then closes it again and clutches me close as we walk up the path, the wind blowing the sounds of the city across our path: racing-car vrooms, the call to prayer, urgent rap from a car stereo, moments of calm. 'How did you know anyway,' I say, 'that Vaz wants me to go away?'

'It's obvious,' she says, a second too late, and I know he must have said something – when she was on his knee, perhaps. There was a moment when she could have changed his plan, moved her hand up his back and round his shoulder and up on to his cheek. A moment when she could have stopped us; me and Vaz. Like I could have stopped her and Ty, in the bookshop at the foot of Greenwich Hill. I could have said it: *Romany, don't go. Don't take that dream away from me.*

But it wasn't a dream, it was a fantasy, so we did right – do right – to keep our mouths shut and live with the aches. We walk arm in arm through the park with the wind buffeting us, upending rubbish bins, churning the thick mats of tiny blue flowers, beech leaves flicked from bronze to black. The sky's darkening but the sun's still strong and the park flashes all around us – rays on jewellery, silver paper, bike mirrors, discarded cans. The gaps ache, the parts that are gone, but we won't let them stop us, move back towards the gate and the copper-bronze sky and the blue-black houses behind.

'You don't just stop loving someone, do you?' says Romany, to no one in particular, to the air and the pavement and the sticky black tarmac. 'Look at Tom and Karen. My mum and dad – I tried so hard to hate them.'

'I thought you really did.'

'You have to let yourself start again.' She says this straight to me. The air rumbles and crackles all around. Lightning arcs across the sky, suspending figures in a flash of blinding white, freezing dogs in mid-leap, stalling birds' swoops, blazing Romany's face on to my retina for ever. Another wordless moment of understanding; we can't always be on each other's side but can always be there, by our sister's side.

'I learned that I could when I came to Mount Street,' she says. 'But . . . however shite it was at that house in Aston there were times when everything fitted. Me and Mum and Dad and the dog and the backyard; even Mum's crazy ramblings had some sense in there, for me, anyway. Your family always felt . . . I don't know . . .'

'False?' I say.

'I couldn't walk without you,' says Romany.

Also available from Tindal Street Press

SCAPEGRACE
Jackie Gay

'A joy to read' *Big Issue*

Birmingham 1976. The hottest summer on record. Alice and her teenage gang are changing as fast as the world around them. As they explore their city outside the familiarity of home and school, they are enthralled by the forbidden – ouija, sex, arson – but unprepared for the fallout.

21 years later, Alice comes home to her mum's flat at the scruffy end of the high street. Will she be able to rekindle her girlhood friendships and reconnect with their shared values of loyalty and trust? The last thing she expects to find is answers in a tin full of creased letters, or her first love Johnny waiting for her amid the bric-a-brac in her old refuge, the shed.

'Amusing and poignant . . . a remarkable rendering of teenage angst' *The Times*

'Lively and acute. Her portrayal of adolescent girls is spooky, amusing and believable' *Lesley Glaister*

'Jackie Gay's narrative is tender, liberating, spiky and defiant' *Big Issue*

ISBN: 09535895 1 X

Also available from Tindal Street Press

HER MAJESTY edited by
Jackie Gay & Emma Hargrave

'Buy everyone you love a copy' *Laura Hird*

Ali Smith, Liza Cody, Amy Prior and Helen Cross, plus fresh, unsung voices from across the UK; here are 21 majestic stories. Adventures of the spirit that illuminate the hidden courage of ordinary people: the everyday splendour of *Her Majesty*.

  This bold, sharp-eyed anthology casts a crystalline light on contemporary lives. Modern dilemmas jostle with ancient themes: fertility, loneliness, survival. Stylish stories from some of the UK's best women writers told with an energy that will dazzle and delight.

'Teeming with life and truth and with a rare quality of intimacy' *Nell Dunn*

'Short, sweet instalments of reality . . . Like an album of heartfelt songs, you are in there somewhere' *Pride*

'A good collection of stories is like a luxurious box of chocolates: variety, texture, surprise. This is one of the most inviting boxes around' *Time Out*

ISBN: 0 9535895 7 9

Also available from Tindal Street Press

WHAT GOES ROUND
Maeve Clarke

'Galang!' Sol said. 'But yuh can only run fi so long an' so far before it catch up wid yuh.'

'Before what catches up with me?'

Sol smiled, dimples inverted commas in his cheeks and teeth gleaming vampire white against black skin. 'Yuh past, Frank. An' Rose . . .'

When Frank returns to Jamaica for Poppa Ben's funeral, he's pursued by Rose, an old flame who's convinced their destiny is shared. Meanwhile, his daughter Jewelle – flummoxed by her daily chores, but seduced by Jamaica's charm – discovers there's more to the island than its beauty. What's 'dis big people business' that no one will tell her about?

'Wonderfully vivid! *What Goes Round*'s rich cast of characters leapt off the page to live on in my imagination' *Suzannah Dunn*

'For lovers of Caribbean literature, a humorous, character-packed account of a man's return "back home" to Jamaica with his teenage daughter' *Bookseller*

ISBN: 0 9541303 3 2